SEASONS'
END

Will North

Northstar
Editions

Published in the United States by Northstar Editions.
Seasons' End / Will North — 3rd. Ed.
Library of Congress Control Number: 2013923021
Cover Design by Laura Hidalgo

ISBN-10: 0-9994347-0-5
ISBN-13: 978-0-9994347-0-3
EPUB ISBN-13: 978-0-9994347-1-0
EPUB ISBN-10: 0-9994347-1-3

:

For Susan

one

AT FIRST HE thought it was a deer.

It was not quite morning on what promised to be yet
another brilliant end-of-summer day. The pre-dawn fog
was just beginning to lift. Not that it actually "lifted."
Not that it was fog, either, come to that. That's just what
islanders called the queer maritime phenomenon because
"marine layer" was too fussy a phrase for an everyday
event. In the wee hours it lay like a lid a hundred feet or
so above the ground in late summer, and as the upper air
warmed, plumes of mist descended and rose, twisting
wraithlike through the feathered branches of the firs that
cloaked the island. Then, at a certain but highly uncertain
point later in the morning—the regulars at the Burton
coffee stand sometimes bet on the precise moment—it
simply disappeared, like steam from the manholes in
Manhattan streets he remembered from his childhood.
The fog didn't move off, the way clouds do. Instead, in a
sort of meteorological sleight of hand, it just vanished.
You missed it entirely if you didn't pay attention.

Colin Ryan paid attention. Though it was only the
first Monday of September, 2012, and the night had been
warm, on this morning's bike ride Colin could already

sense the coming autumn chill. It was there in the sharper tang of the air that swept in from the Pacific and in the subtle shift in the quality of the light as the transit of the sun took a lower, more southerly route across the sky. It was there in the way the echoing honks of migrating geese began to replace the shrieks of laughter of the children who summered on the beach. It was there in the way the leaves of the alders and broad-leafed maples on this mostly evergreen island would, in a matter of a few weeks, not so much change color as slowly lighten as they died, reverting to the pale greens of spring, as if the movie of the seasons was playing backward. Summer didn't flame out in the Pacific Northwest as it did in Colin's native northeast, it slipped gracefully offstage. And here in the middle of Puget Sound, surrounded by the perpetually snowcapped Olympic Mountains to the west and the Cascades to the east, Colin thought this perfectly appropriate. Flash was unnecessary when grandeur was everywhere. But in the thin half-light of dawn he could tell the end was approaching, the gathering autumn already sucking the marrow from the fat bones of summer.

There were still warm days, though, and he was taking full advantage. He was nearing the end of his pre-dawn ride, an eight–mile circumnavigation of the southern half of the island, something he did every morning before opening the clinic as long as the weather held. It had been nearly two decades since he'd moved to the island to take over the local veterinary practice.

Colin was hunched over his handlebars and speeding down the steep, sinuous stretch of the Vashon Highway just south of the little hamlet called Burton, the tires of his touring bike hissing over the dew-damped asphalt like tape being ripped from a dispenser, when he saw the dark mass ahead in the middle of the road.

Deer were a year-round menace on Vashon Island, but the danger worsened as fall approached, as if in their frenzy to pack on as much weight as possible to carry them through the winter, the beasts became senseless to danger whenever they saw an irresistible patch of grass. Given the dark canopy of the conifer forest, many of these irresistible patches were along the sunny margins of the island's narrow roads.

The "highway" was nothing more than a two-lane blacktop that stretched from the ferry dock at the north end of the island to its opposite number on the south end, some thirteen miles away. The rather grand title of "highway" dated from the time, not so long ago, when the south and north end ferries were finally joined by a continuous paved road, a measure of progress and a point of local pride requiring a suitably proud name. Whenever Colin looked at a road map of the island, which he did a lot when making farm calls, the pattern of perpendicular side roads branching off the Highway reminded him of the spine and ribs of a deboned salmon.

Vashon's deer population was something of a tourist draw. Placid as slender cows as they munched picturesquely in front lawns, in apple orchards, in family gardens, and along the roadside, graceful as ballet dancers on point when they moved; the deer were photo fodder, as if they'd been placed there for visitors' viewing pleasure by the Chamber of Commerce. But the deer drove locals mad with frustration, since the cost of erecting and maintaining high, deer-proof fences around home vegetable gardens often outweighed any budgetary advantage they might have gained by growing their own produce. The two species—deer and residents—waged a sort of endless existential battle; the deer trying to get into the gardens, the residents trying to keep them out, scheming to a draw. It didn't help any that the deer reproduced like rabbits and that their only apparent predator was the automobile—that and the occasional crazed urban hunter who took the ferry from Seattle in the fall and thought nothing of shooting across fields and yards at anything that moved.

COLIN SQUEEZED HIS brake levers hard and slid to a stop on the slick pavement a point where the road leveled out along the north shore of Outer Quartermaster Harbor. In the dim light just pearling the sky in the east, he noticed a Great Blue Heron hunched on an arm of driftwood at the water's edge, motionless as an undertaker. He unclipped from the pedals, leaned his bike against the guard rail, and crossed the road, his cycling shoes clicking on the pavement like a metronome.

In another half hour, traffic for the morning's first Tacoma-bound ferry at the south end of the island would pick up and, even though it was Labor Day, the now-deserted road would get busy. Colin knew he'd have to drag the deer to the side of the road so there wouldn't be another accident. It wasn't the first time he'd done it. He wondered what had happened to the car that hit the beast. At this hour, it would have been an old beater of a pickup belonging to an island laborer, the kind of fellow least likely to be able to afford repairs, the most economically vulnerable to any accident, whether personal or vehicular. They often had a well-loved old dog who rode with them; Colin took care of their animals when they were sick, often for nothing.

As he came closer to the inert carcass on the asphalt, though, he realized, even in the dim pre-dawn light, that there was a problem with this particular deer. Instead of the usual flea-bitten russet coat, this one was wearing a short black cocktail dress. And silver high-heeled sandals. And wasn't a deer.

THE BODY LAY on its back but the head was turned away, the face curtained behind a swirl of sun-streaked ash blonde hair. The slender tanned limbs lay splayed like a child's pick-up sticks.

He didn't need to see the face. He recognized the dress. He'd admired it, and the woman who wore it, only hours earlier at the annual beachside party the old summer families always held the night before Labor Day, the day before they all left the island for the winter.

The body belonged to Martha Petersen Strong, known to everyone on the beach as "Pete." He'd known her and loved her for more than twenty years.

two

COLIN RYAN MET Tyler Strong at a flat-letting agency on Regent Street just off London's Piccadilly Circus on a drizzly late Friday morning in September, 1984. The agency was on the floor directly above the street level Tourist Information Centre. The narrow stairs opened to an airy office with pearl gray walls and high Georgian windows that flooded in light from Regent's Street. The floor was covered in tight charcoal commercial carpet and a long black counter much like a bank's, with openings like tellers' windows, ran across one end of the room. Colin was at one of the windows going over a list of cheap bed-sits, as the British called a studio with shared kitchen and bath, with a perky young leasing agent with big, deeply kohled brown eyes and an even more deeply scooped blouse, when a perfectly modulated voice behind him said,

"I say, old man, here's a thought: Why don't we go in together on someplace more seemly?"

Coming from someone who, by his accent, was most certainly American, the fogeyish British mannerism was ridiculous, but when Colin turned, he found himself facing a grinning young man about his own age who clearly was making fun of the fact that they were both, as the English would say, "from the colonies." The guy had sandy hair, a long narrow nose that put Colin in mind of an Afghan hound, and was unusually tall, easily six inches taller than Colin.

A hand shot out: "Tyler Strong," the young man said, as if Colin should recognize the name, which he didn't. The brown-eyed leasing agent's attention shifted instantly.

COLIN RYAN WAS in London to become a veterinarian. It was an admittedly strange way for an American to become a vet—strange, that is, unless you figured in the cost. The kind of kid who dragged home stray cats, he'd known he wanted to be a vet for years and he'd dreamed of getting his degree at Cornell. But his widowed mother didn't have the money to send him there and, thanks in part to the chaos of his childhood, he hadn't gained the grades in high school to earn a scholarship. But his school guidance counselor, who had also been his biology teacher, believed in him. With a little digging she discovered that with the British pound at an historic low against the dollar, Colin could enter London's Royal Veterinary College for roughly half of what Cornell would cost. He got in, was halfway through his last year at the school, and had been living in a flat in Harrow, way out on the Metropolitan Line of the Underground. The disadvantage was a long commute to the city; the advantage was it was cheap. But his landlord, a fussy curator at the Victoria and Albert Museum with fantasies of becoming a real estate mogul, had jacked up the rent and Colin could no longer afford the place. He was looking for something smaller and closer.

Colin and Tyler stepped out of the queue at the agency, crossed Regent Street, and walked a block up Brewer Street where they found a corner pub called The Crown.

"Name your poison," Tyler said as they approached the bar.

"Pint of London Pride would suit," Colin said, "but it's my shout."

"Nonsense; I'm the one who hauled you here."

Colin shrugged. "Fair enough."

The pub was dense with a lunchtime crowd of office workers. Colin watched in amazement as the aging peroxide blonde behind the bar lifted her head above the punters lined three deep in front of her and yelled to Tyler, "What'll it be, luv?"

"Couple of pints of Pride, my dear lady!"

"Right you are!"

Colin wondered if it was Tyler's height that caught the woman's eye, but there were other tall men in the crowd as well. No; it was just something about the fellow, something that caught people's attention and held it. Had Colin been the one ordering he'd still be standing at the bar, hand in the air, angling to get served.

The pints appeared, the dimpled glass mugs brimful. The barmaid winked. Tyler paid, told her to keep the change, and they drifted away from the crowd.

"Come here a lot?" Colin asked as they touched glasses.

"Here? Never. Not my sort of place; no history, no atmosphere. That's one thing I can say for Oxford—great old pubs. And younger barmaids!"

They'd established where they were from and why they were in England before they'd reached the pub. Tyler was doing a term at Oxford before heading to law school.

"So what's your proposal?" Colin asked finally.

"Simple. Oxford: great school, aforementioned great pubs, but otherwise deadly boring. The action's all here. I need a London base."

"Someplace 'seemly,' you said…"

"Exactly. And my thought is that, while two can't live cheaply as one, they sure as hell can pool resources and get a better place to live than each of them could separately. Landlords rip off singles in this town."

Colin looked at Tyler. The fellow was wearing a Harris Tweed jacket in a herringbone weave of fall colors, a cream-colored rollneck sweater that looked to be cashmere, pleated gray flannel trousers, and cap-toed brown suede shoes that looked almost new. Colin had on jeans, sneakers, a faded black T-shirt, and a badly pilled black cardigan he'd picked up at an Oxfam charity shop in Harrow.

Tyler read his eyes. "Look, I heard the price range you and that lovely agent were discussing. I'd go at least double that. And I'll cover it for the extra few months longer you're here than I'll be."

"Why?"

Tyler smiled. "Because I can."

"Fine. But why pick me out of the queue?"

"Besides the fact you're a fellow Yank?"

"Besides that."

Tyler paused, pushed back an errant shock of hair, and smiled. "I have a few useful skills: I know which woman in a crowded room will sleep with me, and I know an honest man. You may sound like you're a capo in the New York Mafia with that accent, but you were gracious and patient with that agent when everyone else was being pushy. And it wasn't an act."

"All that and a shilling still won't get you on the Tube," Colin said.

"The shilling's extinct, and gentlemen nearly so, my friend." Tyler's smile was irresistible. "So, do have we an agreement?"

Colin smiled, raised his glass to Tyler, and nodded.

"Deal."

In short order, back at the agency, Tyler had negotiated a "seemly" furnished two-bedroom flat atop a carriage house just off the King's Road in fashionable Chelsea, as well as the comely agent's phone number. Colin watched him operate with quiet amazement. It was clear that Tyler Strong was used to getting his way, and to doing so without breaking a sweat. He combined a certain boyish charm with a languorous self-possession bordering on diffidence that, Colin would soon learn, drew women to him as if they were spellbound.

And though a chasm of class difference yawned between them, Tyler and Colin turned out to be, for the most part, "best mates" that winter. It didn't hurt that Tyler spent weekdays at Oxford and Colin had the flat mostly to himself.

PETE ARRIVED A month after he and Tyler moved in.

Early one Saturday morning in October, as the hand-sized, yellowing leaves of the plane trees outside his window began carpeting the cobbled pavement below, Colin was awakened by the downstairs doorbell. He assumed it was Strong, too hammered, as usual, to find his keys. He struggled into a shirt, padded downstairs in his undershorts, threw open the door, and was already turning back toward the stairs when it registered that the person at the door wasn't, in fact, Tyler, but a wisp of a girl standing beside a massive knapsack. Her face, delicate and angular, was slightly elongated, as if it had been shaped by Modigliani. Her eyes were the color of seawater, shifting between blue and green in the morning light as if tidal and flecked with gold like sunshine on wavelets.

"Hi, I'm Pete!"

Colin stared. He wasn't actually awake yet.

"I'm Tyler's girlfriend? From Seattle?"

"Oh. Right…" he said, though he hadn't a clue why. Tyler hadn't mentioned a girlfriend in Seattle. "Um, I think he's still up at Oxford."

He'd just realized he was standing at the open door, in front of a luminously beautiful young woman, without his trousers. This did not seem to faze the girl in the least.

"May I come in?" the sylph asked.

"Jeez, I'm sorry! Of course you can; I'm a little slow in the morning." This was an understatement; Colin barely had a pulse in the morning, at least until he'd had his second cup of very strong tea.

"Let me take your backpack; we're just up the stairs."

He groaned as he lifted the pack, wondering what in heaven's name she had in it and how so small a woman, only a couple of inches over five feet, had ever managed to get it here from Heathrow.

"I'm sorry to be so early," Pete chirped as she closed the door. The apartment was above a space that once had stabled horses and now cosseted a perfectly restored red

MG-TC roadster, complete with wire wheels which belonged to their very rich, very spoiled landlord, a lesser Saudi prince.

"It's just that the overnight flights from the States get in practically at dawn and I didn't know what else to do."

Colin's attention, at this moment, was fixed upon the rear elevation of the perfectly proportioned, almost doll-like woman climbing the stairs ahead of him. She was wearing a nearly ankle-length skirt with small floral print on a straw-yellow background, a waist-length cotton cardigan the color of French vanilla ice cream, and saddle-tan flats. As she ascended, there was a very slight hitch in her right hip, an asymmetry that gave her a delightful bounce. Long blond hair, almost as pale as the cardigan and parted in the middle, shimmered like a shaft of sunlight between her shoulder blades. Why hadn't Tyler told him this lovely creature—this "girlfriend"—was coming to visit?

Colin stashed Pete's pack in a corner of Tyler's room and settled her on the sofa in the bay window that overlooked their shady cul-de-sac—a "mews" was what the English called it. After he'd pulled on a pair of jeans, he put on some music and went to the kitchen to make tea. When he returned with their mugs the girl was fast asleep, curled like a ginger cat among the worn cushions of the couch. He watched her sparrow-like chest gently rise and fall, her porcelain face childlike in repose. There were the faintest freckles scattered across the bridge of her nose. Her right hand cradled her cheek and the slender fingers of her left hand, the nails neatly manicured but unpainted, draped limply over the seat cushion like tassels. He had never seen anything or anyone so perfect in his life.

He knelt and touched her arm. She jerked awake.

"Oops," she said, rubbing her eyes and smiling sheepishly. "Jet lag."

He stood, then handed her a mug of tea.

She peered into the cup and sniffed. "No coffee?"

"Um, no; you're in England now. The choice is very bad coffee or very good tea. Go for the tea every time; no use trying to resist."

She smiled. "And it cures jet lag?"

"Actually, no. There is only one known cure."

"A nap?"

"Wrong. A walk. Daylight affects the melatonin in your brain, which in turn tells you when to be awake or asleep. Your melatonin is someplace over the mid-Atlantic, where it's still dark. You need to let it catch up.

"With a nap," she repeated, snuggling into the pillows again and giggling.

"With a walk and lots of sunshine which, uncharacteristically for October, seems today to be in ample supply, though I doubt they call it 'Indian Summer' over here. A nap, you see, would only worsen your jet lag."

"What are you, a doctor?"

"Sort of. But the science is very clear on this." *What's more, I should very much like to spend the rest of the day while you're in a conscious state,* Colin thought to himself.

"So I have a modest proposal," he continued.

"Didn't Jonathan Swift have one of those?" the girl said, giggling again. Her laughter reminded him of sleigh bells.

"That was several centuries ago, and I'm not Swift."

"Oh, I don't know; you're doing okay so far…"

Colin was caught off guard.

"And your proposal was…?" she prompted.

He collected himself. "I propose we head out and see what London has to offer us this fine day, while we await Tyler's return." He listened to his own words and heard how formal his address had become after a few years in London, how incongruously thick his New York accent still remained, and it flustered him even more.

But the girl sat up and grinned as if it were Christmas. Then her look turned serious.

"May I just ask you a question?"

"Sure."

"Who are you?"

"Huh?"

"I mean, you know. Who are you? What's your name? What are you doing in Tyler's apartment?"

He had no idea why his roommate had never mentioned him to his girlfriend—any more than he knew why he'd never mentioned the girlfriend. Or that she would be visiting. Or that he wouldn't be here when she arrived. And yet it didn't entirely surprise him, either. He'd learned that Tyler Strong, while affable and generous, was chronically unreliable. It often seemed to Colin as if Tyler was perpetually distracted by a narrative that was running parallel with the one in which he appeared to live but attended to only fitfully. Often it was amusing… when it wasn't annoying. Today, it was annoying.

Colin shook his head, smiled, and introduced himself. They had their tea. And after Pete freshened up in the bathroom they stepped out into the crisp autumn streets, strolled through Chelsea, and played boulevardiers as they passed the designer shops along Fulham and Brompton roads, until they reached Knightsbridge. Colin guided Pete into that vast brick-red terra cotta palace of luxury, Harrods, and bought them a picnic lunch in the department store's sprawling ground floor Food Halls, with its acres of cheeses and fish and game and meats and fruits and vegetables and breads, all presented so artfully you'd think the same people who merchandised the designer clothing upstairs did the food floor as well. They ate on a Hyde Park bench beside the long, gently curved lake called the Serpentine.

"How long have you and Tyler been dating?" Colin finally asked.

Pete looked at him and, to his surprise, just shrugged.

He squinted. "What's that supposed to mean?"

She watched the swans which, like icebreakers plowing through floes, cut wedges of open water through the fallen leaves papering the lake's surface.

"It means I don't know."

"You don't know?"

"No, not really. The thing is, we've just always been together, since childhood. I really don't know when the 'dating' began. You know what I mean?"

Colin didn't, but said he did.

"He was always there; I was always there. We were always an 'us.'"

"And you never had a second thought?"

She turned from the swans and looked at him. "No. Not till now."

He had a momentary rush of hope before she added, "Why's he not here?"

COLIN KNEW FOR a fact that his roommate had spent the night before with an expensively-dressed and exceptionally well-preserved middle-aged woman who, as it transpired, owned the new pub they were trying out on the edge of West Kensington: the Bunch of Grapes. The woman sat alone under an arch at the softly-lit far end of the bar. A tiny pin light above her head tipped her spiked black hair with mercury, etched her high cheekbones, and shone on a single strand of pearls that led like lanterns along a narrowing path to the declivity between her breasts. She wore a black taffeta jacket with padded shoulders and plunging, knifelike red lapels and, though the lighting kept her eyes in shadow, the angle of her head made it clear she was watching them. She steadied a half-empty martini glass with three manicured fingers.

"Power dresser," Tyler mumbled. "She's wearing Thierry Mugler."

"Huh?" Colin said.

"French designer. Very big now."

A moment later the barman brought a round of unrequested refills and tilted his shaved head in the woman's direction.

"Compliments of the Guv'nor, gents."

Tyler nodded in the direction of the arch and lifted his pint. When the barman called last orders an hour or so later Tyler was in the power dresser's bosomy embrace.

COLIN GLANCED AT Pete, then out across the Serpentine.

"Oxford's not like schools in the States, you know," he said, making it up as he went. "There aren't regular class periods or anything. I'm sure he's just hung up with some windy don going over some essay, Pete. That's all."

He looked up again. He hated lying to her.

After lunch they walked south on Sloane Street. On their way back to Chelsea, amid the ever-colorful crowds thronging the pavements along the King's Road, Pete slipped her arm through his. He knew it was to keep them from getting separated, but it felt sweetly intimate as well. They talked and laughed and he absorbed her enthusiasm like oxygen.

It was dusk when they returned to the flat; Tyler was asleep in his room. There was no sign he'd even noticed Pete's backpack. Pete looked in on her inert boyfriend, then found Colin in the kitchen, staring into the fridge.

"I've got leftover take-away Indian curry. Only two days old!" There was a limp white cardboard box in his hand.

Pete smiled and shook her head. "I'm practically asleep on my feet, Colin; can't fight the jet lag another minute. But I had a wonderful day with you." She pulled his sleeve, got up on tiptoes, and kissed his cheek.

"You're a good man, Colin Ryan."

Colin shrugged. "Welcome to England, Pete."

He watched her close the door to Tyler's room, dumped the curry into a saucepan, snapped on the electric hob, and stared out the window to the courtyard below.

Terrific. I'm in love with my roommate's girl.

three

COLIN KNELT BY the body in the middle of the road. The mist-thick Northwest forest around and above them was so quiet he could hear the blood pumping in his ears. Somewhere far across Quartermaster Harbor he could hear the high whine of an outboard running south from Dockton to the deep water channel beyond, where the salmon were running. Along the roadside there was a bank of overripe wild blackberries that, in the dewy air, breathed the fragrance of cassis. Even the gulls were quiet, as if the fog were a blanket beneath which they slumbered.

He leaned forward and placed his hand at the top of the bony corduroy of ribs radiating from Pete's sternum; he had never done anything so intimate with her before. He marveled at how a woman who had borne three children could still look delicate as blown glass. Her skin was cold, yet he thought he felt a heartbeat.

He placed two fingers lightly on the carotid artery in her neck and her eyelids, smudged with mascara, fluttered open like bruised wings. He jerked his hand away.

"Jesus, Pete! I thought you were dead!"

But the seawater eyes never focused. "Pete" Petersen Strong was not dead, but she was nearly comatose and, he guessed, now that he was close enough to smell, dangerously drunk. Gently, he opened her slack jaws and checked her throat for vomit. The principal cause of death in cases of alcohol poisoning, he knew, wasn't the alcohol; it was asphyxiation. Alcohol suppresses the gag reflex. Her throat looked clear. With an uneasy sense of intimate invasion, he felt her limbs and torso in the dim light for signs of injury and found none obvious. He stared at her dark form for a moment and shook his head. There was no reasonable explanation for her to be here on the double yellow line of the Vashon Highway, no reason except intention.

Colin slipped his arms beneath her shoulders and knees and, as if lifting a large dog at the clinic, pulled her toward him and rose in one fluid movement. He carried her across the road to the shoreside verge, leaned her back against the steel guardrail, then removed a light rain shell from a holder behind his bicycle seat. He'd just begun to slip her arms through it when, in the gathering of the light from the east, he noticed bluish bruises ringing her birdlike arms just above her wrists. He zipped up the jacket, tried to make sense of the welts, and could not. A few yards away, its vigil disturbed, the great blue heron unfurled its vast smoky wings and hauled itself into the air, skimming low above the harbor's surface and croaking loud complaints to the dawn.

Pete's breathing was slow and shallow, but not irregular. He had no idea how long she'd lain in the road and he knew he needed to get her to someplace warm and safe. *Someplace safe.* He looked again at the wrist injuries. Almost certainly, they were bruises of restraint. But why? How? He couldn't imagine Tyler hurting his wife, and yet he couldn't imagine who else could have caused those injuries in the very few hours since he'd seen the two of them last.

Fury rose in his throat. No wonder she'd fled. He knew so much about them, and yet so little. What could have happened? Why would she choose this end? For years, he'd been made to feel a part of their family, an intimate. But he knew nothing, really, about this woman he held dear to his heart, nor about the husband he thought a friend.

He knew nothing. He was, as he always had been, an outsider.

IT HAD BEEN the traditional Madrona Beach Labor Day weekend ritual, one Colin knew had changed little for generations. Three families—the Petersens, Strongs, and Rutherfords—owned half of the dozen or so houses and cottages scattered across the gently rising ground above the water. Each family had, over the years, established its own compound. But the families only summered at the beach; the rest of the year the houses lay empty, staring blank-eyed out over the water and shuddering through winter storms that flung salt spume over their lawns and ripped shingles from their rooftops.

Labor Day weekend was the end of the two-month rolling house party that was "The Season" among the summer people. They arrived just before the Fourth of July and departed on Labor Day, their various SUVs and minivans crammed to the roof with children, dogs, cats, beachwear, and sports equipment. It had been, in most respects, the usual last night boozy bash: the careening children, the overindulging adults, the hours-long communal dinner, and the end-of-season fireworks on the beach, a melancholy echo of the July Fourth festivities that started it all.

But this year it seemed to Colin there was something else, an edginess like distant atonal music the source of which he'd not been able to identify: sarcasm over cocktails, discord during dinner, as if the season had lasted a bit too long and too much sun had left everyone tender and cranky.

And now there was this. He placed a hand on the livid wrist of the unconscious woman beside him and wondered what extremity of hopelessness had brought her to this point.

"Jesus, Pete," Colin whispered. "Why didn't you say something?"

COLIN COULDN'T LEAVE her to get help and tried to will an early pickup truck to pass so he could flag it down, but the road was empty and quiet. He knew the sensible thing was to get Pete to the island's medical clinic a few miles to the north. But he also knew that if he did so, the news of Pete's attempted suicide would race across the island like a forest fire and the Strongs and Petersens would be furious. Even in an emergency—and wasn't this one?—they would consider it a betrayal. And yet he certainly couldn't take her back home to Tyler. Not with those wrist bruises.

He looked at his watch. Another twenty minutes before the ferry traffic picked up. He put his arms around the woman he had never quite stopped loving and tried to warm her. There was no response, not a sound, not a reflex. In the east, the sky was brightening and, as the sun began to slice shafts through the drifting mist, Colin heard what sounded like the low gurgling engine of an antique Chris Craft motor cruiser coming from the direction of Burton. Fog had a habit of making ventriloquists of any noise source and it seemed to him this old yacht was motoring right down the Highway instead of across the outer harbor.

The anomaly resolved itself moments later when an ancient white Cadillac Coupe de Ville rumbled out of the brightening swirl and came to a halt beside them. To say the automobile was white was a stretch. It had spent decades parked beneath an ancient cedar and in the tree's perpetually damp shadow it had developed a patina of green algae that blotched the vast sheet metal expanse of its hood and trunk like a pox. The once glacially white vinyl roof now supported colonies of native mosses, as if the vehicle were a traveling exhibit of local flora.

Colin recognized the car immediately.

Edwinna Rutherford, known to everyone on the island as "Miss Edwinna," pressed a button and— miraculously, given the age of the mechanism—her window descended. The elderly driver nodded once and said, "I thought so." Then she negotiated a lurching three point turn in the middle of the road, pulled beside them, activated the passenger window, and said, "Get her in."

Colin lifted Pete from the roadside and laid her on her side on the burgundy crushed velvet rear seat. Then he swung his bike into the Caddy's cavernous trunk and joined the driver in the front seat.

"Good morning, Miss Edwinna," he said.

"The hell it is," the woman snapped.

Edwinna Rutherford favored purple as a wardrobe color of universal utility and appeal. She was wearing a faded purple terrycloth robe and had a patterned purple silk scarf wrapped, turban-like, around her head. She'd had cancer years earlier and her hair had never grown back with its former luxuriance, so she'd shaved her head and wrapped it in scarves ever since. She was a large woman with a face as weathered as lichen-crusted roof shingles. Despite her advancing years—Colin guessed she was easily eighty—she had a sharp mind and an even sharper tongue.

"Goddamned nuisance is what this is." She gunned the engine and the car vaulted through the drifting feathers of the fog. The mist would burn off early this morning.

"Were you on the way to the ferry?"

The driver shot him a look. "No, I *saw* her. I hate getting up at this ungodly hour."

"Where did you see her?"

"In my dream, you imbecile; where did you think?!"

"She was trying to commit suicide, Miss Edwinna."

"Does that give her the right to wake me? People are so inconsiderate..."

Colin had treated Edwinna's cat Desmond for years. Desmond was a loving, but somewhat neurologically-challenged giant of a feline, a Maine Coon cat to whom Miss Edwinna, her protests to the contrary notwithstanding, was devoted. Edwinna lived at the far eastern end of Madrona Beach in a simple bungalow that thirsted for paint like a man lost in a desert did for water. And though the Rutherfords owned two of the cottages on the beach,

Edwinna lived apart from them and was seldom recognized as one of the clan. This was partly because Edwinna had married into the family and, in short order, made known her opinions of its members. But the thing that really made Miss Edwinna troublesome was that she "saw" things. Edwinna Rutherford was genuinely clairvoyant. It unnerved people, and frankly it annoyed her, too. So she kept to herself, using isolation like psychic insulation.

"You saw this?" Colin asked as Edwinna rocketed through the twenty-five mile per hour beachside stretch of highway just below Burton.

"No, I just like to take impulsive pre-dawn drives when visibility is zero. Although with my old eyes it hardly matters..."

"Would you like me to drive?"

"Don't be impertinent."

She took the curve up into Burton wide and fast, pounded the brake pedal like she was trying to stamp out a fire, and managed to bring the automobile to a shuddering halt at the blinking red light between the Harbor Inn and the Burton Mercantile general store.

"Where to, doc?"

"You're the psychic; you tell me."

"And you're a New Yorker. Does wise-ass just come in the water there with the fluoride, or are you special?"

"Jeez, Miss Edwinna, cut me some slack. I don't know where. The health clinic is out; the families would go ballistic. And we can't take her home like this.

"No shit, Sherlock. Not with those wrists."

Colin looked at her. "You saw that, too?"

"No, I just make this stuff up."

The old lady stared at him and drummed her bony fingers on the steering wheel, waiting.

"No. My place is out."

"Though that's where she belongs..."

"What?"

"Don't 'what' me, young man. You know damn well 'what.' You love her. Have for years. Not that it did a damned bit of good, because she's never understood the first thing about you. I don't know which of you is dimmer, you for still loving her when it's hopeless, or her for never seeing it. Lame, the both of you are."

"I gave that up long ago, Edwinna."

"Bullshit."

"Not to mention she's married..."

"To a three-legged table."

"Excuse me?"

"Unstable."

"Tyler?"

"She got another husband I don't know about?"

"I've known him more than twenty years; he's okay."

"Okay men don't abuse their wives, Doc."

A car horn honked behind them; the first of the south end ferry traffic had arrived. Edwinna lowered her window and gave the impatient driver behind her the finger. No one honked on this island.

Colin leaned his head on the dusty dashboard. "All right, my place."

"About time, is what I say."

"Miss Edwinna, with respect, what you say isn't always right."

"The hell it isn't." She gunned the big V-8 again and roared away from the light, which continued blinking as if it had simply been marking time while they argued. A mile farther north, just past the Judd Creek Bridge, she swung the Caddy right onto Quartermaster Drive. Just after the narrow neck of fill called "the portage" that connected the main island to its little sister, Maury Island, she yanked the car left and up the hill to the bluff overlooking Tramp Harbor.

"How do you know where I live?"

The old woman just stared at him.

"You're scary, Miss Edwinna."

"You know it. Keeps people on their toes."

four

COLIN WOULD REMEMBER that first weekend in London with Pete and Tyler as if it had been bound in an album of sepia-toned snapshots. That was partly to do with a trick of the October light. The weather was clear and the combination of the low autumn sun and the ever-present moisture rising from the Thames made every feature in the cityscape look like it had been overlain with gold leaf. There was an unnatural softness, as if he were viewing the city through gauze. Yellowing plane tree leaves rattled and whispered as the three of them shuffled through streets busy with walkers out to savor the last clement days before the winter's wet and dark set in. The gleaming enamel-painted facades of Victorian terraced town houses, normally the color of clotted cream, glowed apricot in the slanting light. The faint tang of coal smoke escaping from Chelsea chimney pots drifted like an acrid but somehow comforting perfume. Forget the clichés of spring, Colin mused as the three of them strolled through St. James's Park that Sunday afternoon after showing Pete Big Ben and the Houses of Parliament; fall is the most romantic time of year, with couples drawing closer as the days grow darker.

And yet on this particular Sunday, the romantically-attached couple with whom he walked puzzled him. As he watched Tyler and Pete together he could not help but think they were oddly matched. Tyler vibrated with antic energy, regaling Pete with curiously lurid histories of the neighborhoods through which they passed: famous murders and the great Scotland Yard detectives who investigated them; Churchill's prodigious drinking as he struggled to outfox the Nazis from the underground Cabinet War Rooms not far from Number 10 Downing Street; the history of prostitution in tony Mayfair's Shepherd Market; Cold War spy intrigue in Whitehall; notorious royal flirtations in Hyde Park.

Colin wondered when Tyler had managed to gather these historical tidbits and guessed some offbeat guided tour. Some men postured and preened before their women, Colin knew, but this was Tyler performing street theater at walking speed, with Pete as the sole audience. Colin felt like he was watching from the wings.

Pete's own behavior was no less mystifying. While she appeared to attend to Tyler's every word, nodding and exclaiming with each colorful new revelation, laughing as her boyfriend acted out his stories, she also shot Colin sideways looks which seemed to telegraph: *This is not me; this is just what I have to put up with.*

Smitten as he was, Colin couldn't understand why she did it; habit, perhaps, a lifelong familiarity with such behavior, an acceptance of this frenetic theatricality as the norm, the baseline from which to measure the rest of her experience with men. If that was the case, Colin thought, he must fall well below the level of Pete's expectations. He was no showman, no Tyler.

The show folded, as all performances do eventually, that evening at their "local," the Cross Keys pub, where they went for a light dinner. Moira Kennedy, one of Tyler's earliest conquests and a woman whose wavy, flaming red hair matched perfectly her fiery disposition, was working behind the bar. Colin watched Tyler lead Pete off to a quiet corner while he stepped up to the bar to order their usual.

"Two pints of Director's please, Moira, and a half of shandy," Colin called.

"Oo's the shandy slut, is what I wanna know?" she snapped.

"Now, now, luv; that's just a childhood friend of Tyler's from the States."

"Seem pretty chummy to me."

"Well, they would be, wouldn't they, Moira; they grew up together."

They both watched as Pete, still jet-lagged, nuzzled into Tyler's shoulder. Tyler had positioned himself so he didn't have to face the bar.

"So how together have they grown, is what I'm wonderin'," Moira hissed as she pulled the pints.

"It's not like that, Moira; they're friends from childhood," Colin lied. He was getting used to covering for Tyler.

"Uh-huh. You three here for dinner, too?"

"We are."

"In that case I'd recommend the haddock in cream sauce for those two," she said, cocking her coppery head in the couple's direction.

"Really? Why's that?"

"Bloody horrible it is tonight, that's why."

Colin laughed and paid for the drinks. By the time he reached their table, though, it was clear Tyler had descended from his daytime high as abruptly as the setting autumn sun. The gloom was palpable.

Tyler grabbed his pint and downed half of it in one go. "Took long enough," he said finally. "They have to brew the stuff first?"

"You're welcome," Colin replied as he passed Pete her shandy.

Colin had seen the pattern before. There were days when Tyler seemed on a seesaw of the spirit, the life of the party one minute and killjoy the next. Something or someone would trigger a blackness that enveloped him like the sooty London fogs of yesteryear. He'd grow short-tempered and argumentative, or simply broody. The mood could last a few hours or a few days, there was no telling. And it was impenetrable. He looked at Pete across the small oak table they shared. She shrugged.

"Shall I get the bar menu?" Colin asked.

"As if we didn't already know everything what's on it."

"Pete doesn't, you know."

Tyler took another long slug and banged his jar on the table. "We're not staying anyway. I'm not hungry and Pete's half-asleep. See you later."

He rose abruptly and headed for the door.

To Colin's astonishment, Pete rose and followed, as if on a leash.

He picked up his pint and Pete's drink and went back to the bar.

"We don't take returns," Moira said when she saw the untouched shandy.

Colin looked at the glass and shook his head.

"What is it that women like you see in Tyler?"

"You mean besides the handsome and rich part?"

Colin nodded.

"Mystery," she said.

"Huh?"

"It's like this. You, for example, are a good and honest bloke, and not bad on the eye, either, if you don't mind me sayin'. What you see is, I'm guessing, what you get."

"Damned with faint praise…"

She waved his comment away. "But your mate there? Something hidden, something unpredictable and mysterious, know what I mean?"

Colin shook his head.

She stared over his head toward the door. "Makes a girl want to get in there and sort it out…"

DURING HER VISIT, Pete, who was an art history major at New York's Sarah Lawrence College, haunted London's galleries and museums while Tyler was up at Oxford. Nominally, at least, her reason for being in Britain was to pursue independent study of the painters who had influenced the French Impressionists. No doubt because of Tyler's presence in England, she'd chosen Joseph William Mallord Turner. She spent hours studying the Turner collection at the Tate. On the museum's late night Fridays, after Colin finished at the vet school in Camden Town, Pete met him at the Pimlico tube station and dragged him to the gallery where she enthused about Turner until Colin pled starvation.

The Morpeth Arms, a handsome Victorian-era pub just upriver on the Thames, was their atmospheric post-Tate dinner stop. While Colin tucked into a steaming plate of shepherd's pie and mushy peas, Pete bubbled,

"I can't get over the pure physicality, the violence even, of Turner's later work. I mean, look, this is a guy who for years did neo-classical or allegorical paintings with the precision of an architect. Where did all that swirling passion suddenly come from?"

Colin looked up. "Um, your salad's getting cold."

"What?"

"Joke."

"I'm serious. Where did he find it?"

She asked this as if Turner's prodigious skills had gone missing at some point or been hidden by his cat.

"Suddenly, out of nowhere, he finds this freedom of expression. First he paints these static—stilted, really—classical scenes and the next thing you know he's painting these wildly emotional canvases—fires, storms, shipwrecks. What happened to him? What unlocked that vision?"

"I heard his eyes went bad. Things got blurry."

She shot him a fumy look. "You heard nothing of the sort. You just like to wind me up."

Colin made a gesture with his laden fork as if capturing her in a picture frame. "You're beautiful when you're wound up."

"Oh, stop. Plus, I know you actually appreciate great painting, even if you do pretend to be the poor, illiterate kid from the wrong side of the tracks in New York."

"The wrong side of the tracks was the Hudson River which, at the time, was inhospitable even to fish."

She paused in her rant, took a sip of her shandy—a mix of beer and lemon soda Colin told her repeatedly was a disgusting thing to do to good ale—and put the half-pint glass down. "This routine you've got—the lightning-quick, witty, self-deprecating remark—it's so clever, and also so distancing. It's like you're dodging something. Maybe you're dodging you."

"Was that meant to stimulate conversation or kill it?"

She narrowed her eyes. "Colin..."

"Okay, okay. It's a fair comment; I'll grant you that much. But here's another. Your fascination with how Turner found his passion...isn't that just you wondering how you can find your own?"

"You're answering a question with another question. And besides," she added with a lascivious wink, "I found my passion."

"Which is?"

"Tyler!" She shrugged as if helpless, a victim of the heart.

Colin put down his fork. "You've known him all your life, right?"

"Right."

"From earliest memory, it's been Tyler and Pete, Pete and Tyler?"

"Uh-huh."

"So is he something you've found, or just something you've accepted as an inheritance? An inevitability? What is he to you?"

There was the slightest blink in the passage of time, as if some official at the Royal Observatory just downriver had made a momentary adjustment to the atomic clock that kept track of Greenwich Mean Time, and then she tossed her head and smiled.

"I think someone's jealous," she said, her laughter thin as frost crystals.

"Who's dodging now?"

"I am, because I need the Ladies.' Where is it, d'you think?"

Colin nodded his head in the direction behind her. She hopped off her low stool, slung her purse over her shoulder, and bounced away, that one hip lifting a little higher than the other, as if she were dancing to private music.

The subject was never raised again. Tyler came and went, like stages of the moon. By mid-month, Pete had christened Colin her "long lost brother." It was not the relationship Colin dreamed of, but he kept his longing to himself and said nothing of Tyler's infidelities. This was how Colin was made. More importantly, it was who he wanted to be. And who Colin wanted to be was a matter to which he attended with some care, although it had a complex pedigree. It rested on a base of the street rules in his old Manhattan neighborhood: stay watchful and never betray a friend. It was layered with the Arthurian legends he'd read as a boy, where the message was: honor the woman you revere, regardless of who she is pledged to, and be her defender. He knew these values were archaic. He didn't care. There was nobility about them, something that resonated deep within him. It was love bonded to respect, desire wedded to an ideal and, of course, fundamentally unattainable.

Besides, he had no choice.

And by November, Pete was gone.

"CAN I JUST ask you a question?" Colin said.

He and Tyler were sitting at a corner table at the Cross Keys, having just celebrated Thanksgiving with steak and kidney pie and a bottle of "claret," as Tyler insisted in calling the Bordeaux they'd ordered. Flame-haired Moira was off and Tyler was in one of his expansive moods.

"I believe you meant 'May I,' and you just did," Tyler replied, grinning. He was well into his second after dinner double whisky, a pricey 25-year old single malt from the island of Islay, in the Scottish Hebrides.

"Are you in love with Pete?"

"Oh, ho! Jealousy rears its ugly green head!"

"Stop being an idiot."

"Being an idiot is one of my many charms."

"Help me out here. What would the other ones be?"

"Ooh, testy tonight are we?"

"It's a simple question."

"One thing I've learned about my roomie is that nothing's ever simple with you. You see layers in any incident, multiple meanings in every otherwise declarative statement. You're an analyst; must be your medical training: the diagnostician."

"Would that be in the manner of a compliment?"

"Oh, I shouldn't think so…"

"Good, because that would be so out of character."

"Impossible. I have far too many characters to ever be out of one."

"Well, how about you see if any one of them can answer the question at hand."

"Why do you wish to know, if not out of rampant jealousy?"

"You're answering a question with a question."

"I've always found that an effective mechanism by which to keep the interrogator off balance."

"Didn't work this time, pal. I'm not unbalanced."

"Well, that's one of us, then."

"Answer the question or I'm sticking you with the entire tab for dinner."

"Okay."

"Okay what?"

"Okay stick me with it."

"You're right. You are an idiot."

"Ah, but only sometimes; one never can tell."

"Actually, one can. You're an idiot for pretending to love Pete and shagging every other woman who comes across your path at the same time."

"Am I getting only every other? That's only a fifty percent success rate. Damn! I'm slipping. Get me another whisky, will you?"

"Not a chance."

"How about if I answer your question?"

"I'll take that into consideration."

"Big of you. Yes."

"Yes, what?"

"Yes, I love her."

By which you mean…what?"

Tyler heaved a theatrical sigh and stared off into the dim light of the saloon bar. The soft light from rose-shaded sconces and table lamps made warm pools on the patterned, predominantly red, mock-Sarouk carpeting.

"By which I mean I can't imagine not being with her, not having her be a part of me. I suppose these days one would say we're 'soul mates.' "

"'Soul mates,' or just old mates?"

Tyler shot him a look. "We're not just friends, you know."

"Yes, yes; you're lovers, too. Big deal. You have lots of other lovers. Where's the distinction? Where's the fidelity?"

"Goodness, I had no idea they had Puritans in the New York Mafia..."

"I'm serious; I don't get that part."

Tyler smiled, leaned back on the rear legs of his chair, and made a grand slice through the smoky pub air, as if dividing the Red Sea.

"One bifurcates," he said. Then he winked, as if he'd just lured a naïf out of innocence.

"As in divide and compartmentalize."

"Exactly."

"So all these other women—the ones who call you from Oxford, the ones you bring home from the pub here, the matron at the Grapes...?"

"One box, as it were."

"And Pete?"

"Quite another. One box holds trash, the other treasure."

"I just hope you remember which box is which."

five

THE FOLLOWING SUMMER, having completed his undergraduate degree in London, Colin moved to eastern Washington to begin his certification work at the vet school at Washington State University. A few weeks later, Tyler invited him to his family's Puget Sound summer compound on Madrona Beach.

He stood at the stern rail of the shiny enamel-white and forest green car ferry from Seattle watching it drag its frothy wake like a bridal train. The air was gentle and warm and gulls hitched a ride on the cushion of air the ferry pushed ahead. As he strolled up the port side toward the bow, the snowy volcanic cone of Mount Rainier loomed impossibly massive away to the south, rising through a low cloud layer and emerging again above and climbing up, up into the cobalt blue sky to more than fourteen thousand feet. Above its summit, a flat lenticular cloud sat like a pale gray beret.

On the green and yellow bus, stumpy as a box car, that met the ferry and chugged south along the road that formed the island's spine, he'd had the queer sensation that the ferry had somehow slipped through a crack in the time-space continuum and he now existed in a parcel of reality that was running some forty years behind the rest of the world. There were kids safely peddling their bikes down the middle of the road, free of the anxious oversight of adults. The drivers of cars passing in opposite directions would wave and even stop to exchange greetings and those behind them waited without leaning on their horns. It was a small island with no room for impatience.

At the heart of the island's compact commercial center the bus stopped at the curb next to a park and across the street from the Thriftway supermarket. Several people got off, others boarded, but the bus didn't immediately depart. In the little park, beneath an open-air shed, local farmers stood behind tables laden with fresh flowers, produce, meat, baked goods, wine, and crafts. A group of musicians played and children danced barefoot in the grass. After perhaps ten minutes several of the riders from the ferry returned carrying bags from the farmers' market and the bus moved on a hundred yards or so to the town's only significant intersection. There, a solitary traffic light blinked red shyly, as if embarrassed to remind people to stop and take care. No one seemed in a hurry anyway. On the corner, there was restaurant called The Hardware Store. He chuckled and wondered if the hardware store was in a building called The Restaurant. A few doors down, opposite the pharmacy, a fellow wearing mirrored blue sunglasses and a weathered baseball cap in matching blue was working with machinelike intensity at sweeping the curbside gutters. Another much older gentleman sat upon an adult-scaled tricycle wearing a red football helmet, smoking and smiling crookedly and chatting up everyone who passed him on the sidewalk.

As the bus inchwormed its way south, stopping wherever anyone needed to get off or on, Colin could feel his jaws unclench, his shoulders unknot and drop. It was an experience that changed him profoundly and that, ultimately, would bring him back to the island a few years later. That wasn't the only draw, but the sense that he'd finally found where he belonged in the world was powerful, something he couldn't ignore. He had found home.

That first, glittering August afternoon, he arrived at the beach where the Petersens and Strongs and their friends had their summer houses and felt as if he'd stepped into an old *LIFE* magazine pictorial of "old money" grandees—those families who, long ago, spent "the season" at sprawling, rustic-chic summer cottage compounds in places like eastern Long Island, Cape Cod, or coastal Maine—"summer cottages" that, in actuality, were cavernous compared to the shotgun flat in which he'd been raised on the lower west side of Manhattan. The beach families seemed perpetually in motion; playing tennis, sailing, swimming, organizing touch football matches, or taking cocktails on the verandah before dinner.

Colin thought this gracious way of life had faded into extinction long before the second World War. And in some remote part of his mind, he'd mourned its loss, the way you might mourn the passing of, say, the original Orient Express even though you'd never made a journey across Central Europe to Constantinople in its luxurious carriages. What he mourned, he supposed, was a certain vision of family he'd never known himself. One crowded with brothers, sisters, aunts, uncles, cousins, and neighbors, all gathered along some broad, sun-blessed beach of the imagination, a beach a universe away from the clangorous and threadbare amusements of the only beach he'd ever known as a boy: Coney Island.

The beach families were gracious and welcoming from the start and treated him as if he were family. But of course, he wasn't. There really was no place in this wealthy patrician stronghold for an Irish Catholic street urchin whose principal family distinction was having owned and lost a bar on the corner of 38th Street and Tenth Avenue in New York's Hell's Kitchen.

The bar had catered to the predominantly Irish firemen from the Ladder 21 Station down the block where his father, Rory, had worked before he was injured in a roof collapse while fighting a fire in the garment district. The guys at the station joked that any time the economy slumped the garment district caught fire. Inventory that had been hanging around too long was destroyed and insurance companies covered the losses. It was as if insurance settlements were the venture capital of the rag trade.

Colin always stopped at the bar on his way home from school. The off-duty fire laddies would slip him a beer in a shot glass and a greasy Slim Jim sausage and tell him stories while his father, Rory, limped around behind the bar. In those days, the saloon was festooned with memorabilia: old photos of the station, framed newsclips of famous fires, insignias, retired badges, and long polished brass hose nozzles. It was an institution, as much a part of the station as the shiny red fire trucks.

In such a neighborhood, and with such a loyal clientele, it took a lot to lose money with a bar, but

Colin's father had what it took, which mostly had to do with drinking up the profits and having entered into a few "business arrangements" with the Gambino family — arrangements which took the form of loans with distinctly favorable terms...for the Gambinos. When Rory eventually, and inevitably, failed to meet his payments, the Westies, a group of Irish-American thugs working for the Gambinos, arranged a fatal four-story fall for Rory from the roof of the tenement that housed his bar. The medical examiner found the alcohol level in Rory's blood to be as high as the building from which he'd dropped and ruled it an accident. No one ever asked what he was doing up there or — given how drunk he must have been — how he got there in the first place.

The Gambinos took ownership of the bar, which was their objective all along. A bar is a splendid business for laundering money. By then, though, the neighborhood had begun to change. Puerto Ricans were moving in, the Irish and other Anglos pushing back against the tide. Bernstein, Sondheim, Laurents, and Robbins turned the years of that sometimes violent transition into the hit musical, *West Side Story*. Colin saw the movie version and found it both wonderful and ludicrous; he'd never seen either the Puerto Rican or the Anglo gangs dancing and singing in the streets. But he had seen them bleeding there, and he had a couple of knife wounds of his own by which to remember his neighborhood.

Colin got out on that classic Irish ticket: wit. He was smart and quick. The guys at the firehouse found his mother, Margaret Mary, a cheap apartment in a rent-controlled building nearby and looked after them. And when the combination of a hard life, a three-pack-a-day smoking habit, and a massive heart attack killed his mother when he was in his first year at vet school, Colin returned to the city for a week, made the funeral arrangements, thanked the guys from the station, buried her next to her husband at Woodlawn Cemetery in the Bronx, and never went back. The remainder of the payout from his father's pension put him through school.

By the time he'd met Tyler and Pete in London, Colin Ryan was well advanced in the process of reinventing himself. It wasn't a matter of creating a false identity—he couldn't escape his West Side accent, for one thing. But he didn't divulge much about his history. He wanted to be taken as presented, a person in the present tense. There wasn't much past worth telling anyway as far as he was concerned.

OF THE BEACHFRONT families, Pete's was the oldest and best established. The Petersen compound, an archipelago of three gabled and shingled houses, sat on flat, grassy terrace at the apex of the beach's half mile-long, inward-curving arc of sand, pebbles, driftwood, shells, and sand dollars. Pete's great-grandfather Neils, a Danish immigrant, had been a shipwright at the big dry dock that operated in the 1890s just across the outer harbor from Burton, in the Maury Island hamlet that naturally came to be called Dockton. He'd helped design and build many of the nimble little steamship ferries that constituted what was known then as "the Mosquito Fleet" that linked the island to ports on the mainland.

At the turn of the century, when a steam ferry pier was built at the west end of Madrona Beach in Burton and the Bayview Pavilion Dance Hall blossomed and ragtime bands came to play, Neils was quick to buy land east of the dance hall, where he built a cottage and rented rooms to weekenders from Tacoma. When the dry dock was sold and floated to Seattle in 1909, Neils set up his own company on the abandoned waterfront and began building coastal fishing boats. He never looked back.

World War I stopped the dancing at the Pavilion, but it didn't stop Neils Petersen. After a fire "of suspicious origin" leveled the abandoned dance hall, he bought up the land and cleared it, more than doubling his beachfront holdings. By the time Pete's grandfather Robbie was born in 1919, Neils had built several extensions to the original cottage. That sprawling, weathered beach house had been an anchor for the family for three generations since.

DURING HIS FIRST visit, Colin often rose early to walk the driftwood-strewn shoreline. There were surprises every morning for a city boy: a family of raccoons ranged in size like kitchen canisters—large, medium, small—waddling hurriedly down the beachfront lane, stopping to make furtive, over-the-shoulder glances to ensure humans weren't following; deer tracks in the sand, as if the leggy animals had gathered in the pre-dawn darkness hours for a communal swim. And, as the light strengthened, he could see, atop an old guano-stained piling only fifty yards offshore, the motionless American bald eagle that spent mornings at slack tide scanning the still water for foolhardy young salmon lounging near the surface. If you were lucky you'd catch that moment when, suddenly, the great bird rose on silent wings, then swooped down toward the surface, talons flared for the ambush. Then it would yank itself airborne again and circle, rising on updrafts, until it drifted off toward the forested shore with its prey, followed by pestering crows and dive-bombing gulls which it utterly ignored.

But it was the silence that stunned Colin, a quiet beyond his experience. He'd never lived anywhere but a city before, a world in which life was measured in decibels. But here, apart from the murmur of wavelets and the wakening birdlife, the screech of the gulls and complaints of the crows, the beach was enveloped in silence as if by a fog. As the day brightened, however, the first cars and trucks, their headlights sweeping the blue-black water as they came up-island from the south end ferry, rumbled northward along the "highway." Their intrusion was like a miniature of the distant dawn thunder of the empty New York Central Railroad freight trains he remembered from his childhood, mile-long chains of boxcars that hammered hollowly north along the Hudson River tracks, bound for what, to him, were the unimaginably exotic lands to the west.

On such mornings, Colin returned to the kitchen of the Old House and often found he had a companion.

"Can you make a decent cup of coffee, child?" the old woman, knotted like old wicker, would shout. It was the same question she always asked. She always shouted because she was nearly deaf and refused to wear a hearing aid. And she always called him "child" because she couldn't quite hold the nice young man's name, though she knew she'd met and liked him. Friend of the family, he was.

"I can, ma'am," Colin would answer, bowing and also shouting.

"Then get to it, boy! Day's a'wastin!"

"Yes, ma'am!"

Solveig Petersen was approaching seventy-five that year. She was Neils Petersen's son Robbie's widow. And though she came from tough Norwegian stock, her mind was failing at roughly the same rate as her hearing. The doctor, Colin knew, had diagnosed advancing dementia, but the family wondered, too, whether Solveig was simply, quietly, modestly retreating from the pain of her losses. If memory fails you, if sounds muffle, it's like being wrapped in a thick down duvet: cushioned, insulated, warm. You could sink into that warmth and let go of the past.

After coffee and before the rest of the family began stirring, Solveig would announce it was time for "their" walk, and Colin would accompany her on a tour of the grounds.

"Did you know Robbie, my husband?!" she'd demand as they descended the porch steps, her hand in the crook of his arm.

"No, ma'am, but I've heard stories about him."

"No? Did you say, 'No?' Well then, let me tell you a story about my Robbie."

"Yes, ma'am."

"Brilliant man, he was, my Robbie. And not just because he had the sense to marry me. Oh, no. Made his

mark early, he did, long before Old Neils died. Robbie—
did I tell you he was my husband...?"

"You did, ma'am; Robbie was your husband."

"Right you are, you clever lad. Well, Robbie—he was
barely twenty, you see—but he could see into the future.
And he got the old man to shift his business from building
dinky little fishing boats to creating a company to ship
freight north to Alaska. Alaska was the future, he said!"

They had completed their promenade along the lane
that paralleled the beach and now turned across the
close-cropped lawns toward a garden that was not much
more than an unkempt tangle of salt- and drought-
tolerant plants and shrubs at the west end of the
compound, a garden which, despite chronic neglect,
provided a profusion of blooms.

The old woman turned a familiar page: "In 1939, ten
years into the Depression, mind you, the crazy kid
persuades the old man to buy two mothballed freighters
at a bankruptcy auction in Seattle. Can you imagine?
Gets them refitted and next thing you know he's running
the Pacific Pioneer Shipping Company."

They'd nearly reached the Old House again when
Solveig pulled Colin's arm down to share a confidence
she shared on every one of their morning walks. "Met
him that year and married him straight away, I did; I
know a winner when I see one!"

"You were right about that, ma'am. You sure were."

"Damn right!" the old woman shouted, laughing and
giving his arm a slug.

Sometimes, at this point, as he led her indoors and
settled her in her chair by the south-facing window,

she'd fix him with a look and say, softly this time, as if to herself, "You're a winner, too; someone will notice."

And then, if no one was there to see him, Colin would bend down and kiss the old woman's forehead. He prayed she was right, but he had no faith in prayer.

"Anything else you need right now, ma'am?"

"No thank you, child. I'll just sit a bit."

Colin bowed and took his leave. He poured another coffee, slipped out to the porch, and settled into one of the Adirondack chairs that were arrayed in a row there like deck chairs on an ocean liner.

Colin knew the rest of the story. It was told in the snapshots bound in a worn leather photo album that stood on a shelf by the fireplace, images that were like stills from "The Robbie Petersen Movie."

World War Two, a cataclysm for the rest of the world, was the making of Robbie Petersen. He was in the right place at the right time. The Aleutian Islands are a thousand mile-long serrated scythe blade of weather-shattered volcanic islands that slices far across the North Pacific, nearly to Russia's Kamchatka peninsula. While World War Two American commanders were preoccupied with the campaign in the South Pacific, the Japanese attacked in the far north, bombing Unalaska Island and the military post at Dutch Harbor on June 3, 1942, and then occupied the westernmost islands of Attu and Kiska. With a presence in the Aleutians, the Japanese were suddenly within a few flying hours of the big military bases and naval shipyards around Seattle.

The United States had not been unaware of this potential threat and, somewhat belatedly, had begun building clandestine military bases, disguised as canneries, at Cold Bay on the Aleutian peninsula, and on Unmak Island, just west of Dutch Harbor.

With the Japanese attack and occupation, a thorny problem emerged: how to protect the native Aleuts. The office of the Alaskan territorial governor and the military debated the subject for months, with the governor arguing, with unusual sensitivity, that relocation to an alien environment in the dense forests of the Alaskan panhandle might cause greater harm to the Aleut population than might Japanese occupation of their barren islands, for the invaders would need the natives' fishing and foraging expertise to survive. Naturally, the military ignored the concerns of the governor and ordered the evacuation of virtually all of the population from the Aleutians.

It was a disaster for the Aleuts, but a windfall for Robbie Petersen. When the federal government commandeered vessels to support the buildup in the Aleutians and evacuate the native population, Robbie's company, Pacific Pioneer Shipping, had a distinct advantage over other Alaskan freight companies which served the more populous mainland communities: his captains knew the vicious currents, the massive tide shifts, the impenetrable fogs, the safe harbors, and the narrow passes between the islands of the Aleutian chain like no others.

It was all there in the album, the mounted photos fading like Solveig's memory: Robbie's freighters unloading Quonset huts, steel Marsden mats used to make instant runways, and other materiel for the

Aleutian Theater of War; ship captains and military officials with arms around each other's shoulders, cigarettes dangling from the corners of their grinning faces, leaning against half-tracks hauling cargo from the docks. New construction everywhere.

But there were no snapshots of those same boats "back-hauling" hundreds of uprooted, confused, terrified native Aleuts to dark, dank, forest-choked internment camps in Southeast Alaska where, as the territorial governor had feared, many had ultimately perished.

Solveig, who was the daughter of Seattle-based fishing fleet owner Ole Sorensen, had been married to Robbie at that point for four years. In the midst of the Aleutian Campaign, their first son Harlan, then three, gained a baby brother, Justin. Years later, after Justin took the company's helm, old Robbie would boast, "That was Bering Sea water in his mama's belly, you know; floated in it nine months before he reached shore!"

It was a salty amniotic fluid to which the young man would return all too soon. In 1973, not long after he came home unscathed from his tour of duty in Vietnam and once again took charge of the family shipping company, Justin was swept overboard and lost while struggling to secure deck cargo during a storm south of the Pribilof Islands.

Old Robbie never recovered; his heart failed a year later.

In his will, Robbie left the shipping company to his wife, Solveig. Day-to-day management was by then in the capable hands of Solveig's nephew, Soren Sorensen, the youngest of Robbie's captains but the only one with a business degree. Robbie's elder son, Harlan, was named chairman, but apart from signing occasional legal documents, he had few duties. If Harlan was disappointed with these arrangements he never let on. For one thing, he was too busy becoming the Episcopal bishop of Seattle.

THE SEA HELD no magic for Harlan Petersen. It took his father away for months at a time when he was a child and it drove a wedge between him and his younger brother when it became clear Justin would be the heir-apparent. By then, however, Harlan, armed with a Doctor of Divinity degree from Princeton's Theological Seminary, had distinguished himself as a battlefield chaplain in Vietnam with two Purple Hearts. The church acknowledged his heroism by hastening his rise through the hierarchy, and soon Harlan had become one of the most senior teaching elders serving in Seattle. There was something deep within him that sought honor through service. An even moderately competent psychiatrist would have understood instantly that this was his way of distinguishing himself from his more colorful seagoing kid brother, and of seeking his father's approval and affection, but by then it was too late: Robbie and Justin were both gone.

It was in the church, and especially as bishop in the cathedral church of St. Mark's on Seattle's Capitol Hill, that Harlan found his place in the world. And it was his wife Barbara, whom he met at a service mission one night in Pioneer Square, who made that place feel like home. Though Barbara had never taken vows, she devoted her life to serving and saving the homeless, the disaffected, the hungry, the abused, the desperate of central Seattle. It was her street ministry that turned the cathedral's weekly Compline Service into a haven for the lost and searching. Every Sunday evening throngs of them filled the cavernous gray stone church, packing the pews and sprawling across the floor and up the altar steps. At precisely 9:30 p.m., fifteen robed men filed into the nave and took their places in the northeast corner. There was a momentary pause and then, following a single note from a pitchpipe, they lifted their voices into plainsong liturgy, the soothing chants rising up, up into the shadows of the domed vault where each note hung in the air for what seemed like an eternity, as if immortal. And in that great, darkened space, for one echoing half hour, those who gathered there found a measure of peace.

But as a mother, Barbara would be as evanescent as the fading notes of plainsong. When their only child, the girl they called "Pete," was only ten, her mother sickened and succumbed to a virulent form of pneumonia contracted, her physician suspected, from one of her indigent converts.

Harlan was devastated. But instead of drawing closer to his young daughter, instead of becoming the new center of her motherless world, he effectively orphaned her, retreating into the ritual certainties of his church. It was as if, after the death of his wife, his father, and his brother, he could not bear to risk giving his heart to his child for fear that she, too, might perish.

It was Pete's grandmother, Solveig, who stepped in to care for the girl. She moved into the bishop's residence and saw to the child's needs while her only son buried himself in church administration, never to emerge fully again. They barely spoke. It was Solveig's decision to make her granddaughter heir to the shipping company Solveig herself wanted nothing to do with.

During Colin's morning walks with old Solveig that first summer, she never mentioned Harlan. Robbie was always "my husband" and Pete was always "my girl," as if Harlan was lost to her as completely as her younger son, Justin.

six

AS EDWINNA'S ELDERLY Cadillac rumbled up the hill toward his house, Colin looked over his shoulder at the woman who lay unconscious on the back seat. It seemed to him that this was how he'd always viewed Pete: at a remove. And from that distance, what did he really know about the woman he'd long cherished?

At the beginning, in London and then later during summers at the beach, Pete had been the most vivid feature in his personal landscape. There was an incandescence about her that seemed to energize everyone who came within her orbit. He'd watched, mesmerized, as Pete organized potluck dinners around some exotic culinary theme, or led children on beach expeditions to find the baby crabs that sheltered under rocks at low tide, or organized driftwood fort-building projects, or invented contests, like who could amass the greatest fortune in washed-up sand dollars in ten minutes.

Sometime in December of that first year, though, when Colin was in Seattle learning a specialized surgical procedure at a leading veterinary clinic, he met another Pete, one he'd never known. She was home from college for Christmas break. They'd had dinner at a Thai restaurant on Broadway not far from the bishop's residence. Afterward, they walked through Volunteer Park, the landscape garden designed by the sons of the creator of New York's Central Park, Frederick Law Olmsted. Snowflakes danced in the dark but, typical of temperate Seattle, melted on landing, as if they'd been an illusion.

To Colin, Pete seemed somehow deflated, a muted version of the woman he knew and loved from the summer.

"Did you enjoy dinner?" he asked, taking an indirect route.

"Yes, of course. Why?"

"I don't know, luv; you just seem different...distant."

"I'm the very same me as always, Colin."

"You're not, you know..."

She looked up at him. "Are you a vet or a shrink?"

"Even a vet learns to observe his patients."

"I'm not your patient."

"No, you're not. You're my dearest friend. I care about you." *More than you will ever know.*

"And what is the doctor's diagnosis?" They were peering into the grow-light illuminated windows of the park's tropical plant conservatory, a fanciful glass and steel greenhouse modeled after the Crystal Palace, built in London in 1851 for the Great Exhibition.

"Depression, I would say—though having done so, I have to confess that I am only qualified to diagnose it in dogs, cats, horses, pigs, goats, and the occasional blue parrot."

Pete chuckled and turned to lean her back against the glowing greenhouse window. She crossed her arms and smiled up at him, the light behind her wreathing her head like a halo.

"I think you're going to be a pretty damn good vet, Colin Ryan."

"Because my diagnosis is so brilliant?"

"No, because you care and you pay very close attention. You're a born observer."

"Thank you," Colin answered, despite the fact that the passivity implicit in 'observer' made his heart hurt.

"But your diagnosis is wrong," she said, pushing off from the wall and walking out into the snow-laced darkness.

Colin caught up with her. "So what is the correct diagnosis?"

Pete faced him, her face solemn, almost pinched.

"What you see is someone who's marking time, okay?"

"Okay, but I don't understand."

Pete turned on her heel and trudged off. He followed.

"Colin, look," she said as they traced the curved lane down toward Federal Avenue East. "Much as you care for me—and I know you do and I cherish that and love you for it—all you know about me is what you saw in London and during two months at the beach. That's—what—a fifth of my year? That beach is life-giving, and I'll be honest: it's all I've ever had of happiness. What do I have beyond that? A mother who is long dead and who was more devoted to the 'down-trodden,' as she called them, than to her own daughter. A father who loves his damned church more than his own kind, has never stopped struggling to 'measure up,' and never will, at least in his own eyes, and certainly not in mine. A boyfriend I've known all my life but who sometimes seems a stranger to me. That's what I have. It's what I've been dealt; it's what's left.

"And let me tell you something, Mr. Diagnostician. What I have to get me through the year is what I get from the beach: the warmth, and the light, and the water, and the birds, and the friends, and the children, all of which is, like a squirrel's acorns, food I store for the winter. Everything else, every day of my life away from the beach, every day I spend in the shadow of that damned cathedral and its bishop, is as dingy and gray as faded fucking churchman's cassocks. College helps, yes, but it's this I return to: lifeless days and nights in 'the bishop's residence' when you feel like you're holding your breath, waiting. Waiting for the summer. Waiting for the beach. Waiting to breath. So don't even begin to tell me I'm 'distant.' You haven't the slightest idea. And it's only *December!*"

Colin expected her to stalk off. Instead, she flung herself into his arms, and he held her there, not knowing whether the cold wetness of her cheekbone against his chin was melting snowflakes or freezing tears.

He stood with her there, in an amber pool of light cast from an ornate streetlamp, for what was, for him, a magical eternity. Eventually, she released him and patted snow crystals, or perhaps tears, from his lapels, as if preparing him for a stage appearance. Then she took his arm and he walked her home.

He heard her voice again now, as she lay across Edwinna's back seat: *You haven't the slightest idea...*

"DON'T STOP. Keep going."

"What?"

"Do it!"

"I am not use to being addressed that way, young man," Miss Edwinna snapped.

"Get used to it; you got this one wrong. Drive past."

Edwinna pulled the Caddy into the shadow of a big cedar over the lip of the hill.

"You didn't see *that*, did you?" Colin demanded.

"See what, you annoying beast?!"

"I'm only annoying because I catch you being fallible."

"I don't follow."

"Don't, or won't? Did you see that bicycle in the driveway…"

"So there was a bicycle. So what?"

"That bicycle belongs to Adam Strong."

"Pete's kid? What's he doing at your place?"

"Well, Edwinna, I can think of two possible explanations. Either he has your prodigious gift and has figured this all out, or he hasn't and he's come to see me, as he often does, because his mother's missing and because we're friends."

"You think you're so smart."

"No, I don't Edwinna; but I also don't think I can 'see' everything, like you. You didn't see this."

"Point taken."

"Good. Now here's Plan B."

"What Plan B?"

"Plan A is shot. Pete's not coming to my place with her son there. We agree about that?"

A truculent pause.

"We do."

"Plan B, therefore, is that you take her to your place."

"Don't be an idiot; that's right under Tyler's nose!"

"Which is the last place he'll look."

Another pause.

"Correct. Damn you."

Behind them, Pete groaned and, for a moment, fluttered her arms before her face, as if fending off something or someone.

"Miss Edwinna, we need to get Pete to your place quickly."

"So it would seem."

"I'll handle Young Adam."

Colin got out and retrieved his touring bike from the Caddy's trunk. As he passed, the passenger side window ghosted down.

"Colin."

"Ma'am?"

"I shall require your help."

"You've got it, Edwinna. I'll be over to look after her as soon as I deal with Adam. I promise. Meanwhile, I imagine she'll be viciously sick when she comes to. So be prepared."

"Young man…"

"Oh, cut it out. We're in this together."

The old woman sighed. "Yes. Yes, we are…Colin?"

"Ma'am?"

"Thank you for loving her all these years."

Colin let his head go as if it were a dead weight. He stared at the ground. "Thank you for 'seeing' her, Edwinna. I don't know what I would have done if something had happened to her."

"Something *has* happened to her, dammit; we just don't know what. I don't see everything. I wish I did, and then sometimes I hope I won't, if you know what I mean. And what I do see is getting unreliable now that I'm in my dotage. But don't tell anyone, will you? They like to think I'm a witch."

"Your secret is safe with me, ma'am."

Edwinna punched the accelerator and the mossy Cadillac flew down the lane and disappeared into the thickness of the forest that clasped Colin's narrow lane in a damp green embrace.

seven

COLIN COASTED HIS bike the hundred yards or so back to his own place. The single-story white house was unprepossessing from the road. He liked that, liked its simplicity. But it had a secret. Inside, it was open, airy, and sleekly contemporary. A kitchen of almost antiseptically white cabinets and gleaming stainless steel appliances opened to an airy dining and living area above which vaulted a soaring, cedar plank-clad ceiling. An overstuffed couch and two big easy chairs rescued from the Salvation Army store in Seattle and slipcovered in natural linen by an island seamstress sat opposite a fireplace faced in sand-colored limestone. Upon the mantle, in a glass case, sat a hand-made wooden model of a bluenose schooner made by an old client who'd bartered it to cover the cost of surgery for his aging border collie.

But what caught the breath of anyone who walked through the front door was the wall of French doors at the rear and the panoramic view they provided of Puget Sound beyond. The house was perched on a bluff eighty feet above Tramp Harbor. On a clear day, you could see all the way to snow-cloaked Mount Baker, the dormant volcano a hundred miles or so north near the Canadian border.

Adam had come around the side of the house and was on the deck in his usual position, searching the blue horizon to the north through the eyepiece of the powerful telescope Colin used to spot migrating pods of shiny black

and white Orca whales. This morning, the air was milky
with moisture, the strengthening sunlight filtered as if
through a screen. Colin's dog was sitting next to the boy
and leaning against him at an angle. He'd named her
"Eileen" for that very reason. She was an orphan, a rescue
dog, and had clearly never received enough attention. Now
she was making up for lost time. Thankfully, nobody
minded her warm body, redolent of dog, pressed against
theirs. Lean and leggy, she was part golden retriever, part
Afghan hound. He remembered learning at vet school that
Afghans were brought to the United States from Europe by
the Marx Brothers and bred by Zeppo. Eileen was goofy
enough to have been one of Harpo's unheralded sisters.
The Afghan genes gave her a long, soft muzzle, Greta
Garbo legs, and big feet that seemed disconnected at the
joints, so that when she walked they slapped the floor as if
she were wearing flip-flops. Her golden retriever genes
gave her a sweet and gentle disposition. All you really
needed to know about Eileen was that she was the kind of
dog that chased her tail without ever quite comprehending
it was a part of her anatomy. Colin called her his dumb
blonde girlfriend. He was crazy about her.

Eileen's head snapped around when she heard him
open the French doors and she rose and bounded across
the deck, limbs akimbo, jumping and barking
ecstatically—a deep and magisterial bark, the effect of
which was ruined by the fact that it always ended with a
ridiculous squeak, as if she'd been a lifetime smoker and
was having a coughing fit. The fact that she invariably
hopped on her forelegs while barking didn't add to her
majesty much, either.

"Adam! What a pleasant surprise!" Colin said as he hugged the prancing dog. "I thought you all were going back to Seattle today."

"Mom's missing."

The boy was still peering through the telescope, as if he might find her somewhere out there in the breeze-fretted channel.

"Since when?"

"Wasn't at home when I got up. Wasn't on the beach."

"Maybe she drove to town."

"Car's in the driveway."

"What's your Dad think?"

"He was still in bed."

"She likes to walk around the peninsula in the morning."

"Walking shoes are by the back door."

"Whoa, you've really been working on this mystery, haven't you?"

He'd known Adam since the day he was born. A bit of an "old soul," Adam was; he could be as noisily antic as any of the kids on the beach, but it wasn't uncommon to find him wandering the tide line alone at dawn or simply sitting on a bleached driftwood stump staring across outer Quartermaster Harbor. He was perfectly happy in the company of adults and had been able to carry on thoughtful conversations with them from about the age of five. And he had a hunger to learn. When he noticed on a walk one day that a section of the beach at the tip of the Burton peninsula was composed of crushed white shells instead of the dark, gritty sand and smooth, tide-weathered stones all the other beaches were, it puzzled him. The fact that he noticed at all made him different from most kids his age, but what he did next was, to Colin's mind, classic Adam. Instead of asking his mother or father about it, he got on his bike, pedaled the four miles to town, went to the island's tiny history museum on Bank Road, and dug through any document he could find about the Burton peninsula until he discovered that the beach was what was left of an oyster shell midden left behind by the S'Homamish tribe, who'd used the site for nearly a thousand years before being driven out by settlers.

Then he pedaled over to Tramp Harbor to tell Colin all about it. When Colin said, "Wow, wait till the other kids hear about this," Adam just shrugged. "They won't care." And he was right.

Adam was eight, but Colin had long teased Pete that her son was born at the age of forty. He often wondered whether the boy's maturity had developed early because, at some perhaps molecular level, Adam understood he was born of despair. The boy with his mother's seawater eyes came into the world on August 15, 2002, almost exactly a year after his ten year-old brother, Tyler II, was killed in a freak water-skiing accident.

Pete's daughter Justine, then fourteen, was at the wheel of the family speedboat, Tyler beside her as spotter, and "Two," as Tyler Junior had always been called, was cutting a wide and expert shoreward arc with his slalom ski through the choppy water perhaps twenty yards off Madrona Beach. With his father yelling, "Go for it, dude," Two jumped the speedboat's wake and grabbed big air, one hand holding the edge of the ski like a skateboard maneuver, to the wildly cheering kids watching from the swimming float nearer shore.

Between the roar of the Evinrude and the cheering, no one heard the distant screams of the old woman running toward them along the beach from the east.

Two landed perfectly, raised a hand in salute, then stopped abruptly, the tow line handle racing out ahead of him. There was debris in the water, something his father should have anticipated. Two's ski had caught the angled branch of a partly submerged log. His lanky body—for he took after his father—catapulted skyward, flipped once, hit the water at high speed and an awkward angle, and never moved again. The impact snapped his neck. He was dead instantly. Edwinna Rutherford stopped running along the beach, dropped to her knees, and curled her body into a ball on the sand, howling. No one noticed her; there were too many other screams.

A month later, when al-Qaeda terrorists destroyed the twin towers of the World Trade Center in New York, killing thousands, the horror barely registered in Pete's consciousness. She had not left their darkened Seattle home on Capitol Hill since the accident and had spoken to no one, except to try to console Justine, who was inconsolable.

Then, in November, in a moment of unexpected intimacy, the kind that occurs when a woman seeks comfort and reassurance from her husband and gets sex instead, a child was conceived. And though she was already thirty-five and hadn't wanted more children, it soon became clear to everyone that the baby would be Pete's salvation.

But Tyler didn't share her joy. When they learned the child would be another boy, something in Tyler's soul disconnected. What Pete saw as a miraculous second chance Tyler saw as a cosmic rebuke; a living reminder of his failure as a father to do the one thing men exist to do: protect their women and children. Two was gone because of Tyler's characteristic carelessness, his willful ignorance of consequences, his chronic immaturity. Two was the recklessly confident athlete he himself once had been. Tyler saw himself reflected in his boy, felt reborn in that young body. Through Two, Tyler thought he could rewrite his own history. Two was his hope.

And hope had died.

ADAM HAD ALWAYS liked Colin and this summer he'd become a frequent visitor to Colin's cottage on the bluff. He'd bicycle around inner Quartermaster Harbor and show up unannounced, like a dog seeking shelter. He'd sit on the edge of Colin's deck, his legs swinging rhythmically, humming a bit to himself from time to time as if waiting, patient as a fly-fisherman, for something interesting to emerge from the water far below.

Colin was never sure why Adam had started visiting. Maybe for the quiet. The family compounds down at Madrona Beach tended to be boisterous, the recreational activities frantically competitive—so different from those of year-round islanders whose weekend ambitions ran to trolling slowly for salmon in the deep channel off Dalco Point, or pulling their crab pots and steaming the meaty Dungeness crabs they'd caught, or puttering in the garden, or, come winter, jigging for squid at night at the end of the Ellisport pier.

One thing Colin was sure of was that Adam didn't visit for the fun. Or the conversation. They hardly talked. They didn't play. Their relationship was affectionate but oddly formal.

"Hey, I'm thirsty after my bike ride and you must be, too. Want something to drink?"

A nod.

"I got juice and lemonade."

"What kinda juice?"

"Cranberry, I think."

"Lemonade." Pause. "Please."

"You got it. How're things down at the beach?"

Shrug.

Colin often wished he'd had a natural aptitude for play. He didn't. Every time the boy visited he felt he'd failed him in some way, by not thinking up games, by not talking in a high, excited, child-energizing happy voice. It wasn't that Colin was depressive. He often thought the happy part of him existed in a state of dormancy, as if his store of joy was like a tight ball of tinder waiting for some external spark to set it alight. He envied those to whom playfulness seemed to come naturally and easily. He wondered what combination of brain chemicals it was, what package of neurotransmitters he'd missed getting at birth that made normal people happy. As for play, he was sure it was a learned skill. If you grew up in an environment that was safe, where there was a certain assured percentage of happiness like a minimum daily dietary requirement, then playfulness grew just like the rest of you. Like your bones and muscles. But if you had a chronic deficit in this nutritional category, you were stunted. Colin was stunted.

As a consequence, when Adam visited, Colin felt stiff and anxious despite his affection for the boy. But while this stiffness plagued him, it seemed of no matter to Adam. Adam was not interested in being entertained. Adam came, Colin guessed, simply for the companionship. Colin respected Adam, was in fact a bit in awe of him. He attended to the boy, took him seriously, talked to him like an adult, and listened. That's why they were friends.

Adam was curled in the lap of one of Colin's big easy chairs, studying the pulp at the bottom of his empty glass as if at tea leaves, as if a solution to this latest mystery lay there.

"Wherever she is, Adam," Colin said, "I'm sure she's safe."

The boy turned to him with a flash of what was either anger or fear. Or both.

"How can you know that? You have no evidence. Things happen. Like *accidents*."

Accidents. They were the family curse; the curse of both the Petersens and the Strongs, in fact.

"I can't say why I'm sure about that, Adam. I just am. I don't expect you to believe me, but I hope you will. Maybe I'm getting like Miss Edwinna."

"Nobody's like Miss Edwinna; nobody else I know, anyway. She knows things. She sees them."

"Yes. She does."

Adam got up, went to the refrigerator, poured himself a second glass of lemonade, and returned to his chair.

"You make good lemonade."

"Thank you, Adam. The secret is I use real lemons; those small ones that are four for a dollar at the Thriftway. They have thin skins and better juice."

"Uh huh."

Adam's eyes rested on the watery distance and Colin let him brood while he changed clothes. When he returned the boy was asleep. Colin lifted the glass from his limp fingers. He wondered if Adam was exhausted, and if so why, or whether in sleep he sought refuge, and if so, from what?

eight

COLIN GRABBED THE phone halfway through the first ring. Adam stirred but slipped back into sleep effortlessly, the way children do.

"You're not so smart, either, mister," Colin heard Miss Edwinna bark. "You didn't think about how I was going to get her the hell out of the goddamned car..."

Colin smiled. "And did you?"

"Do you have any idea how old I am?"

"I would not presume to guess, Miss Edwinna."

"Too old to haul inert bodies around, I can tell you that!"

"So she's still in the car?"

"Don't be an idiot; I carried her, fireman style, into the house. The girl weighs less than a bird. Then, by way of thanks, she vomited over my shoulder and all over the kitchen floor."

"Better there than the bedroom, Edwinna."

"Go to hell. When are you coming to sort this all out?"

"I still have Adam here."

"Well, get rid of him."

Colin's phone beeped once: an incoming call, which he let go to voicemail.

"So she's conscious now?"

"Enough to throw up."

"Keep her on her side, Edwinna."

"Why?"

"So when she throws up the next time she doesn't choke."

"I'll choke you if you don't get over here, pronto."

The beeper in Colin's pocket went off. He pulled it out.

"Shit!"

"I beg your pardon?"

"Look, Miss Edwinna, I've got an emergency at the clinic; you'll have to attend to her a while longer. I'll be there as soon I've taken care of this. Try to keep her comfortable in the meantime. Gotta go."

He hung up before she could protest and then roused Adam.

"Sorry, pal, but I've got to get to the clinic. Time for you to head home anyway. Want a ride part way? I've got the van."

"What about Mom?"

Colin sat on the arm of Adam's chair and roughed up the kid's sun-bleached hair. "Like I said, I'm sure she's fine."

The boy looked unconvinced, shrugged, and stood. "I'll take a ride to the Highway, okay?"

"You got it. Bike in the van. Let's roll. Eileen? In the car, sweet girl."

The gangly dog plodded out the door Colin held open, looking more like an imperious camel than the graceful animal she truly was. That was part of her charm. She had no idea how lovely she was.

AT THE END of Quartermaster Drive, where he let Adam out just before turning north to town on the

Highway, he pulled out his cell phone and retrieved the message he'd missed while talking with Edwinna. As he'd expected, it was Patsy, his British vet tech. Because it was Labor Day, she'd been on call, which meant anyone calling the office would automatically get bounced to her number. They were a small practice and he and Patsy alternated who'd be called on days the clinic was closed. On her days, Patsy screened the calls and let him know when there was a real emergency. It was an unusual arrangement, but Patsy had trained at London's Royal Veterinary College just like Colin, though several years after he'd graduated. But when it came time to take a scalpel to an animal she had hit a wall and dropped out. Short of surgery, though, there wasn't anything he wouldn't trust her to do.

He slammed his fist on the steering wheel.

"You idiot, you should have taken Pete to *Patsy's*." Patsy, who knew him better than he knew himself, who was like an extension of himself at the clinic. She'd have known how to take care of Pete. And now there was an emergency. Or, rather, yet another.

AFTER SHE'D ABANDONED vet school, Patsy had fallen for, and stupidly gotten pregnant by, a charismatic Scottish drummer who'd subsequently immigrated to Seattle to be a part of the grunge music scene. She followed but realized after a couple of years that he'd never be anything but a marginal session player, while groups like Pearl Jam and Nirvana hit it big. Ian had talent, even a certain presence, but no ambition. More importantly, he had no long-term vision for himself, Patsy, or their four year-old daughter, Emma.

Patsy Ashton didn't have a lot of patience for slackers, and what patience she'd had with Ian had finally passed its expiration date. She hadn't clawed her way out of London's East End only to be dragged down again by someone somewhere else.

She was at the Seattle Library branch on Capitol Hill with Emma one morning, scanning the *Puget Sound Business Journal* while her daughter enjoyed story hour — the cheapest babysitting service in Seattle — when she saw an article about a new vet taking over the clinic on Vashon Island from a husband and wife who were retiring. When she read that, like her, the new vet had trained in London, she made her move. On the day Colin was scheduled to take over the practice, she and Emma caught an early bus to West Seattle, boarded the ferry to Vashon, and were waiting at the front door of the island's clinic when the new vet arrived.

"Dr. Ryan?"

"Yes?"

Patsy extended a slender hand and shook his with a strong, confident grip. "Patricia Ashton. Your new assistant."

"I don't have an assistant."

"You do now."

Her smile was so bright it was like looking directly into the sun.

"We just had a ferry ride!" the little girl beside her said, hopping on one foot.

Colin looked down at the child with the bouncing red curls and freckles, looked back at her handsome mother, laughed, and invited them both in. Patsy had her state veterinary technician license in no time and they had worked together ever since.

Patsy was a natural. She had a warm and genuine word for everyone who came into the clinic and an uncanny way of putting animals at ease...and owners as well. Though the practice was kept busy principally by the ailments and injuries of pets, the mostly rural island also supported a wide and occasionally strange array of farm animals needing assistance: horses, cows, goats, sheep, chickens, geese, pigs, llamas and alpacas, ostriches, and peacocks, among others—not to mention an organization that rescued abandoned or abused farm animals, and another that cared for injured or ill wild animals. On any given day, it was just as likely for Colin and Patsy to be treating an injured North American bald eagle or a sick wolf as someone's overfed cat.

Patsy was happiest on farm calls. Her urban upbringing notwithstanding, she was the kind of woman who thought there was nothing more delightful in the world than standing in the pouring Northwest winter rain with her arms up some cow's uterus, the water pouring off her nose while she waited patiently for the doctor to fetch the right suture thread. That was exactly the condition in which Rebecca Johns found her one February afternoon. Rebecca, a stocky, graying, non-nonsense woman, ran "Nibbling Nubians," a herd of goats she hired out like green mowers to chew through land choked with wild blackberry and other noxious shrubbery. She'd been driving by a farm in her pickup when she caught sight of Patsy kneeling in a field in the rain, next to a prostrate cow. She hit the brakes, pulled to the roadside, and jogged back along the fence.

"You okay there, Patsy?" The rain was strong and stubborn, not the usual island winter "mist."

"Never better!" Patsy shouted.

"What the hell are you doin', girl? You'll catch your death!"

"Waiting on Dr. Colin."

"Where the hell is he?"

"Needed umbilical tape, he did; went back to the clinic for it!"

"And left you holding the bag?"

Patsy laughed. "Literally! Cow just calved and I'm protecting the uterus!"

Rebecca shook her head.

"You sure you're all right?"

"Oh yeah; at least I'm not on my feet at the clinic!"

This was true. Patsy was kneeling in bloody mud the consistency and color of catsup.

"He'll be back in a few minutes; I'm fine, really..."

Rebecca threw her hands up, trudged back to her truck and yanked open the door just as Colin rounded the bend in the van. She slammed her door shut again, stood directly in the van's path, and, when Colin stopped and rolled down the window, said,

"I was wrong about you, Colin Ryan; I thought you were a gent, but you're a beast like all the other men."

Colin laughed. "Hey, I offered to send her but she said she wanted to stay!"

Rebecca looked back at the woman kneeling in the mud and chuckled.

"Doesn't surprise me in the least. Take care of that girl, Colin, you hear? One in a million, that one."

"Promise. On my honor as a beast."

"WHAT HAVE WE got, Pats?" Colin said to his tech as he came through the back door of the clinic.

"And good morning to you, too, Doctor Ryan," she said, looking up from a whimpering Jack Russell terrier.

He stopped, let his shoulders relax, and smiled.

"Good morning, Patsy. I'm sorry your holiday has been interrupted."

"Yours, too..."

"It's my job."

"And mine."

Colin shrugged. "Fair enough."

"Where's Eileen?"

"In the van. She likes to pretend I'm her chauffeur. It's like '"Driving Miss Daisy,'" except I'm not as sanguine about it as Morgan Freeman. The window's open; she'll be fine. What's happened to ruin our day?"

"It's the usual, Doc. Owner backs out of driveway right over sleeping dog. Owner disconsolate. Dog supremely pissed off at owner."

"Have you sedated her yet?"

"She's a 'he,' unless you're referring to the owner."

Colin looked at the dog and then at Patsy.

"Oh God; don't tell me..."

Patsy flashed a wicked smile. "Uh-huh."

"It's Otis."

"And his murderous mistress, 'Queen Jean,' your best, most devoted client."

"Shit. Just what I needed this morning. All right, let's have a look. What've you found so far?"

"Only a probable fractured right tibia."

Colin checked the terrier's eyes for signs of shock and then, with characteristic gentleness, murmuring to the dog as his did so, palpated its torso and limbs. The right hind leg was already swollen.

"I expect you're right, Pats; let's get x-rays."

"While you console Queen Jean?"

"Sure you wouldn't like to handle that for me?"

"I'm just a vet tech, doctor."

"And a sadist."

Patsy shrugged. "Not my problem there's some on this island think you're a hunk. Mystery to me, though."

"It's nothing to do with that; the lady's been trying to off that dog for years."

"Don't we know it! Let's hope he keeps outsmarting her; she's probably essential to our cash flow."

He took a deep breath, left the treatment room, walked down the hall and turned the corner to the reception area.

Jean Forrester launched herself into Colin's arms, her musky perfume engulfing him like the earlier morning fog.

"Oh my God, Doctor Ryan, what have I *done*?!"

Colin detached himself from the woman's embrace.

"Let's just calm down now, okay? Why don't you make yourself comfortable in that chair and we'll have a chat."

"I didn't see him, Doctor Ryan; I thought he was in the house!"

"Sit."

She obeyed immediately.

"Do you have a doggy door, Mrs. Forrester?"

"Please call me Jean."

"Do you?"

"Well, certainly; I can't be expected to be at his every beck and call, now, can I?"

"No. No of course not. I had no idea you were so...busy."

"My life is so full, Dr. Ryan."

"I'm sure it is." Colin knew Jean Forrester was the widow of a massively successful software engineer who'd worked himself into a stroke in his mid-forties, been severely paralyzed and cognitively impaired, been placed in the island's nursing home, and had finally succumbed a few years back. He had left her a great deal of money and, unfortunately, a great deal of spare time. He had also left her Otis.

"I was backing up when I heard the beast yelp..."

The woman in the chair pulled a tissue from her purse and dabbed at nonexistent tears, her makeup unblemished. Jean Forrester was a California native who'd never sunk, as she would put it, to Northwest fashion. No flats or fleece for her. He guessed she was pushing fifty, but it was hard to tell. Henna-haired and just a bit on the wrong side of voluptuous, she went everywhere in heels, never was seen without makeup, and took great care to reveal just a bit more plush, sun-tanned décolleté than was strictly necessary outside of, say, a burlesque hall.

To judge from the number of appointments she logged at the clinic, her robustly healthy Jack Russell was perennially at death's door. Ever since the dog had snapped at her, three years back, for some no doubt perfectly understandable reason, Jean had been concocting dire conditions that would require the blameless animal to be "put to sleep." First it was cancer, according, she said, to a vet on the mainland. Terminal. Best to focus on quality of life and euthanize him...though she'd misplaced the vet's paperwork. Then it was that the little dog repeatedly attacked small children in town, though there were no confirmed reports.

Olivia Mukai, Colin's unflappable Japanese-American receptionist, answered Jean's frequent calls with perfect grace and handled her in-office histrionics with the unearthly calm of a Buddhist monk. For this alone, Colin promised Olivia she would have a place in his practice forever.

"Otis will survive, Mrs. Forrester. You're very lucky...or rather Otis is. May I suggest you look behind the car first the next time you go for a drive? You could easily have killed him."

She twisted the tissue in her hands. "Are you sure we shouldn't put him out of his misery? You know, like in Oregon—that physician-assisted suicide thing...?"

"You're forgetting one thing Mrs. Forrester."

Her eyes widened. One darkly-penciled eyebrow lifted.

"The terminally ill patient makes that decision, not the patient's owner."

"But he can't speak for himself!"

"Precisely my point."

He shot her a look but she was rummaging in her purse for another tissue.

"Perhaps you'll excuse me while I attend to him?"

Radiant smile accompanied by heavy breathing. "But of course, Doctor Ryan."

"PATSY, LET'S SEE that x-ray!" he barked as he reentered the treatment room.

His assistant emerged and handed him the image. He slapped it up into the clips on the light board.

"In a hurry?" Patsy asked.

"What? Oh. Yeah. Kinda."

She looked at him while he peered at the image.

"Simple fracture. No displacement. No need for surgery. Let's wrap it."

"Colin?" Patsy seldom called him by his first name. Not in the clinic, anyway.

He looked away from the light board.

"You okay?"

And suddenly, Colin felt so heavy it was as if he couldn't support his own weight. He bent over and leaned on a stainless surgery table.

"That's sterilized, that is…"

He straightened and removed his hands.

"Sorry."

She smiled. "What's up?"

"What?"

"No, that was my question. Don't turn this into a Monty Python routine…"

"Nothing."

"Nothing, except that you don't have the time of day for this dog."

"That's not true."

"Sure?"

He leaned back against a counter and closed his eyes.

"Pete tried to kill herself this morning."

"*What?* Where? How? Bloody *hell*, Colin!"

"I found her lying in the middle of Vashon Highway south of Burton, just before dawn. Unconscious. She picked that sharp curve so no driver coming north would see her until it was too late."

Patsy stared at him for a moment, then shifted her gaze to the middle distance while she followed her racing thoughts. Finally, she refocused and said, "Or picked it because she knew you'd find her first."

Colin's head jerked up.

"Huh?"

"Half the people on this island know your morning routine. I'll bet Betty's got your cycling schedule posted by the door at the Mercantile, next to the bus and the ferry schedules."

"Patsy, she was unconscious!"

"Were her fingertips blue?"

"I don't remember. Maybe."

"What was her rate of breathing?"

"Very slow, but regular. What's this about?!"

"Those are the signs of acute alcohol poisoning."

"I'm a vet, not a doctor, Pats; how the hell would I know that? How do you know, for that matter?"

"My ex; it was an all too common condition."

"And your point is...?"

"If those were her symptoms, she was in big trouble; if they weren't, she was waiting for you to rescue her."

"That's nuts, dammit!"

"Colin?"

"What?!"

"Who are you really angry with?"

Colin looked out the window to the clinic's parking lot. Eileen was staring blank-faced out the side window of the van, as if watching television. He felt the antagonism seep from him as if into a drain in the floor. He turned back to his tech. "Not you, Patsy. Lord knows, not you."

Patsy smiled at him, a smile that, had he any sense at all, he would have recognized as enduring affection.

"Colin, you were born to rescue wounded creatures. I suspect that's why you went to your father's bar every day after school, as if by being vigilant you could keep him sober and turn him around. But then the Mob took the matter out of your hands. You fought your way to vet school, partly to be able to support your mother, but then she up and died before you could rescue her, either.

"You've been rescuing ever since, but with animals; it's why you're such a bloody brilliant vet. Hell, animals can't even tell you where it hurts, but that only makes it more challenging for you. You're neurotic as all get out, but you've figured out a way to make it pay the bills."

Colin looked up and shrugged. "Thank you. I think."

Patsy regarded her boss for a moment. *The guy's an original, hopeless and wonderful all at once.* She shook her head. Then something occurred to her.

"Who was on call at the medical center?"

"I didn't take her there."

"*What?* Where is she? Don't tell me you left her at your place in that condition!"

"No. She's with Miss Edwinna."

"Rutherford?"

"The one and only."

"That woman's batty!"

"You're wrong about that. Look, use your lovely head for something besides a hat rack: the Petersens and Strongs would go ballistic if word got out that she'd tried to commit suicide."

"I can't believe this."

"What?"

"That you're more concerned about the bloody reputations of the bloody summer people than you are about Pete's life!"

Colin stared at her.

"That's bullshit, and to borrow a phrase, who are you really angry with?'"

Patsy clamped her hands on each side of her head, as if containing an explosion. "*You!* You're risking your reputation as a doctor for their reputation as...what? Pillars of Vashon society? They don't even live here but two months of the year!"

"Like I said, I'm a vet, not a doctor, and besides, there was something else."

"Now what?"

"There are bruises around both her wrists: signs of forcible restraint, or a fight. I don't know which and it hardly matters. I thought she needed someplace safe."

Patsy stood as if flash frozen. Just as quickly, she thawed, reached across the surgery table and took his hand in both of hers. His was cold, from anxiety. Hers were warm.

"Colin. You did the right thing. I didn't know it was so ugly. I'm sorry I railed at you. What can I do to help?"

"Wrap that pup's leg and let me slip out the back door? Just tell Lizzie Borden out there I had a farm call."

"You got it, buster."

Colin stepped forward and surprised her with a hug.

"I don't know what I'd do without you, Pats," he said quietly. And he held on.

She shrugged him off to conceal her surprise. "Go on, get outta here; some of us have work to do."

When the door closed, she mumbled, "Damned shame nobody was around to rescue him when he needed it..."

nine

PATSY ASHTON CRUISED west on Cove Road in her aging Subaru, heading home. It was still early and the sun had yet to hit the tips of the summer-dried grasses on the slopes and meadows on the west side of the island. That would come later, in the afternoon, when the day would wane and the slanting late summer light would illuminate every mote of pollen and dust in the air and make this part of the island look gilded.

Home for Patsy Ashton was the Colvos Store, a lovingly restored one-story structure with a two-story façade like something from the main street in a dusty Wild West town. It had been built in the early nineteen twenties as a general store to serve the daily needs of the largely Scandinavian families who'd settled this part of the island. They'd emigrated and found on Vashon a water-girt, conifer-clad world not unlike their homeland, but without the brutal winters. They cut timber, cleared land, and farmed this side of the island, eventually specializing in egg production and orchard fruits. The old store still had a wooden boardwalk that ran the width of the building, designed originally to protect customers from the mud and horse manure in the forecourt where, to this day, a solitary and ancient gas pump stood, the kind with the glass face showing the level of the fuel, now long gone dry; a sentinel reminder of simpler times.

When the shiny new Thriftway supermarket opened in the center of town, the little store struggled on for a few years, battling against the currents of change like a salmon thrashing itself upstream. When it finally came up at auction, there were few bidders; Patsy was the highest. Where others saw a relic, she saw a home as quirky and individual as she was.

Over the years, she'd pulled down the old horsehair and plaster walls and ceilings and replaced them with insulation and sheetrock, rewired and re-plumbed, traded the drafty single-pane windows for double-glazed ones custom-made to preserve the building's character, sanded and finished the old end-grain fir floors so that they glowed warm and mellow as the flesh of butternut squash, repainted, hung curtains, restored the wood-fired cooking stove, and added a modern Propane stove as well. It had taken years and with every stage of the project, as she mastered the skills required, Patsy grew stronger and more self-reliant.

Not that self-reliance ever had been her objective. She would much rather have had a partner or husband to handle such chores, but she didn't. And it wasn't for lack of suitors. Patsy was a radiant, leggy blonde with an easy laugh, and even now, with her daughter grown, she still turned heads at the supermarket. In fact, it was hard for her to get through the store in under an hour if she stopped in after work, because half the customers, people she generally knew only by their pet's name, would chat her up. That included any number of available men, none of whom interested her.

She knew there was talk on the island about her and Colin, but talk was all there was. Though their friendship was long and strong, built on trust and shared experience, theirs had never been more than a working partnership.

Not that there hadn't been opportunities. On the clinic's first anniversary, they'd closed the door at five and opened an obscenely expensive bottle of Dom Pérignon that a grateful customer had given them. Colin had gotten uncharacteristically mushy after the last fluted glass was emptied and invited her to his house above Tramp Harbor for dinner. Patsy had declined. She was already paying overtime for Emma at the nursery school, about which Colin knew nothing, and she was afraid. She was afraid of how much she loved him. She was afraid that, if she revealed herself, he'd pull away. The thought of the two of them alienated, their exchanges stilted afterward at the clinic, ruining everything they'd built in the preceding months, terrified her. She'd given him a hug and told him to drive carefully on the way home.

She'd rued that decision ever since. No, that wasn't entirely true; it was the right decision, then. He wasn't hers to be had; he was still Pete's, not that she'd ever have him. Oh, yes, Pete loved him, in her way, but her way did not include straying from the path that had seemed set for her almost from birth, the path that connected the Petersens and the Strongs, that tied pliant Pete to handsome Tyler, the path that bound their histories as certainly as their real estate. She didn't know either of them well, had only been to a few of their beach parties, but it seemed to her that Pete wasn't the kind of person who made things happen; she was the kind who had things happen to her. Tyler had happened to her. Patsy didn't believe Pete had either the imagination or the courage to choose for herself.

Patsy pulled into the gravel forecourt of the Colvos Store just as her cell phone began playing its salsa ring tone.

"Damn, not another emergency." But when she flipped open her phone she knew the caller.

"Emma!"

"Mom! Guess what?!"

Patsy smiled. "Okay, let me guess: you've found the love of your life, you've hit the Mega Millions lottery, you've got a new piercing, or tattoo or something, you've..."

"Mom..."

"I'm listening."

"I'm in! They found the scholarship money. I'm going to med school at the University of Washington!"

"It's Labor Day; you got mail?"

"Email. One of the scholarship students pulled out; I was next. I start in a week!"

"Oh, Emma, I am so thrilled! Truly! But to twist in the wind waiting for word on financial aid so long...I'm so sorry I couldn't afford to send you..."

"Mom, stop. You got me to this point, okay? All on your own. You're my hero and I don't want to hear any apologies. Just cheers."

"Okay, I'm cheering. And I'm very proud."

"I love you, Mom."

"I love you too, kiddo. But I didn't do it all on my own."

"I know. Will you call Colin?"

Colin had been bewitched by Patsy's daughter from that first meeting at the door of the new clinic the day he opened. And over the years he'd been a devoted "uncle"—helping with her homework at the clinic after school when he could, going to her science fairs, being in the audience at her school plays, and finally mediating battles she'd had with her mother when she'd hit her teens. But before he was ready for it, she was grown; a fiery redheaded version of her own strong, smart mother.

"No, Emma, I won't. I think he'd want to hear the news directly from you."

"Yeah, you're right. I'll call him."

"But maybe not just now."

"Is he on a farm call?"

"No."

"Then...?"

"He's dealing with an emergency. With Pete."

"Oh, Christ, what the hell is it now?"

"Emma!"

"Okay, okay. But Jeez, Mom, sometimes it's like she has him on a leash or something, like he's her pet. The Mascot of Madrona Beach!"

Patsy sighed. "Look, sweetie, it's dead simple, okay? He loves her."

"You know what, Mom? I don't believe that. I don't think you do, either. Maybe he did once. Maybe they were soul mates once. Okay, I get that. But after all this time I think it's just a habit with both of them. And not a good one."

"Emma, he found her at dawn, unconscious, in the middle of Vashon Highway. She was trying to kill herself."

"No way."

"Way."

"No, I mean there's no way she would kill herself; she's too self-absorbed."

"You planning on going into psychiatry?"

"I'm serious. Look, Colin taught me to swim on that beach, right? I spent a lot of time with those people. I watched her, partly because it seemed to me they all led a kind of charmed life. Pete...she's like the scion of the Petersen clan, upholding...well, I don't know what. And she and Colin are close, it's true. But it seems pretty one-sided to me. I mean, you know... Pete gets someone thoughtful and caring to talk to, at least for two months in the summer, but what's Colin get out of it? I can't figure it out. It's like she lives off of him. Like an emotional parasite! And he actually wants to be the host body."

"That's ridiculous. And rude."

"Come on, Mom. Don't tell me it's never occurred to you. Hell, I'd live off Colin, too, if I was married to Tyler Strong."

"What's got into you today?" Patsy had never heard Emma be so outspoken before, especially about Colin, who she knew her daughter loved. Maybe it was the newfound financial independence and her dream of a life in medicine coming true. Or maybe she'd just made another of her developmental plateau-jumps, like she did as a child, and this time she'd gone from being daughter to advisor.

"Mom, Tyler Strong's a letch! He was after me the moment I got boobs. Don't you even notice these things?

The fact that Pete continues to live with him and put up with him tells me she's just plain lazy. Or in denial. She doesn't want to upset her cushy life."

"She lost a son, for heaven's sake, Emma. Maybe she's had all the upset she can handle."

And as she said this, Patsy wondered whether she'd been wrong about doubting Pete's attempted suicide. Maybe Pete had simply had enough.

"Okay, forget about her," Emma continued. "Look what she does to Colin: here's this guy who's one of the sweetest, most centered men on the planet, and then, in July and August, it's like he's been taken over by aliens."

"I think you've been watching too many science fiction movies…"

"You don't see it? The way he gets all anxious and hyper-vigilant about her?"

"That's enough, Emma! That man has been as good as a father to you. Maybe better. He loves you. You have no idea…"

"Yes, I do, and I love him, too. That's why this makes me crazy! It should make you crazy, too!"

It did, of course. Colin's relationship with Pete drove Patsy quietly, seasonally wild, year after year, the way that the Mistral, that summer wind in southern France, was said to make people crazy. For years, her strategy had been simply to wait the season out. Come autumn, he'd become his gentle, caring self again. You could set your watch by it.

"Why should it make me crazy?" she lied. "It's his life."

"Because you love him even more than I do, Mom."

"We're not getting into that."

"Why not? Why do we *never* get into that? You said it yourself; he's been like a father to me. Why aren't you his *wife*?!"

"I'm hanging up."

"No, you're not."

"I am. I'm really happy about your news, sweetie; I'm over the moon. But it's time to say bye-bye for now."

"Mom, this is important! This is about *you*! Honestly, I don't know which of you is crazier…"

Patsy hit the red "End" button on her phone. The sun had cleared the island's center ridge and it was hot as a sweat lodge in her car. Still, she didn't move. And she didn't pick up when, almost immediately, Emma called back. She'd listen to the rest of the rant on her voicemail. Patsy would kill for her daughter, but she couldn't tolerate being lectured to by her. There were times she wondered whether Emma had ever truly left behind that "My mother is an idiot" phase that seemed to have started, like an alarm clock going off, the day after the girl's thirteenth birthday.

She sat in the baking heat and thought, for the millionth time, about Colin Ryan. He was a brilliant and intuitive veterinarian. But he was dim as a post when it came to women. Pete wasn't the only woman about whom he was blind, oh no. And it didn't help that he had no idea how attractive he was to women. Patsy saw it every day. They sensed his gentleness as if it were a fragrance in the air; those who were clients saw it at work with their animals. But he never relaxed his professional distance, never let anyone too close, as if he could not separate the personal from the professional. Or didn't want to.

He'd done that once, Patsy knew. And it nearly did him in.

Eight years after he'd taken over the veterinary practice, Colin had been sitting on a high stool at the end of the bar at the Hardware Store bistro early one summer evening, finishing off a fragrant bowl of local mussels steamed in white wine with apple, bacon, thyme and shallots, and was savoring a perfectly chilled bottle of Oregon Pinot Gris that sat in a condensation-beaded metal ice bucket beside him. Dinner at the Hardware Store was a present he gave himself every Friday after he closed the clinic. He liked the warm light, the babble of voices as the weekend got started, the clients and friends who stopped to chat with him on their way to a table. On these Fridays he could almost believe he knew everyone on the island.

He was just pouring himself a second glass when a voice at his elbow said,

"You gonna monopolize that bottle?"

Colin looked to his left to find a petite woman of about thirty standing by his chair. Her hair was dark brown and cut in a bob that angled up and back from her chin to a point high on the nape of her neck. He remembered that the Japanese believed that the nape of a woman's neck was deeply erotic, and, in this case, he agreed. Hers was smooth and pale, with fine wisps of hair that caught the gleam of the spotlights above the bar. Her creamy skin was emphasized by the standing collar of her quirkily geometric jacket in white rayon that was folded and pleated like an origami sculpture. Below the asymmetrical tails of the jacket, she wore narrow black

Capri pants and strappy, high-heeled sandals, also black. There was also a black and white ikat weave scarf rolled and tied, pirate-style, around her forehead, its tails cascading down to her left shoulder. She managed to look simultaneously unorthodox and fashionable.

"It is, after all, mine," he answered finally. "Unless you are my date."

"Were you expecting one?"

"No, but one is ever hopeful of good fortune."

"Does fortune follow you?"

"On occasion."

"Then perhaps this is one of those, but a gentleman would offer the lady a glass of his wine."

"Am I a gentleman?"

"That remains to be seen."

"Are you a lady?"

The woman stood on a rung of his chair, hoisted herself over the counter, and grabbed a clean wine glass from the drying rack behind the bar.

"Only when I have to be," she answered, taking a seat beside him and holding out the glass.

It took him a moment to recognize that he knew the woman. He had encountered her some weeks earlier while he was kayaking on the mirror-still water of outer Quartermaster Harbor just before sunset. She was in a single rowing shell, pulling hard on the oars, intent on her form. She was also on a collision course with his kayak.

"Hey!" he'd yelled to the rower.

A pretty head turned. "Oops! I guess I was just in the zone!"

"That's what I don't get about rowing," he called, maneuvering his kayak out of her way. "You can't see where you're going!"

"It's not about the view; it's about the workout," the rower cried as she sped past him, never missing a stroke. Within moments, she was a hundred yards distant and pulling away fast. He let her go.

Now, at the bar, he eased the pale straw-colored wine down the inside slope of her glass.

"I trust you will find this Lange Estate Reserve Pinot Gris an exemplar of its type: refreshing acidity and hints of apple, kiwi, and pear. That will be nine dollars."

"What? That's robbery!" Her eyes, green with flecks of gold, flashed like sparklers.

"No, that's quality. In life, you get what you pay for. Or do you make it a habit to badger strangers for free drinks?"

"You're not a stranger; you're that vet."

"How can you be sure?"

"Your picture is in the island newspaper this week; you brutalize quadrupeds."

It was true. The paper was running a series on island businesses. A reporter had followed him for a day and taken pictures as he neutered a pair of goats on a farm call. The reporter was male and left early, pale and unsettled by the procedure.

"And you're no stranger to me," Colin countered.

"Oh?" She paused, one delicately sculpted and deftly shaded eyebrow lifted in skepticism. But he knew he had her.

He ducked his head and leaned toward her. "I have certain powers," he confided, "and these powers tell me all your secrets."

Then he sat upright, took a sip of his wine, and returned to his dinner.

She watched him. He waited.

"Meaning?" she said finally.

He put down his fork, finished the wine in his glass, and signaled to the bartender, Bert, who owned a slobbering black Newfoundland with a penchant for eating whatever household items might be lying about—in short, a regular customer at the clinic.

When Bert arrived with the fresh bottle, he poured a measure into both their glasses.

"Show me your hands, palms up," Colin ordered. There was a trace of boredom in his voice, as if he did this all the time.

She thrust them toward him as if in silent challenge.

Colin took the hands, noted the absence of a ring, turned them over and back again, and then closed his eyes, as if receiving information from the cosmos. Finally he let them go.

"So?"

"You wish me to tell you what I know?"

"Only if it gets me more wine."

"Very well." While he topped her glass she snagged a crostini from his plate.

He was having a wonderful time. "I may be frank?"

"Of course."

"You are a lady of taste." Here he lowered his voice and leaned toward her. "But also of reduced circumstances."

He sat back. "And you are not from the Northwest."

"That's preposterous."

"Is it?"

Colin may have left New York City and London behind, but he hadn't left behind his appreciation of urban fashion, or of beautiful women. He elaborated:

"You are wearing a highly unusual jacket of exquisite tailoring. It is, I believe, an Issey Miyake original or, if not, an excellent copy. It is also, I might add, a perfect choice to pair with those pencil-thin slacks: architecture above, simplicity below, nothing to draw attention from the main event. However, Miyake has not had a collection in that fabric for nearly a decade and the edge of the right cuff is frayed, suggesting either that you have been careless with something beautiful, or that you acquired it second-hand. I suspect the latter since, judging by the way you hold your glass, you are left-handed. And by the way, a woman born and raised here in the Northwest would never appreciate the artistry in that jacket, as it is made of neither fleece nor Gore-Tex. I compliment you."

The woman smiled, but said nothing.

"And then there is the matter of your heels: very high quality sandals—from Nordstrom's Rack, I suspect—and very possibly Blahniks. But the lifts are worn almost to the shank. Carelessness? Neglect?"

He regarded the hands again. "Your manicure, by the way, is perfect, and, thankfully, free of those gaudy inserts that seem the rage among a certain class of women these days. You have had a pedicure, too. These are, to my mind, quiet signs of taste and visible expressions of self-respect. What's more, manicures and pedicures are an inexpensive indulgence, well within your budget. Shall I continue?"

"I should probably have slapped you by now, but I haven't, so do go on…"

"I believe it is also the case that you are an athlete of some kind. Let me think about this."

He gazed over her shoulder for a few moments, feigning concentration.

"You are trim, your shoulders square, your posture upright. Though petite, I suspect you are strong. Your sport involves your hands," he continued. "Your fingers, while graceful, are calloused. You are, I believe, a rower."

He dropped her hands, took a sip from his glass, and waited.

The woman beside him set her glass on the bar, leaned on one elbow, cupped her very slightly dimpled chin in one hand, and squinted at him.

"Who the fuck are you?" she said, her voice barely audible above the rising clamor at the bar.

"The vet?"

"You know what I mean."

Colin smiled. "I'm the guy in the kayak you tried to run over in your rowing shell a couple of weeks ago."

"You cheated!"

"Isn't it more important that I remembered?"

"You have a point. You're gonna tell me how you worked out all the rest of this stuff, right?"

"Right."

"At my place?"

"Sure."

"Now?"

"If you wish."

"I do."

Her name was Morgan Madison. She was born in Chicago, raised in Seattle, and went to Evergreen State College, a "progressive" school in Olympia, Washington, where she studied sociology and art. After two years, she dropped out and moved back to Seattle, where she made and sold costume jewelry and worked part time at a succession of leftist "social change" organizations. When she finally got bored with causes, she married an older and quite successful surgeon who practiced at Seattle's Children's Hospital and also did volunteer work. Six years and no children later, her husband, Rory, left to volunteer for a month in Somalia.

"Rebels shot him dead the first week," she told Colin in bed later that evening.

"I'm sorry," he said, pulling her closer.

"Why? You didn't shoot him."

"I'm just sorry you had to live through that."

"That was the least of it."

"What do you mean?"

"Apart from a small life insurance policy, he'd left all his money to Médicins San Frontières."

"Doctors Without Borders?"

"Yeah. Very high-minded, he was. I had to sell the house on Queen Anne. I came to Vashon to visit a girlfriend, liked it, found a bungalow I could afford off Beall Road, and went back to making jewelry. Haven't you seen my booth at the Saturday market?"

"Saturday's a workday at the clinic."

"So that means you'll be leaving early in the morning?"

"Um, yes."

She climbed on top of him. "Then stop talking and make me scream again."

While they lived together, Colin paid most of her bills so she could pursue her art and invested thousands of dollars in renovating and expanding "their" house. A year later, Morgan announced she was moving to Vancouver, British Columbia to live with a resort-builder she'd met while on a skiing holiday with her girlfriends at Whistler Mountain.

She sold the house, walked away with all the accrued equity, and threatened under Washington's common property statute to take fifty percent of the income Colin earned during the year he'd supported her if he ever tried to reclaim the money he'd spent on her house.

Patsy thought later that Colin's fiery relationship with Morgan was like being catapulted into the empty sky by a trebuchet, only to fall to earth again. The ascent was thrilling, the landing crushing. It took more than a year for Colin to recover, and Patsy ached through all of it. What he obsessed over, when he said anything, was the deception's one-two punch: the infidelity and the theft. Why hadn't he seen it coming?

One day, she answered him.

"Look, I know you loved her, doc, and you wanted to save her. Only one problem with that."

Colin looked at her.

"She didn't need saving; you did. She knew what she was doing."

She watched as Colin shook his head in disbelief.

"Sometimes I think you watched too many of those *Lone Ranger* shows on TV when you were a kid," she said. "You're always trying to ride in on the white horse to save the day. But you know what? While that works fine in medicine, it hardly ever works in life. And you know something else?"

Colin looked up.

"They didn't call him the 'Lone' Ranger for nothing. Like the song says, *His horse and his saddle were his only companions...*"

Colin smiled at last. "He had Tonto."

"I'm sure that was a great comfort on cold nights."

ten

"COLIN!"

It was the second summer after he had met Pete and Tyler, and he had been summoned to the beach compound again, this time for a ceremony.

Though he had just turned away from his car, Pete was already airborne. He caught her in mid-air, and swung her around in a wide circle of joy. She was in tennis togs.

When he lowered her to the grass, she bounced like a child.

"I *knew* you'd make it! It wouldn't be right without you!"

"It," was her wedding to Tyler Strong in mid-June. The families had come to the beach early for the event, two weeks before the Fourth.

His own feelings for her aside, Colin never really had any doubt that Tyler and Pete would marry, though perhaps not quite this soon. That the wedding would be held at Madrona Beach also seemed foretold.

Colin wrapped Pete in a hug, kept her there for longer than was perhaps appropriate under the circumstances, then held her away from him. He was surprised to see her tears shining in the sunlight. But she was smiling.

"How are you, little cub?" he asked.

They had evolved nicknames. Colin, from black Irish stock, a descendant, his mother had claimed, of a Spanish nobleman washed ashore in Kerry after the defeat of the Armada, had matured to become a big-boned six-footer with a dark, neatly-trimmed beard and a helmet of close-cropped, curly brown hair. His chest was a mass of inky curls as well, a source of embarrassment to him, as if he hadn't quite fully evolved, but also an odd source of attraction to certain women. Pete had taken to calling him "big bear." He called her "little cub."

She took his arm and led him across the lawn.

"Bored is how I am! I'm waiting to play doubles, but Tyler and Rob have been at match point forever!"

He stopped and looked at her and she finally understood.

"Oh! And happy! Really, Colin. It's what I've always wanted."

"Good. Yes, that's good. I'm glad."

He turned toward the tennis court.

"That's Rob March?"

"Yeah, I know, he's gained a lot of weight since last summer. Tyler was killing him, but Rob's caught up. He works harder than Tyler, despite the weight, but Tyler's better-trained. They've been cycling between advantage and deuce for twenty minutes and neither will yield."

"I'll go over and be a distraction."

"Colin?"

He turned to the tiny tanned woman with the chiseled chin beside him.

"I am so glad you're here. You have no idea."

He disengaged his arm, patted her shoulder, and walked toward the fenced tennis court behind the Old House.

Pete watched him cross the lawn. Instead of entering the fenced tennis court, he chose to stand quietly in the shade of a hawthorn tree and watch. She knew Colin didn't play tennis. Tennis was a country club brat's sport and country clubs, she guessed, would have been thin on the ground among the tenements on Manhattan's West Side where he'd grown up. But she knew that wasn't why he stayed outside. It was his natural reticence, a kind of modesty—not weak, but strong. Unlike Tyler, Colin did not need to prove himself, did not need to be the center of attention.

For the hundredth time since their meeting in London she thought, *he loves me. I love him, too. Such a good man. But it's too late now.*

She turned away and headed for the old Petersen house. *It was always too late, dammit. Preordained. And nothing I can do about it now, anyway.*

WATCHING THE TWO tennis opponents, Colin was struck by the stark differences in their playing style. Though Tyler's shirt was drenched with sweat, his strokes were fluid, almost effortless. He appeared, as if by magic, in just the right spot to return Rob's shots. Rob, on the other hand, was all effort. Grunting on his serves, and groaning with each return, he stalked the court like a beast after prey.

Colin liked Rob. The summer before, Rob had become the newest young lawyer in Old Adam's firm. He was the son of Adam's late partner, Eli March. There was something in the gentle giant's nature that calmed the turbulence that occasionally rippled across the surface of the beach families' relationships. The surviving members of the three families—the Petersens, Strongs, and Rutherfords—were so tightly knit that it was as if they had a blood connection. But old childhood rivalries occasionally flared among both parents and offspring. When they did, it was Rob, the newest member, who was the oil cast upon the waters that made it possible for sparring friends or warring partners to let go of their ancient hurts and get on with just being.

The Marches had no summer home on the island, but Old Adam invited Rob to the beach because he saw depth in the big man. He wasn't a member of the beach families, but he was a member of the firm's family, and that was good enough for Old Adam.

When Colin had met him the summer before, Rob had reminded him of the slightly pudgy kid in high school who never quite fit in but always could be counted on to help you with your homework. Earnest. Seriously smart. There was a pretty blonde girl, a relative of the Rutherfords called Peggy, on whom Rob had his eye that summer and Colin wondered if she had been invited to the wedding too.

He returned his attention to the game.

As he watched from the shade of the hawthorn, Colin began to see Tyler's strategy: he was running Rob around the court to wear him down enough to make mistakes. Once again at deuce, Rob rocketed a predictable passing shot down the line. Tyler let it go, conserving his energy.

"Advantage!" Rob crowed.

A condescending nod from Tyler. *I'm toying with you, you idiot, and you don't even know it.*

After his next serve, Rob charged the net and Tyler popped a short lob over Rob's head and out of reach.

"Shit!"

"No, I believe that's deuce again, old man." Smirk.

Colin left the shade of the hawthorn, entered the court, and sat on the slatted green wooden bench at the sideline. A nod of recognition from Rob; nothing from Tyler. Tyler was aware of only the court. Rob's next serve was an ace that left Tyler flatfooted when the ball nailed the far corner. Rob danced briefly, like a circus bear.

"Advantage, Rob," Colin now called from the bench.

"No shit," Tyler snapped.

Rob served again, softly this time to catch Tyler off-guard. But Tyler swept his racquet just above the rubberized green surface of the court, lobbed the ball over Rob's head, laughed dismissively, and waved his racquet, as if saying, "Bye, bye!"

But Rob lumbered back, reached, reached, connected, and executed a blind forehand return over his left shoulder. Tyler, so confident Rob would fail, didn't even turn to follow the arc of the ball, and thus did not see it drop, with a puff of dust, just inside the baseline.

"That's game," Colin called.

"What!?"

"It fell inside. Just."

Rob whooped and pumped his racquet in the air.

Tyler slammed the edge of his racquet on the top of the net over and over until the wire cable supporting it sang. Colin was stunned by the ferocity. Tyler whipped around toward Colin.

"That was your fault, bastard!"

"Uh-huh, and thank you for that gracious welcome, loser."

Tyler stalked to the sidelines, dropped onto the bench, and stared at the dirt as the sweat from his forehead left spots as black as blood on the court surface. "Why did I invite you to this wedding? Remind me."

"You didn't; the bride's family issues the invitations."

"True. Never saw your attraction, to be honest."

Rob arrived, Colin shook his hand and turned back to Tyler.

"There wasn't any, Tyler, and you know that. She was always yours, my friend. To be honest."

THAT AFTERNOON, OVER drinks on the porch, Colin watched Tyler. Knowing him as he did, he had expected an anxious jauntiness, a mix of groom's day-before jitters and Tyler's characteristic bravado. Instead, his friend seemed oddly subdued. Colin put it down to tennis exhaustion initially, but as the afternoon wore on, it seemed to him that his friend was like a man in slow motion, slogging as if through hip-deep mud, not toward the matrimonial altar but toward execution. A dead man walking. Colin put himself in Tyler's place: if he'd been about to marry Pete, he'd feel only elation. He'd be over the moon. But would he ever have put himself in Tyler's place? Would he ever have asked Pete if she loved him, asked her to marry him? No, it wasn't his place to do so. It would never be his place. He was not one of them.

After dinner, in a spasm of traditionalism, Pete banished Tyler from her sight until the morning's ceremony. It was bad luck, she said, for him to see her again until she was in her wedding gown, approaching the minister—her own father—on the arm of old Adam Strong, Tyler's uncle.

As the dishes were being cleared, Pete appeared at Colin's side.

"I need a walk on the beach. Will you come?"

"Of course."

She smiled and took his arm.

The two of them sloshed along the tide line for a while in companionable silence. To the west, the sun had dipped behind the fir-clad hills and the cobalt blue sky began fading to the color of robin's eggs. Across the outer harbor and beyond the low hills of Maury Island the almost iridescent white cap of "the mountain," as everyone here called towering Mount Rainier, had turned the color of pale Spanish sherry. All around them the visible world seemed to slip from three dimensions to two, the low hills flattening to a navy blue screen.

Colin finally spoke. "You okay, luv?"

Pete squeezed his arm against her side and smiled but said nothing.

A little farther on, looking out across the darkening water, she said, "It's what was meant to be. All along. This is where it's all been going."

"This wedding?"

"Well, marrying Tyler, anyway."

"You act as if it was inevitable."

"I wouldn't say that."

"What would you say?"

She paused. "Preordained. I think that's what I'd say... *preordained*."

"As in, not a choice?"

"As in part of the plan, part of the natural order of things."

"I never took you for a fatalist."

"I'm not.

"Then...?"

"Life is what you're given; this is what I've been given."

"That's bullshit. Life is what you make of it."

To his surprise, she giggled.

"What?"

She hugged his arm again. "If I'd been given as little as you were, I'd believe life was what I made of it, too. But I have had a certain degree of privilege, haven't I?"

"With no mother and an absentee father?"

"No, with the interwoven safety net of the Petersens, the Strongs, and, to a lesser extent, perhaps, the Rutherfords, not just here on the beach but in town, too. We're like a tiny galaxy, held together by our own form of gravity. That's part of what draws Tyler and me together, what keeps us together."

"The weight of history?"

"No. Or at least not just that. Something else, but I think it's related. We are known to each other. Do you know what I mean? I think everyone, deep down, longs to be known—truly known—to someone. There is such a comfort in that. I think that's the foundation of love. Tyler and I, we've always had that."

Colin wanted to argue with her, but there wasn't any point. He'd never pressed his case and this wasn't time to start. He nudged the conversation off on a tangent.

"If that's the case, what's up with Tyler this afternoon? Where's the dazzled groom?"

Pete said nothing for a moment. She used the soles of her feet like paddles to spray seawater out ahead of her as she walked through the shallows. Finally, she spoke.

"I think it's his mother. She's not coming."

"Mother? He's never said a thing to me about his mother."

"No, I don't suppose he would have."

"Meaning?"

Again, silence.

"Tyler's dad, Richie Strong?" she said finally. "He was a famous pilot."

"So he said, but he's never told me much about him, either."

"He seldom does. But I will. You deserve an answer. Tyler's dad was something of an aviation hero. Went to Billie Boeing's flight school down in Oakland before the war. He was maybe twenty. Came home with a commercial pilot's license and a wife, Amanda James. She was a secretary at the school; I don't think she was even eighteen yet. American Airlines, which was only a couple of years old, had already heard about Richie from Boeing and they snapped him up."

"Wow."

"Yeah. And then, in World War II, the president of American Airlines, a guy named C. R. Smith, was made head of something called the Air Transport Command. Their job was to ferry planes filled with equipment and soldiers back and forth across the Atlantic. Tyler's dad was one of the first pilots Smith commandeered under the war powers. Apparently, Smith already had Richie on his radar screen. Tyler's uncle..."

"Old Adam?"

"Yeah, well Old Adam told me Smith used his brother for all kinds of top secret missions. One story is he took General Mark Clark, who was tight with Eisenhower, deep into North Africa to oversee the campaign against Rommel there. The plane he piloted was flanked by a dozen fighters."

"Impressive."

"Yeah. Old Adam's crazy about his kid brother. It's very sweet. Anyway, after the war, Richie went back to American Airlines. He was already one of their most senior pilots and he was only thirty. Flew for them from then on, from prop planes to jets. Then he was killed.

"What, he crashed or something?"

"Yeah, he did."

"Oh, man..."

"In a car."

They'd reached the far west end of the beach, where the sand gave way to sharp, barnacle-encrusted rocks. When they turned, they could just see the tip of Rainier, above the hills across the harbor, glowing as if aflame.

"For years," Pete continued, "everyone said it was an accident; Richie was driving his car, a convertible, too fast. Hit a telephone pole. Nineteen sixty-two."

"Shit. All those years in the air and he dies on the ground. That's so ironic."

"And wrong."

"Yeah, that too."

"No, I mean it didn't happen that way."

"What?"

"Tyler's father killed himself."

Colin stopped and stared at her. "Jesus, Pete!"

"It's all about Amanda."

"Tyler's mom?"

"I got this from Old Adam, after several bourbons, okay? Tyler doesn't know I know. Please don't say anything."

"Okay. Promise."

"Old Adam and his wife Emily made room for Richie and Amanda at the beach house, right here, after they'd married. Emily was the only daughter of Silas Wolfenden, the founder of Wolfenden Industries, the timber giant, and Silas gave Adam and Emily the land here on the beach. Silas had cut all the timber decades before and it was all new growth then. Old Adam's got a big heart; he built the smaller Strong beach house next door to his own for his brother and Amanda. But Emily never trusted Amanda. Figured Amanda had seen that Richie was going places and just latched on to him for the ride."

Pete paused and looked out over the darkening water.

"And?" he said after a few moments.

"And she was right. American Airlines based Richie in Chicago. Richie was gone a lot, building a career, and Amanda landed a job as a stewardess. For the next ten years they both flew, though not together, and put off having kids. Adam said word was Amanda was a quite a party girl. In 1950, when Amanda was twenty-nine, Jamie was born. But she didn't settle down."

"Okay, I'm not following here. I thought they were married a long time. They had two kids."

"Yeah, Jamie…"

"And Tyler."

"Right, but Tyler came along much later, when Amanda was nearly forty."

"And Tyler's father killed himself? I don't get that."

"Old Adam told me his brother Richie came home early from a trip, found the house empty, Jamie with a sitter, and went looking for his wife. Found her at her favorite bar, right there in their neighborhood outside Chicago. She was wrapped around the bartender. Not the first time, either. Richie turned around, climbed in his car, headed out fast into the countryside. Police figure he drove straight into that pole. Died instantly. Or maybe he really died back at the bar, you know? I mean, how can someone who has a kid commit suicide? I think some part of them has to be dead already to do that."

Pete had stopped, and, reflexively, Colin put his arms around her. She did not withdraw.

"Man; that must have been hard on Tyler."

Pete pushed away and continued walking.

"Tyler wasn't even born yet. He came along eight months later."

"Wait. Was Richie even Tyler's dad?"

"Good question."

"He doesn't know?"

"He believes he's Richie's son, the son of a hero and flight pioneer; it's Amanda who doesn't know."

"Shit."

"She swears he is. Problem is, as Old Adam tells it, the math doesn't work. Richie couldn't have been the father; he was away, flying."

"This is tough."

"But Amanda wasn't done."

"What's that mean?"

"It wasn't enough for her."

"What wasn't?"

"Having a dead hero for a husband. She wanted a son who was a hero, too. She wanted a fucking parade of heroes, if only to put the spotlight on her mothering instead of her adultery."

"You've lost me."

"It's simple; when Richie died, she pushed Jamie to live up to Richie's legend. The kid joined the Marines first chance he could, got sent to Viet Nam, and was so gung-ho he'd already been made a company commander by the time they sent his unit to Khe Sahn. The battle of Khe Sahn, which was at the end of his tour, was a bloodbath. A week before he was to be discharged—he already had a Purple Heart by then—Jamie dug a hole, climbed into it, and issued orders to his company from it. He didn't want to get shot just days before going home."

"That makes sense."

"Yeah, except he took a direct shell hit instead. Nothing left of him but the dog tags."

"Jesus."

They were now nearly parallel to the Petersen compound. Pete stopped and looked at her friend.

"So Amanda drilled it into Tyler that he had two heroes to live up to, his father and his brother. And she never let him forget it. He hates her."

"Hates her but invited her to the wedding?"

"Oh, yes. His mother, after all. A chance to prove he's made good. Except she couldn't care less. Plus, she knows what Old Adam thinks of her. She sent Tyler to boarding school for years and left him in Adam's care for the summers. Showed up here once with a boyfriend. Adam gave them both the bum's rush. She hasn't been back since."

"Where is she now?"

"She had a string of 'gentlemen friends' and finally married the richest one, a Detroit auto parts dealer. Lives in Florida, now.

"And isn't coming."

"Right.

"And Tyler's upset?"

"Right. Except he hasn't figured out that's the reason. Thinks it's just jitters. You know how he always seems to need to be in the spotlight, like he's on stage? That's Amanda's influence, too. It's like she's always in the wings, watching to see if he measures up. So everything's a performance for him. It's why he flirts so much, too. He keeps searching for admiration, appreciation."

"Doesn't that bother you?"

"Uh-uh. But one of these days, soon, he'll stop trying so hard to be someone who has to impress, to be someone he isn't. He'll understand that the someone he is, is just fine. That's the man I am marrying: the Tyler on the inside."

Try as he might, though, Colin saw only Tyler's capriciousness, his serial infidelity, his curious disconnect from day to day reality. In the end, he put this all down to jealousy. He loved Pete. He was not a reliable judge.

Seven and a half months later, when Pete called to say she'd just given birth to their first child, Justine, Colin understood the precipitous marriage. He worked the months backward and they spelled, "Spring Break Mistake." It was typical that the families' code of silence had been maintained until it could be held no longer.

There were so many secrets.

Tyler, Colin later learned from Pete, had pressed for an abortion. He argued, he said, the case of reason: they were too young; he was still in law school (at New York University, conveniently close to Sarah Lawrence College); she hadn't finished her undergraduate degree.

The truth was that despite his lifelong connection to Pete, monogamy terrified him. And then there was the baby. What Tyler understood all too clearly was that he'd never had to be responsible for anything, including himself. And to the extent that he reflected at all on the prospect of having a child, what he struggled with was the near certainty that he did not have whatever it took to be a father. How could he? He'd never known his own.

Pete struggled, too, but not with the decision to have the child. Though eventually, in 1994, the Seventy-First General Convention of the Episcopal Church would endorse a woman's right to "reach an informed decision about the termination of her pregnancy," in 1986 it was still opposed, and so was she. She never even presented it as an option when she told her father she was pregnant. Her father was now so deeply engaged in church matters and disengaged from his daughter's life that the announcement of her pregnancy occasioned little more than a raised eyebrow and a question: "Who...?" Informed that Tyler was the father, he merely nodded, as if this was a foregone if nonetheless premature conclusion, and returned to his paperwork. He had every confidence in his daughter.

No, what Pete struggled with was Tyler. That Tyler did not want the baby cracked the topography of their relationship like a tectonic shift. If he was not the man she'd thought he was, if theirs was not the love she believed it was, then in what reality was she living? How could they have known each other all these years, how could they have been lovers, without her knowing this about him? And what did it mean? That he didn't love her? That he was weak? Or just that he was frightened? In the end, she chose to believe the latter, loved him all the more for it, took charge of planning the wedding, and shouldered the task of reassuring and encouraging him — a job that, in time, she would come to understand was her permanent employment.

It would be years before she would realize she'd been right on all three counts. By then, it was too late.

eleven

AFTER HE LEFT Colin at the intersection of Quartermaster Drive and the Vashon Highway, Young Adam pedaled fast southward past the marina on the inner harbor and coasted downhill to the blinking light in the middle of Burton. Apart from Vashon Village, the commercial center of the island, the hamlet of Burton was the only other spot with a palpable sense of community. Elsewhere, settlement was dispersed and largely rural.

Burton, though, as far as most locals were concerned, had it all—or at least what you needed in a pinch. There was a Unitarian church, the kind of place where the hymns tended to be vaguely reverent folk songs sung to guitar accompaniment and one of the highlights of the worship year was the annual "Blessing of the Pets" at which cats, dogs, birds, the occasional potbellied pig, and, in one case, a little girl's pet barnacle did their best to behave and be blessed. There was a branch post office so small three customers made a crowd and a satellite fire and rescue station whose volunteer vehicle drivers had the good sense to keep the sirens off until they'd cleared the immediate neighborhood. Sharing a low building that housed the post office was a shop called "Found Objects" run by two woman with unerring eyes for the sorts of antique or simply used things you never knew you needed until you saw them there and then you had to have them, although actually getting them was made difficult by the shop's somewhat whimsical hours of operation. Across from Found Objects was the Burton Texaco Station, which, unlike most service stations, actually repaired cars. Somewhat perversely, though, Burton Texaco did not sell Texaco gasoline, or any other brand for that matter, and hadn't for nearly two decades. Attempts by the owners to change the name accordingly had been notably unsuccessful; everyone still called it "the Texaco." On the northwest corner of the intersection, housed in the historic old Masonic Hall, was the Quartermaster Gallery, an exhibit space that served the island's unusually large population of fine artists and was typically the highlight of the island's monthly "First Friday" gallery tour, in part because there was always cheese and wine. In its shadow was the walk-up Burton coffee stand, which functioned as the neighborhood's al fresco gathering spot thanks to the excellence of its coffee, the unpredictable and therefore ever-entertaining mood shifts of its alternating baristas, the dogged loyalty of its zany regulars, and the addition of an awning to keep out the rain. The chill of winter was made infinitely more bearable thanks to an outdoor propane heater one of the customers had found on Craigslist and given to the comely proprietor.

On the southwest corner stood the rambling, vaguely Victorian but actually fairly new Harbor Inn, which boasted a large and friendly dining room and a few bright rooms upstairs for overnight visitors. On the southeast corner directly across from the Inn was the Burton Mercantile, the indispensable general store that anchored both the intersection and the community. The Merc, as it was known, was the kind of place you could find almost anything you ever needed short of clothing and fresh meat or fish, and if it wasn't there you probably didn't need it: hardware for your boat; building supplies for whatever may have broken at home but was too small to go up to town for; gardening tools; canned, packaged, and frozen groceries; basic fresh produce of the sort you'd need if more people invited themselves to dinner than you'd planned for and you needed to stretch the menu; cleaning supplies, should you ever be motivated to clean; beer and wine (a remarkably sophisticated selection); gourmet ice cream (because Betty Walsh, its beloved Irish owner, had a sweet tooth and couldn't tolerate anything less than the best); newspapers and magazines; free coffee and a well-worn couch for regulars to sit on while they drank it; free biscuits for any dog who happened to wander in, with or without an owner; and free advice from Betty on almost any subject—political, financial, or personal. The Merc was open every day but Monday and most holidays too, though Betty closed early at Christmas and New Year's Day. She closed completely, of course, on St. Patrick's Day.

YOUNG ADAM LEANED his bike against the wall outside the store, drifted through the double doors set into the corner of the old wooden two-story building—Betty lived upstairs—and scanned the Merc's narrow aisles.

"You looking for something special there, Young Adam?" Betty called from behind the counter.

"Mom."

"Well, now, moms are special, all right, but I don't stock them anymore. Never could unload the inventory before the sell-by date. Turns out most folks have a mom, you see. No real demand."

"Very funny, ma'am."

"Don't you 'ma'am' me, wise guy; makes me feel old!"

"Yes, ma'am..."

Betty barked a laugh.

No one in Burton had a clue about Betty Walsh's age, nor had the courage to ask. Neither young nor old, she was a compact bundle of apparently inexhaustible energy. She'd been around long enough to know everyone's secrets and also to know to keep them to herself. Her hair was a close-cut brown helmet with flashes of gray. Her face seemed set in a permanent look of impending and inevitable mischief-making. It was known that she had a husband in Montana and that that was just exactly where she liked him to be. She visited him once a month and came back each time swearing—colorfully—that this visit would be the last.

The Merc was the kind of place with signs behind the register that said things like, "I have an attitude and I know how to use it!" and "The deadline for all complaints was yesterday!" It was rumored that the Mercantile was up for sale, but the rumor was itself an antique, at least a decade old. If you asked Betty directly, she'd say, "Sure! Make me an offer!" But most people doubted any offer would be good enough. Not to mention that if she ever made a move to leave, the entire population of Burton would almost certainly throw their bodies across the Highway to block her exit. Even if the store remained after her departure, Burton would have lost its soul.

Betty was besotted with Adam and had been since he toddled up to the counter all by himself one summer's day at the age of perhaps three and spoke two of the words he'd learned so far: "ice cream." After she stopped laughing, the first thing she did was phone the frantic Strongs, who'd been searching the beach for the little boy. The second thing she did was give the kid an ice cream bar. Ever since, the highlight of each summer for Betty was the first day Young Adam burst through the door yelling, "Ice Cream!" It was their running gag.

"So, your mom's gone missing, then?" Betty was teasing the boy.

Adam looked at her with a face as bleak as a shattered World War I battlefield, shrugged, and slipped out of the store as quietly as he'd entered.

Betty walked to the door and watched the boy ride east along Burton Drive toward the peninsula. From the couch behind her, Flo, a silver-haired widow who spent part of most days in the store to keep Betty company, though Betty knew it was actually the other way around, said, "Odd boy, that one."

"No, Flo, you're wrong; nothing odd about that kid at all, except this morning. And that's what's odd…"

ADAM HESITATED AT the turnoff that would take him down to the beach and the summer houses and decided to keep going straight instead, standing on his pedals to pump his bike up the hill to the T-junction at the top where the two-mile loop road around the knob of the Burton Peninsula began and ended. He wanted to go home, but he wanted to go home and find Mom there. And because he was not, by nature, an optimist, he didn't go home.

At the top, he turned right, sat back down on the bike seat, and pedaled slowly as he caught his breath. It was too late to see morning deer, but the air was thick with birdsong and the fragrance of cedar and fir, all second growth, that had flourished after his great-grandfather had logged over the area. As he passed the old Baptist summer camp that occupied a segment of the peninsula, he heard the keening cry of one of the many bald eagles that perched on the high snags over the harbor, watching for fish. Many of the cottages along the loop road still had apple orchards, a half dozen or so trees, in their yards. Gnarled, unpruned, and choked with sucker branches, they were nonetheless thick with just-ripening apples now, despite the neglect. The abandoned apple trees had troubled him awhile back. It had been Uncle Colin's receptionist, Olivia, who'd told him the stories of those days before the Second World War when Japanese American families like hers, and a few stubborn Scandinavians, had turned the little island into a fruit basket bulging not only with apples, but stone fruit and berries too. Olivia's grandfather had built a thriving business canning island fruit and shipping it all over the country. All that changed a few months after Pearl Harbor, when the Japanese farmers and their families were "evacuated" from the island, first to a holding area near Tacoma and then to a dusty desert camp at Tule

Lake, in California. After that, the fruit farms never really recovered. The remnant apple trees, clustered in ragged rows, were like orphans; they looked as if they longed for their families to return and look after them.

At Jensen Point Park, he coasted down into the parking lot, stopped by the big doors of the boat house, punched his kickstand down, and ducked his head into the barnlike building where the rowing club's shells were stored—shining, sleek, and looking fast as white barracudas.

"Hey, Adam! When we gonna be able to recruit you for junior crew, fella?"

It was Amy, one of his mom's pals, a broad-shouldered lady—kinda young, but he could never work out ages—who had a couple of kids who sometimes came down to the beach. She was rinsing the salt off her rowing shell. She had close-cropped dark hair and a face that seemed sad until she smiled, when it suddenly became radiant. It always amazed him.

"Soon, Amy," he answered with more confidence than he felt. "Maybe next year."

"You'll be ace, kid," she said, returning to her shell.

He hoped he would be.

He was proud that his mother rowed. Because she was little and light, she was often pressed into service as coxswain in the long boats, the eights. But in her own single shell, she flew. Early in the morning, before the wind kicked up, he'd watch her streak across the glassy surface of the outer harbor, reaching and pulling, reaching and pulling, smooth and regular as a machine, and marvel at how strong she was.

He looked up and saw her shell, racked in its normal place. It was dry.

He wandered out to the beach and sat on the edge of the barnacle-encrusted concrete boat ramp. On the bow of the crew instructor's outboard skiff, anchored just offshore, a cormorant, black as a nightmare, perched with its wings spread wide. He knew the birds did this to dry off in the sun after diving for fish, but it always seemed to him as if the bird were signaling, "Don't shoot; I'm unarmed!"

As he sat there, it suddenly occurred to him that he'd gone to Colin's hoping his mother would be there. Why did he think that? Sure, Colin was a family friend and had been for as long as he could remember, at least in the summer. But his mom had lots of friends and relatives on the beach. Not to mention her girlfriends in the rowing club. Why Colin?

He thought some more. The funny thing about Colin was that being around him made everything better, in a quiet, easy way. Not like his own father; at the beach his dad was all frantic movement: running around hustling up a game of tennis, or softball, or touch football, or dragging everyone out to go swimming or fishing. Adam had read someplace that sharks had to be constantly on the move just to stay alive. That was like his father. Except, of course, when he was glum or angry, and you could never tell when those moods might take him over. If his mom was around, she'd put a finger to her lips and whisper, "Bleakies..." It was the family signal to steer clear.

And then there were the weird, unpredictable things his dad did, especially out here on the beach—like swerving the fishing skiff when you least expected it so you got thrown off balance, or pushing you off the swimming platform when you weren't looking, or getting you lost on walks in the Burton Woods. You didn't expect that kind of thing from your dad. But eventually, Adam did.

Earlier this summer he'd been sitting on the porch reading Sherlock Holmes stories when he heard their neighbor, Peggy March, laughing at something his dad was up to with the other kids out on the lawn. Mrs. March was sitting on the steps beside his mom. "Tyler's so playful, so full of energy," Mrs. March had said. "My Rob is such a stick in the mud." Adam looked over at his mother, but she said nothing. Then, a moment later, mostly to herself, she said, "I rather think 'erratic' would be more accurate." But by then Peggy had gone off to be with Tyler and the other kids.

twelve

THE FRIDAY BEFORE Labor Day, Soren Sorensen stood in front of the printer in the shipping company's office as it scrolled out his letter of resignation. Outside at the dock, one of his freighters sat idle. The ship was seaworthy, but hardly pretty. Streaks of rust stained its formerly white hull like dried blood. The dock, normally a noisy storm of semi-organized chaos, was quiet as a grave. He had shipping orders, but he couldn't fulfill them. Pacific Pioneer no longer had credit at the Ballard Locks fuel dock. His two other vessels were impounded over at Harbor Island, the shipping center on the south end of Seattle's Elliott Bay. He was dead in the water.

He'd always loved the way the south-facing windows flooded his office with light and sent ripples from the surface of the shipping channel dancing across the ceiling. He sat at his desk and signed the letter. Three and a half decades of service as Pacific Pioneer's general manager and this is how it was ending. Such a terrible, stupid waste.

He set the letter on top of a thick stack of copies of older letters, faxes, and emails, slipped the entire package into an envelope, and left it at the door for the legal services messenger company. The Labor Day weekend was here and he thought about the irony. For the first quarter century after Robbie Petersen put the business in his hands, managing the shipping company had been a labor of love, as rewarding to him as seeing his kids grow. Sure, there were always problems in the cargo business, especially when you worked in an environment as hostile as western Alaska—storms, rogue seas, breakdowns. But he'd loved the job. "The perfect job for someone with a ten-minute attention span," he'd often joked with his wife, because something was always coming up. The crewmen who had come and gone had been like family, and many still kept in touch.

He wondered what Robbie would have thought about what was happening now. Old Robbie; now there was a true gent. His heart and soul had been in the business until his son Justin was killed. Robbie's older brother Harlan became chairman after Robbie himself died. Fact is, though, the Bishop couldn't have cared less; Soren had run the show from then on. Then, when Pete married and Harlan handed over the reins to Tyler Strong...well, that was the beginning of the end, wasn't it?

The economics of coastal shipping had changed by then too. By the 1990s, break bulk shipping—the kind of soup-to-nuts mixed cargo Pacific Pioneer had always carried to the remote ports of western Alaska, the Aleutians, and the Pribilof Islands—was struggling. Container ships had captured the most accessible bulk markets, air transport costs had dropped, planes were more efficient than old ships at handling specialty goods, and shipboard labor and fuel costs had risen sharply.

In competent hands, these market shifts would not have been insurmountable. Soren had seen it coming. He'd warned Tyler, but the lad had done nothing. Then, a little over a year ago, SeaFresh Fisheries, the fresh and canned salmon company in Yakutat that always filled their hulls for the back haul to Seattle, canceled its long-standing contract. It seemed Japanese consumers, worried about reports of diseased farm-raised Coho salmon from Chile, had created a spike in demand for wild, flash-frozen Sockeye from Alaska—Pacific Pioneer's principal backhaul—and SeaFresh decided to ship exclusively to Japan, via newer and cheaper Japanese refrigerated vessels. Though Pacific Pioneer still had clients for northbound shipping, Soren knew the company could not survive by returning empty to Seattle.

Immediately, Soren had called Tyler's office. He received no response and left increasingly urgent messages. Finally, via registered letter, he wrote to propose a solution. The company, he urged, should be restructured:

I believe it is time for Pacific Pioneer to abandon the break bulk cargo business and establish retail supply store outlets to serve the West Alaskan fishing industry in ports like Dutch Harbor. No such service currently exists, and, because we are known and trusted, this could be the company's salvation. Our own vessels can supply the stores and the margins provided by selling at retail will stabilize our financial situation. Unless we take this bold step, Pacific Pioneer will not survive.

It was two weeks before Tyler responded:

I will not oversee the downgrading of my wife's family's shipping firm to a chain of retail stores. I suggest you redouble your efforts to ensure the company's profitability by seeking new customers and cutting costs. That is the general manager's responsibility.

Soren looked at the letter and what he saw was Strong creating a paper trail to cover his own butt. Then, to Soren's amazement, Tyler took out a major capital equipment loan to pay for overhauling two of their vessels, plunging them further into debt. It wasn't until Soren received a copy of the new loan agreement from a bank they hadn't dealt with before that he discovered how Tyler had swung the deal: his wife's signature pledged her personal assets as collateral.

For a while, they limped along. But an old, established company dies by a thousand cuts: long-time customers—any company's "cash cows"—cancel long-standing repeat orders because of economic reversals in their own sectors and go under. Demand for certain products in the target market either declines or shifts and shipping orders drop off. Fuel, parts, and labor costs skyrocket and net revenues decline as costs climb. Payments to fuel suppliers and repair companies get postponed, and very quickly, credit tightens. Deferred maintenance causes ships to break down in remote locations, necessitating expensive emergency repairs. Banks providing capital and operating loans note the declines in both orders and revenues, find the company in violation of performance covenants in loan agreements, and call in the loans.

All of it was happening to Pacific Pioneer. With each reversal, Soren wrote to Tyler, who was both chief executive officer and chief financial officer. Sometimes he got belligerent replies; mostly he got none. On a couple of occasions, Soren appealed to Pete's father, Harlan, but the Bishop simply forwarded the correspondence to his son-in-law, which only further infuriated Tyler.

Finally, when two of their remaining three ships, the M/V ATKA and M/V COLD BAY, were seized by the U.S. Marshall's Office in Seattle on behalf of unpaid creditors in August and the crews were let go, he'd had enough. He'd given his life to Pete's family's firm; he would not oversee its collapse. That belonged in Tyler's lap. He spent the next few weeks organizing paperwork and then he was done.

There'd never been a pension program, of course, but Soren had set money aside for retirement. He wanted to say goodbye to Pete, whom he'd known since she was a toddler, but decided if anyone was to tell her that her grandfather's legacy was lost, it should be her own husband.

thirteen

TYLER STRONG, BAREFOOT and wearing only his boxer shorts, stood at the railing of the long waterfront porch at the Petersen Old House on Labor Day morning and tossed back the remainder of a screwdriver that might as well have been a vodka martini for all the orange juice it had in it. It was nearly nine o'clock and the sun turned the face of every wavelet on the incoming tide searchlight bright. His eyes hurt. His head hurt. The vodka was designed—if any form of conscious design could be attributed to him this particular morning—to medicate his hangover and, in some even less conscious effort, to smooth away the jagged state of his mind.

He was having difficulty patching together the present moment, as if it were a puzzle to which too many pieces had gone missing. Pete was one of the missing pieces. His children were some of the others.

Pete should be here packing. Kids, too. Justine and Two are old enough to know better than to disappear on Labor Day morning; too much work to do. But nothing's been touched. Where are they? Why is it so quiet?

He heard a phone ringing and was surprised to discover a cell phone in his other hand. He flipped it open.

"Yes?"

"This is the King County Sheriff's Office on Vashon. I believe you called 911 to report a missing person?"

"I did?" *Did I?*

"Is this Tyler Strong?"

"Yes, of course it is."

"Well, sir, according to the call center in Burien, someone named Tyler Strong called to report his wife missing at eight thirty-one this morning and left this phone number. They forwarded the message to the island office, you see."

Tyler stared east across the shimmering water as if by doing so he might find answers there.

"Mr. Strong?"

Tyler focused on the phone at his ear. "Yes?"

"Is your wife there?"

Tyler looked around. "Um, no."

"And did you call 911 to report her missing? About a half hour ago?"

"Well, I guess I must have."

Sherriff's deputy Chris Christiansen had been an island-based King County police officer for nearly forty years. And this morning, he was thinking that in all those years he'd seldom had an odder conversation than the one he was having right now with Tyler Strong, whose family he knew well.

"That would be Martha Petersen Strong?"

"Yes. Pete."

"And when did you discover she was missing, Mr. Strong?"

At some level, Tyler knew this should not be a difficult question. Obviously he'd called 911. Because Pete was missing. She wasn't in the house. No one was but him.

"She wasn't here when I woke up this morning," was all he could think to say. *Is that right?*

"I see. And when was that, sir?"

"A couple of hours ago, I guess." *Was it?*

"A stroll to the Burton coffee stand?"

"She doesn't like caffeine."

"I understand they have decaf now."

"She doesn't drink coffee."

For a man who'd lived on coffee most of his life, this was nearly incomprehensible to Chris Christiansen, but he soldiered on.

"Her car?" he asked.

Tyler peered around the corner of the porch. "Here."

"I see. So, she's been gone for a couple of hours."

"I don't know; maybe more." Tyler was getting irritated by these questions, and by how much seemed so broken up in his head.

"Maybe more? You don't know?"

"It was the Labor Day weekend beach party, Officer; I haven't had much sleep." *It was, wasn't it? Just last night?*

"Yes, of course; and now you're closing down the cottages for the season, I imagine, heading back to Seattle?"

"Yes. And she's not here." *Where are any of them?*

Christiansen decided to take the neighborly approach. "I certainly understand your concern, Mr. Strong; I felt the same way when my late wife Harriet disappeared, God rest her soul. She did once, you know. Oh, yes. Remember it well. November 1980, night of the presidential election. I was watchin' the results on television, you know? When I looked around, she was gone. Figured she was in the kitchen or something, but no. Not in bed either. Strange, huh?"

"Strange," Tyler repeated.

"You'll never guess what had happened," Christiansen continued.

Tyler was trying to make this conversation fit with the other pieces of reality that lay scattered like broken shards around the inside of his skull. He said nothing.

"Well, I'll tell you. Seems she was pretty steamed Reagan was winning by a landslide so she took off to cool down. Scared me silly!"

"Uh-huh."

"See my point?"

"Um...yeah." Tyler wasn't really attending to the conversation; he was scanning the beach for his kids.

"Your missus could be anywhere. Perfectly innocent. Who knows what women get into their heads anyway, am I right?"

"Sure..."

"You've checked the other houses on the beach, I'm guessing, Mr. Strong? Called her friends?"

"Uh-huh." *Did I?*

"I see. Well, I can understand your concern, Mr. Strong. I certainly can. But here's the thing: the county has a policy on missing persons. We don't investigate until forty-eight hours have elapsed."

"What?"

"So many false alarms, you see."

"But anything could happen in forty-eight hours!"

"Actually, sir, what we've discovered is that almost nothing does. They nearly always show up, safe and sound."

"What about my children? They're gone, too!"

Chris Christiansen stared at the phone in disbelief. Strong must be drunk; that was the only explanation.

"You mean young Adam, sir?" he asked.

But Tyler Strong had hung up.

HAVING SEEN TO Mrs. Forrester's dog, Colin was driving the clinic van south on his way to Edwinna's when a cavernous emptiness opened in his stomach to remind him he hadn't eaten anything yet this morning. In another half hour, hunger would leave him the gift of a knife-in-the-temple headache. He pulled over at the Cemetery Road intersection, let Eileen out, and followed her up the worn steps of the Coffee Roasterie. It was like stepping back half a century. The old wooden building with its broad front porch was home to the state's oldest coffee roaster, a big copper and steel antique still in use roasting—naturally, on this right-thinking island— "Organic Fair Trade" beans.

The darkly made-up, partridge-plump younger woman behind the register grinned broadly as he approached. "The sun has just risen on my day!" she exclaimed.

Colin smiled and shook his head. The day was young and he was already tired.

"Morning, Cyn."

"Like I'd ever be 'your sin!' What'll it be, doc?" She pulled a dog biscuit from a jar and slipped it to Eileen.

"A large drip and one of your luscious muffins, thanks."

"There's a large drip in here, all right, but he can forget about my luscious muffins," she teased, adjusting an ample bosom.

"That's what I like about you," Colin said. "You're totally about customer service."

Cyndy Blessing was a bit too old to get away with the Goth look anymore; Colin guessed late-thirties. But the spiked hair dyed raspberry, the steel eyebrow stud, the layered, lacy, torn, and curiously sexy black clothes that both covered and accentuated her zaftig figure, and the platform soled, patent leather "bother boots" she sported all suited her somehow and added a certain theatricality to the scene. The one thing she couldn't darken was her eyes, blue as sapphires rimmed with stars; their iridescence was only accentuated by the heavy black eyeliner.

Cyndy was a single mom with a son who was a freshman in high school and who helped out at the clinic sometimes. He was a straight-arrow honors student and she was quietly but immensely proud of him.

"How's that boy of yours?" Colin asked.

"Jean-Paul?"

The father wasn't French; the father was unknown. She'd named the boy after the existentialist, Sartre.

"Do you have others hidden in the attic?"

"No way; one was enough. The latest is that he's gonna be in AP classes this year." She shook her head as if she'd have much preferred he'd been arrested for petty theft.

"You sure about your muffins? I'm ravenous, and in a hurry."

She gave him a theatrical sneer. "That's just like you men; always in a hurry with my muffins." Pause for effect, then, "I've got a blueberry left."

"Sold. You say hi to J-P for me, okay? Tell him he's always welcome at the clinic. That boy has a nice touch with animals."

"You're just trying to get on my good side."

"All your sides are good, Cyn."

She waved him away with a smile and Colin took an empty cardboard cup out to the vacuum-press coffee dispensers on the porch, pumped out a pitch black organic French roast, and added half-and-half.

He sat on one of the benches in the sun, fed bits of muffin to Eileen and stared at the traffic. He knew he should hurry on to Edwinna's, but he needed to think. Patsy had been right: he wasn't thinking clearly this morning.

Colin Ryan had the sort of mind that, without effort, was always three or four steps ahead of wherever he was at the moment. It was a distinct advantage in medicine, but in life it kept him perpetually in advance of the present and therefore only dimly aware of it. It was a skill he'd learned as a teen, a way to anticipate and prepare for whatever danger might await at home, where the heat of his father's anger or the cold of his mother's anxiety could never be predicted and you had to be ready for anything. He'd come back after an evening out prowling the neighborhood or just hanging out on a stoop with his pals, stand in front of the olive drab door to his family's apartment, stare at the brass doorknob, and sort through the alternative conditions that might exist on the other side. Before he turned the knob, he had mapped out two or three strategies: what reactions his arrival might cause—sullen silence, volcanic rage, drunken confusion—how he would respond, what the likely next step would be, and so on out to several iterations.

But he hadn't anticipated Pete's attempted suicide and he felt he'd somehow failed her. At the same time, he was struggling to come to terms with his own emotions about her attempt. He was angry with her, just as Patsy said—Patsy, who he realized he relied upon for much more than her professional skills; Patsy, who cared enough to tell him the truth.

Absently, he tossed another piece of muffin to Eileen. Unlike most dogs, she never simply snatched food in mid-air. No, she'd let it land and, if absolutely necessary, move her body to approach the morsel. Then she'd sniff at it awhile with a certain suspicion, as if, like some royal, she wished her official taster were present to demonstrate its safety.

He was angry with Tyler, too, incandescent with anger and struggling to get it under control. He'd experienced his friend's odd volatility for years—his manic energy and petulant fury during otherwise friendly games, his tendency to say provocative things at inappropriate times, his need to attract the attention of women, his descents into surly silence. But he'd never imagined Tyler might hurt his wife. And yet how else to explain those wrist bruises?

There was a part of Colin—a somehow broken part, he now understood—that had believed for years that Pete would one day reward his fidelity. But it never happened. How ironic it was that she would rather be abused by a husband, and even attempt suicide, than seek his comfort and protection. And how pitiful. Who was he angry with? Himself, more than anyone. He was a fool. But a caring fool with work to do. He tossed the coffee cup in a bin.

"Come on Eileen, let's go see our patient."

fourteen

MARTHA "PETE" PETERSEN Strong retched into the big aluminum stockpot for what seemed to her like the hundredth time. She was empty, drained dry, and wished she wasn't, because the reflex would not stop. It was as if her body, having rid itself of the poison, was now punishing her for poisoning it. She wasn't even fully conscious. She had no sense of time or place; her only reality was sickness.

Edwinna Rutherford wiped Pete's forehead with a cool, damp washcloth. When the spasm subsided, she pulled the younger woman to a sitting position against a bank of white linen pillows in her bed. Beyond the window, through the glossy green leaves of the red-barked Madronas, a rower in a single shell white as a gull's breast skimmed over the surface of the outer harbor, trailing molten gold in the slanting light each time the oars came out of the water.

Pete's eyes struggled to focus.

"Edwinna."

"That's me, toots."

"Where am I?"

"Be it ever so humble: my place."

Pete made to shake her head but it felt like there were razor blades inside it. "I don't understand."

"Doesn't surprise me. Drunk as a skunk, you were. Probably still are."

"Sick," Pete said.

"No kidding. Drink this ginger ale. It'll help your blood sugar."

"Don't like it."

"Do it anyway, dammit!"

"Why are you being so mean?"

"Because you annoy the shit out of me, Martha Petersen, that's why—and because despite that, I want you to get better. For one thing, that's my bed."

Pete sipped some of the ginger ale and promptly threw it up. When the nausea passed, she sank into the pillows, exhausted. Edwinna's cat, Desmond, leaped onto the bed and wobbled over to his keeper. Edwinna adored his nervous ticks; he walked like a drunk, often misjudged distances, and was given to unpredictable fits of manic activity. It was as if he was possessed by demons. Given her own paranormal moments, she thought this made him a perfect companion. The cat peered at Pete as if trying to place her, gave up, made a lightning fast tour of the tops of several pieces of furniture, and then vanished down the hallway, yowling as if tortured.

"How did I get here? The last thing I remember…"

"Yeah, the last thing was you were choosing a good place to die on the Vashon Highway. Couldn't you have found someplace less public? Appalling judgment."

Pete took this in and tried to make sense of it. "No," she said finally. "No. I was home. At the beach house. On the terrace. With Tyler."

"Right. And I abducted you."

For a moment, Edwinna thought Pete was going to vomit again. Her abdomen contracted several times and the older woman was about to pull her yet again to the edge of the bed when she realized Pete wasn't being sick. She was sobbing, tearlessly, and staring at her bruised wrists.

Edwinna stroked the younger woman's hair. "Hey girl, I tell you what," she whispered. "I'll tell you how you got here if you tell me how you got those welts."

But Pete turned away, her body shuddering silently like an old, badly tuned car dieseling away long after the engine has been turned off.

EDWINNA WAS A Rutherford—not that she'd ever had much to do with them. They were, in island terms at least, relative newcomers to the beach. She'd married into the family and rued the day almost ever since.

Edwinna Fry arrived in Seattle at the age of sixteen just as World War II was drawing to a close. Her father, Benjamin, a scientist and a Jew, had taught at the Technical University of Berlin and been an early architect of rocket propulsion systems in Germany. Werner von Braun was his star pupil. Despite his professional credentials and strategic importance, though, Fry became increasingly certain his family would not survive in Hitler's Reich. When the Nuremberg Race Laws eliminated the rights of Jews, Fry took advantage of a scientific conference in London and fled there with his daughter Edwinna and wife Rachel. Once settled, he continued to teach but also served quietly as an advisor to Britain's Secret Intelligence Service.

But though he and his family found refuge in England, Fry's intuition about their future proved accurate: he and his wife were vaporized by a V-1 rocket that hit their Chiswick home in 1944. Edwinna had been at school that day. Just before the lunch break, she had bolted from class and burst into the headmaster's office screaming that her house was going to be bombed. The headmaster took it to be war stress and tried to calm her, but her fear turned to fury. She fled the school, raced toward home, heard the distant explosion, and a few minutes later found only brick rubble and a smoking crater where the center of her life had been only hours before.

Shipped off to an aunt in Seattle in 1946, Edwinna left home a year later and found a job as a stenographer in the King County Superior Court. She lied about her age and her British accent made her seem mature and sophisticated. During trials, she knew instinctively who was guilty or innocent. She could see their stories even before she heard the testimony, but she kept this to herself. In time, she met Jack Rutherford, a rising young court reporter for the *Seattle Post-Intelligencer*. Within a year, and against his family's wishes, they'd married, rented a tiny house on the west side of Queen Anne Hill overlooking Elliott Bay, and were looking forward to starting a family.

Instead, only a month after the United States entered the Korean conflict, Jack was drafted. Six months later, a week after he was deployed, he was dead. When she received the news, all she said was, "I didn't see this coming."

No one understood what she meant.

Jack's father Hank was a contractor. He'd prospered building and expanding the military facilities that ringed

Seattle during World War II, then switched to subdivision development during the post-war housing boom. He also built a summer home on Madrona Beach, just west of the Petersen compound. It was large and, like his subdivisions, cheaply built, but the family loved it.

Edwinna never crossed its threshold. Her inheritance was enough for her to buy a parcel of land of her own on the Burton peninsula and to have a small house built— but by local builders, not her father-in-law. This, of course, did little to endear her to the Rutherfords, but she could not have cared less. Hank Rutherford had kept his other son, Jeff, out of Korea by engineering a "critical trades" exemption for him and making the ridiculously young and stunningly incompetent man a vice-president of the firm. Edwinna despised Jeff Rutherford—not because he avoided serving in Korea, but because he'd never earned a thing he'd been given.

When, after Jeff had been married for a decade and a half, and his society wife, Katie, caught wind of rumors that her husband had something more than friendly relationships with the real estate agents, male, who sold the houses in his father's developments, she sued for divorce. Thanks to the doggedness of the first female lawyer Adam Strong had taken into his firm, Katie secured a settlement that included not only a sizable monthly alimony payment but also both their Bellevue and island homes. Edwinna congratulated her.

Katie and Jeff's one child, Dylan, dropped out of high school in the mid-Sixties soon after his father was exposed and headed east, fetching up at Tolstoy Farm, an agrarian, anything goes, so-called "intentional community" west of

Spokane named after the place Ghandi had studied non-violence in South Africa. Eventually, and perhaps inevitably given the culture of the commune, he fathered a daughter named "Twilight," and then, when drafted to serve in Vietnam, slipped over the nearby Canadian border and was never heard from again.

Twilight's mother, "Dawn," had never really committed to the commune's generally wholesome values and died of a heroin overdose in a Spokane alley when her daughter was ten. The girl was subsequently raised by the others in the commune, educated somewhat sketchily at their alternative school, and—at the first opportunity—had the great good sense to change her name legally from Twilight to "Margaret," a name she chose from the directory hanging in the public phone booth in the Spokane County District Court building where she filed the application. She liked the way the twinned triplet syllables—Margaret Rutherford—rolled off her tongue.

Several months later, after she'd tracked down her only remaining relative, her grandmother Katie, she accepted an invitation to visit the family's Madrona Beach compound for the first time. She and Katie hit it off instantly, and Katie and her second husband, Mike Foley, a retired neurosurgeon, took her in.

That's when she met Edwinna, and changed her name yet again. That was Edwinna's doing. She took Margaret aside, showed her a photo in an encyclopedia of the jowly, double-chinned British actress of the same name, Dame Margaret Rutherford, and suggested "Peggy" as a substitute. It suited, Edwinna thought; she was the kind of girl whose name should end in "y": cute, lively, and none too bright.

Had Colin known of Edwinna's initial assessment of Peggy's potential when he met the girl during his first summer visit to the beach, he would have been stunned. The Peggy Rutherford he met—the product of Edwinna's sharp prodding and Grandmother Katie's gentle nurturing—was a questing and confident young woman, and a lovely one at that. Like Pete, her hair was streaked blonde by the sun; unlike petite Pete, she was taller than average and rather lushly upholstered: a Greek goddess to Pete's Parisian gamine. And when Peggy Rutherford emerged from her countercultural past and began to blossom, Rob March was there, courting her with the kind of quiet persistence that, like running water, wears down even the hardest rock. Still, it came as a surprise to almost everyone, except Edwinna of course, when Peggy ultimately succumbed and she and Rob married.

Like a frog who'd charmed a fairy princess, Rob devoted himself to Peggy's happiness, and his wife flourished. When children arrived, gentle, affable Rob was always on hand to care for them. And as he prospered, Peggy's life gained both the luxury and respectability, like carefully applied layers of thin gold leaf, that she had never imagined possible. Even now, years later, you could sometimes catch Rob watching his wife and shaking his head, amazed at his luck.

EDWINNA ADORED PEGGY, but she loved Pete almost desperately as the daughter she'd never had. But the truth was, she was afraid of her affection for Pete Petersen, afraid that one day she would "see" tragedy in the young woman's aura.

So Edwinna kept herself at a distance, and what she saw of Pete from that remove had evolved over the years from joy to disappointment. She'd watched the eager-to-please, motherless daughter of an emotionally unavailable father—a cleric, no less—bob along like driftwood wherever the tide of her life took her. As a girl, Pete had been bright, inquisitive, courageous, athletic—a tomboy all the other girls on the beach strove to emulate, the girl everyone wanted as her best friend. What dismayed Edwinna was how, as Pete matured, this promising creature became the image of her own long-dead mother: passive, accommodating, apparently satisfied with meeting the demands of whomever needed her—Pete's ambitious but absent father, then handsome but feckless Tyler, and finally her children. It was as if she'd become a blank screen against which other people's dramas were projected. Edwinna had expected more. And what was worse, she knew there was more in there: an intelligent, capable woman who was, for all intents and purposes, coasting. She wondered what it would take for Pete to finally take charge of her own life.

More recently, really since Two had died, she also worried about Pete's health. She'd watched the girl go from slender and graceful to wiry and rail thin. Pete had always been a runner, but now she ran for what seemed to Edwinna like hours. She ran as if she were trying to run something out of herself, as if the pounding physical effort could cleanse her of...what? Grief, perhaps. Or guilt.

Lately Pete had taken to stopping in at Edwinna's on her runs, ostensibly to refill her water bottle, but the visits often extended into discussions. The visits puzzled Edwinna until one afternoon, as the two of them sat quietly on the back porch, Pete said, almost in a whisper, "It's so peaceful here, Edwinna. Thank you."

"Well, of course it's peaceful," Edwinna cracked. "Not a damned thing going on, except me falling to pieces!"

"Not true. There's love here. I've always felt it, and been thankful for it, and wondered why you'd always stayed away. You would have made a great mom."

And for once, Miss Edwinna Rutherford was speechless.

AS PETE DOZED, Edwinna leaned back and thought about how frightened she'd been when she "saw" Pete lying in a road but could not make out where or why. Her visions were a mixed blessing. Long ago, when they began to get in her way, she'd researched the phenomenon. She learned there were certain people who literally heard the voices and conversations of distant individuals. That was called "clairaudience." There were people who felt things emotionally about others they did not know. That was "clairsentience." And there were people, like her, who saw things before they happened or as they were happening at a distance. That was "clairvoyance."

The seeing and the knowing had always come to her simultaneously. But lately, she felt her gift, or curse, or whatever it was, failing. Her visions had once had a cinematic brilliance: sharply focused and glowing with an otherworldly light. More recently, it was as if someone had smeared Vaseline on the lens of her second sight. It had taken her twenty minutes to find Pete. She could see her where she lay, but not the larger picture. She couldn't see how the girl had got there or how long she'd been there. She couldn't even nail the "there," except that she knew it was a road near water. It was almost an accident she'd found her at all, and by then Colin had taken over, thank God.

That Colin. What the hell was wrong with him? Good-looking chap. Successful, in an Island sort of way. Smart. Sensitive. Anyone could see he and Pete had a visceral connection. They weren't lovers, though; Edwinna would have seen that. No, what she saw was his longing and Pete's blindness. Colin was like some Arthurian knight, serving and worshipping his Guinevere from afar. Hopeless. Ridiculous.

Edwinna wondered whether she wasn't being too hard on the woman who now lay in her own bed. What you do when a child disappoints you? Do you extend trust and understanding like lengths of rope? Is love like that: like an infinitely extended safety line? Surely, you needed eventually to reel that line in. But she didn't know. She had no experience from which to draw. This mother of three, this adult in her bed, was not her child. No one was. She looked at the figure asleep before her, fragile as an autumn leaf, and didn't know whether to hold her tight or slap her silly.

What she did know was that she needed to get to the bottom of those bruised wrists.

fifteen

CHRIS CHRISTIANSEN LEANED back in one of the two worn vinyl office chairs behind the desk in the island's tiny squad room. The spring on the chair was so weak that he was forever at risk of flipping backward. The bare-bones police headquarters was tucked away in back of the part-time county government branch office, just off the Vashon Highway a mile or so south of town. Like thieves on an inside job, officers skulked in through a code-protected door lock. There was a window, but the dusty Venetian blinds were perpetually down.

Behind Christiansen, the police radio hissed in the same way that the complete silence of wilderness hisses when your ears are searching for any sonic signal. From Christiansen's point of view, it had been a blessedly uneventful holiday morning. The graveyard shift had had a domestic violence complaint on the north end of the island that, like most domestic violence complaints, was roundly denied by both the man of the house and the wife, or partner, or whatever she was, who'd first called it in. Once the officers got into the couple's mossy single-wide trailer off Cove Road, they found no wounds, no obvious bruises, just a few sticks of furniture upended, the cloying smell of poverty and despair, and the wailing of a small child. Since then? Silence.

Then there was this Tyler Strong call. Something about it troubled him, but he couldn't put a finger on it.

He chewed on it as if on his favorite snack: smoked salmon jerky.

First of all, he said to himself, the summer people never called the police. It was as if they lived in a different, more elevated sphere of existence from the regular folks who called the island home, a world apparently unsullied by conventional civil or domestic distress and immune to crime, their off-island wealth serving like thick batts of fiberglass insulating them from more common human frailties and tragedies. He wasn't so naive as to think they did not suffer like everyone else, not at all. Certainly Pete had suffered when that boy of hers was killed some years back. Horrible loss, that was; sudden, utterly random. For a few weeks everyone on the small island seemed to feel it and talk about it, he remembered, even though few of them knew the family well. The story was in the island newspaper—there being so little real news to report apart from the occasional break-in or traffic accident. Yes, Christiansen said, nodding to himself; the summer people suffered, too. But they kept it to themselves.

And that was the second problem: it was awfully early in the morning for Strong to become alarmed and file a missing persons report. Yes, it was a day for packing and leave-taking, for going back "over town," as people said of Seattle; the end of the season, a melancholy time. Maybe, if you were one of them, you'd linger, saying goodbye to your friends over a cup of coffee or herbal tea, putting the moment off as long as possible. Maybe, if you were a private, contemplative sort, you'd go for a quiet and solitary barefoot walk on the beach.

Christiansen thought about that for a moment, then rose, the springs of his chair screeching at its release, and checked the tidal chart on the office wall. The morning high tide had just peaked and was beginning to ebb. Madrona Beach, he knew, had a broad, shallow shelf that stretched out several hundred yards into the outer harbor before dropping off. A careless sailor thinking distance from shore equaled a safe depth could easily run aground there. When the incoming tide arrived, the swell slipping in to the harbor moved so quickly you could watch the water advance across the shelf almost moment by moment. And when the tide finally turned, it retreated just as quickly—there one minute, gone the next; gone so far, in fact, that a stranger could be forgiven for wondering if it would ever return.

So, even an hour before high tide, Christiansen reckoned, there would have been plenty of beach for walking. Then again, long as it was, you couldn't walk shoeless very far along Madrona Beach, even at low tide; the east and west extensions of the beach were studded with hillocks of rock encrusted with barnacles and mussels that would cut up your feet. And the beach itself was mostly stony with chunks of broken brick from the day, long ago, when a factory operated there fashioning bricks from island clay for the building booms in Tacoma and Seattle. Every day, the tide unearthed what seemed like an unending supply of brick from beneath the sand and gravel strand.

He poured another cup of tepid black coffee from the office's stained and elderly "Mr. Coffee" machine, still staring at the tide chart as if it were a window giving onto the beach. He nodded to himself: a long barefoot beach walk was out. So Pete must be out visiting. Probably at old Judge Strong's place, or saying her goodbyes to the March family in the old Rutherford place. Tyler had said he'd checked, but Christiansen was skeptical; the man seemed barely *compos mentis*.

YOUNG ADAM WANDERED along the beach beyond the boat ramp to the place where the sand gave way to crushed oyster shells he'd learned were ancient remnants from before the time of American settlers. It was a special place for him, a place that, on account of his discovery about it at the history museum, he liked to claim as his own. He came here often during the summer. He loved to skip oyster shells across the water and watch the boats swing out of the inner harbor where the yacht club was and beat for the open water of the outer harbor and the Sound beyond. He especially liked the sailboats—the sloops and ketches and yawls and schooner rigs. It was his older sister, Justine, who taught him how to tell one from the other and who also got him to recognize the difference between the snub-sterned newer fiberglass boats and the older wooden boats with their low, sleek cabins and graceful swan-tailed sterns arching out over the water like a second wake.

But he didn't honestly expect to see many boats on Labor Day morning, despite the clear sky and light breeze from the north. The rich people, Justine told him, were the ones with the fancy yachts, and the rich people were leaving because the season was over. For the next ten months, those graceful boats would lay at anchor or in their berths at the club, bobbing like driftwood. It didn't seem right to Adam; they were living things, in his mind, meant to race across the surface of the outer harbor, heeled over with the downwind rail buried in the water, sails taut and snapping, wakes frothy, like the whipped cream that came atop his hot chocolate at the Burton Coffee Stand. One day, Adam promised himself, he would have such a sailboat, and it would never be left like an orphan at a yacht club dock. He'd sail it all year. He'd call it, he decided, *Silver Heels*, for the froth it left behind.

In the absence of sailing craft on this Labor Day morning, young Adam attended instead to a gull busily poking among the mussels that encrusted the side of the concrete boat ramp. After a bit of jerky effort, the bird prized one mollusk free. Then, its find clutched in its beak, it rose high above the parking lot on its stiff white wings, hesitated a moment, and then dropped the shellfish to the pavement below. Immediately, it dove to the asphalt to yank the fresh meat from the shattered blue-gray shell. When it had finished, it returned to the boat dock and repeated the process.

At school, Adam's favorite teacher had said that human beings were distinct from other living creatures because they alone made tools. But it seemed to him that the gulls on this island, at least, were clever enough to use the asphalt as a shell opener. That was pretty cool and way smart.

Much as he cherished this place, his special place, Adam knew he was hanging around here to avoid going home. He was happy sitting quietly in the warming morning sun and watching the light sequin the open water. But it was a struggle to keep away the scary stuff from the night before. It was a struggle not to hear the voices, the shouting, the anger.

Adam had been asleep, wrapped in a quilt on the chipped white wicker day bed that faced the water on the upstairs sleeping porch, open to the night, when the noises awakened him.

sixteen

"DO YOU HONESTLY believe, in that booze-pickled, hopelessly narcissistic brain of yours, that I don't know where you've been?"

It was Adam's mother's voice. She was on the brick patio below where Adam slept.

"You're drunk." His father.

"Damned right I'm drunk. And I intend to get drunker!"

The boy heard ice rattle into a glass.

"And besides, who are you to talk?" This was his mother again. "You can barely walk. How'd you even get it up?!"

"Shuddup."

"Let's see, now. Would that be, 'Shuddup, I don't want a noisy confrontation?' or 'Shuddup, I don't want to hear the truth?' or 'Shuddup, she's nothing to me,' like all the others? or 'Shuddup, *you're* nothing to me and never have been?'" She was splashing something into a glass.

"Just shuddup. You don't know what you're talking about..."

"Oh, don't I? Maybe you're right! I wouldn't be the least bit surprised; I probably don't even know the half of it! Not a tenth of it! But what I do know sickens me. You wanna know what I know? I know what I smell, and the next time you decide to fuck one of the neighbors, have the smarts to take a swim afterwards to wash off her signature perfume. You reek of that woman's cloying 'Lauren.' It's revolting."

More sloshing into a glass.

"You've had enough."

"Enough? I've barely started!"

His mother laughed, a harsh, rasping sound the boy didn't recognize. "Here's a little bit of fashion insight for you and that whore: did you know that glamorous "Ralph Lauren" was just a little schmuck from the Bronx whose real name was Lifshitz?! Started out peddling neckties out of suitcases. Classy, huh? But it figures she'd drench herself in that swill; she thinks 'cause it's expensive it's chic, like she'd even know, because let me tell you, you bastard... Peggy March isn't even '"Lauren'" perfume; she's drug store toilet water, and I don't mean the stuff that comes in a bottle!"

"You're disgusting..."

"I'm disgusting? Oh, that's rich. No, I take that back. Wrong. That's what shrinks call projection, that is. You're the one who's disgusting. The thing is, I can't even imagine what you see in her, apart from those pneumatic breasts — which, by the way, are as phony as 'Ralph Lauren.' But wait! I get it now! You're as much a fake as she is, and you don't even have silicone to blame! You're like a two-dimensional theater scrim, an illusion of depth where there is none. You're all show and no content. Inside, you're like a vacuum chamber; it's a wonder you don't implode..."

There was a crash, followed by more derisive laughter — again, his mother's.

"Well, isn't that typical. You're crude enough to take a swing at your own wife but too drunk or incompetent or both to pull it off! I can't believe how pathetic you are; look at you, you can barely get up!"

Adam heard the clink of a bottle on glass again.

"Thank God for the honesty of gin!"

Another pause and then Adam heard a shriek.

"Let go of me!"

"'Let go of me?' Like you'd ever let me near you anyway, frigid, fuckin' ice queen..."

A struggle and another crash, then his mother's angry voice again.

"Ice queen? Oh gosh, when could that have begun? After your first infidelity? Your second? Your umpteenth?"

"Bullshit! I'll tell you when. August 2001, 'xactly. Two died and so did this marriage. When that happened, you crawled into a hole and disappeared. Wife? Sorry, mine's gone AWOL."

"Oh, so your infidelities are *my* fault?! Like they only began with Two's death? How many holes have you crawled into since then, eh Tyler? Fuck you! Fuck *you* and everything you've spoiled. I can't believe I ever believed in you, you feckless, unfaithful bastard! I don't need you, I don't want you; I have gin, and that's a damned sight more reliable than you are. More than you've ever been."

Glass on glass and then another scuffle, followed by a scream of surprise. "Let go! You're *hurting* me!"

"Don' you ever count Tyler Strong down, bish. You want gin? Fine, have it all...!"

A muffled scream. The sound of choking.

Adam bolted from the summer porch, dashed through his parents' adjacent bedroom, took the back staircase two steps at a time, threw open the back door, and ran off across the front lawn, curving toward the beach. He knew the way; he'd done it before.

His parents often fought. Late at night, usually. Nothing new about that. Then, in the morning, they acted as if nothing had happened. It was confusing. Sometimes it was hard to know which reality was real: what he'd heard, or what he saw later. Over time, he'd learned to listen and watch and trust only what he experienced, not what he was told.

But tonight was different. Tonight was crazy.

He reached the beach, flew over the tops of several massive driftwood logs white as cadavers in the moonlight, hit the sand, and kept on running when he heard a shout.

"Adam! You scared the shit out of me!"

He stopped. "Sis?"

Adam's big sister, Justine, was wrapped tight in a blanket in the lee of a big log with someone Adam couldn't see. There was a tiny flare of orange; it looked like they were smoking.

"Smoking's bad for you, sis."

Adam sometimes had trouble thinking of Justine as his sister. She was fifteen years older, for one thing. She'd been his live-in babysitter until she left home, when he was three, but he only knew this from his mother; he had no memory of her care. What he did know was that when she reappeared in his life during the summers when the family moved to the island where she now lived year-round, she'd become his best friend. He didn't exactly know why she loved him so, but he thought maybe it was because she'd been there when their other brother died—the ghostly Two, the boy who wasn't there but was everywhere: in framed pictures, in conversations cut short when he entered the room, in angry fights like tonight. Two; the boy who died but lived forever, as real and tangible and immortal to some people as the ebbing and flowing of the tide in the harbor where he'd been killed.

Adam knew how Two had died and that Justine had been at the wheel of the speedboat when it happened. He knew this because Justine told him. That was one of the cool things about his sister: she was straight with him. Not like his parents. Whenever he asked about Two, they changed the subject so quickly you wondered if you'd even asked. When he told Justine about that, she'd said, "They hide it from you because they hide it from themselves." Adam thought that made a ton of sense.

It was hard for Adam to stay connected to Justine except in the summer, and the older she got the harder that became. Part of the reason was geography: she was on the island but he was in Seattle ten months of the year and she didn't visit much, except sometimes at Christmas. The other reason was that it seemed like she'd been in trouble a lot and Mom and Dad hardly spoke of her. He'd picked up enough between the lines to figure out that she'd barely made it out of high school, had been admitted to Seattle University only because grandfather Harlan made a personal appeal via his church to the Jesuits who ran the school, and she had been thrown out only a year later, though Adam didn't know why. Now she had her own place on the island and worked at a bar in the village. Mom didn't approve of that either but Dad didn't seem to care. "She's old enough to make her own decisions, even bad ones," is what Adam heard him say one night.

The strange thing, when he thought about it, was that his sister, who was supposed to be a screw-up, was the only one who seemed to make sense in the family, the only one who treated him like he had a brain, the only one who told the truth—and he loved her more than he knew how to say.

Justine disengaged herself from the nearly inert body beside her and dashed across the beach toward the boy. She was wearing a black Harley Davidson T-shirt long enough, but not quite, to be a dress. The silver-winged insignia flashed in the light from the houses. She lifted and spun him in an affectionate, dizzying circle until they collapsed on the sand.

He wriggled free.

"They're fighting again," he said.

"There's a surprise..."

"No, Sis, I mean really; I think they were, like, you know, punching and shoving and stuff."

"They were probably just falling down drunk. Nothing new there."

"Yeah, Dad said Mom was drunk, but it sounded like he was the one falling over. She was really angry."

Justine reached out an arm and pulled her little brother in like a salmon on a line.

"So what were they fighting about, baby brother?"

"Don't call me that."

"Right. Right. We had an agreement. Sorry."

"Thank you."

"So?"

"Mrs. March."

"Peggy?"

"Yeah."

"What about her?"

Adam looked out at the star-studded water.

"Okay, never mind. I get it." She gave him a hug and they both stared at the water a while.

After a few moments she said, "Can I tell you something I've learned?"

"Sure. What?"

"Adults? Parents? They don't know as much as we think they do. They're not like teachers in school who know all the stuff in the textbooks. Parents are basically just making it up as they go along and hoping for the best. And they make a lot of mistakes."

"So who knows stuff?"

"Hardly anybody. I think we're meant to discover it ourselves."

"What's that supposed to mean?"

"It means you have to come to your own conclusions. You have to pay attention to what's happening around you and then decide things for yourself. I don't mean to say Mom and Dad are stupid. It's more like they're...I don't know...what? Cartographers, maybe. Know what that means?"

"They make maps."

"You amaze me."

"Whatever."

"Okay, so they're map-makers, right? But they're like the first cartographers—the ones who really didn't have a clue what the world looked like and were guessing, based on legends and hearsay and stuff, because they still wanted to help voyagers, keep them from sailing off the edge. So parents...it's like they draw the imagined boundaries of what they think is known, or acceptable, or legal, or something, but then you have to explore the blank spots all on your own. You have to fill them in, figure out what's really right or wrong, true or untrue, come to your own conclusions."

"Like Sherlock Holmes."

"Huh?"

"Yeah, Holmes; I took a book of his detecting from Old Adam's bookshelf."

"You can read that?"

Adam shrugged. "Mostly. Anyway, so this Holmes guy, he's so cool: something happens, right? Like a murder? And he looks at the evidence, but he doesn't accept the conclusions of other people—you know, like the police. No way. That's just like his starting place. Then he starts thinking—'deducing,' he calls it—and he throws out the stuff that maybe other people think is important but it really isn't, and then he lasers in on the stuff that's left. But here's what's the coolest thing about Holmes: when the stuff that's left makes no sense, he doesn't let it go, even when people make fun of him. Uh-uh. He's got this thing that what's left has to be what's right and the only problem is you haven't figured out yet *why* it's right. In one of his stories, he says something like, 'When you rule out the stuff that cannot be, whatever's left, no matter how improble...'"

"Improbable?"

"Yeah; I looked it up. It means 'unlikely.'"

"Right."

"So, 'whatever's left, no matter how unlikely, is what must be.' You ever read him?"

"Adam, he's not a real person, you know…"

"Yeah, yeah, I get that. But he should'a been."

"I hear you."

"Wanna know what else I learned from him?"

"Sure."

"I learned to pay attention."

"Huh?"

"You know…listen to what's going on. Pay attention. Not zone out. Sometimes he solves things without ever leaving his chair. And you know what else?"

Justine nodded and smiled. "You tell me."

"A lotta what people think and say makes no sense."

"No way!" She had to suppress a giggle.

"Way! It's like, they say things or think things and you can't figure out how they got there, you know? And I'm like, 'Where's your evidence?'"

She wrapped her little brother in a hug as warm as a duvet. "You blow me away, kid," she said into his neck.

He twisted away. He loved her hugs, but maybe not here in public, right here on the beach. Even in the dark.

"Hey, I have an idea!" Justine said.

"What?"

"It's way late and I'm beat. I'm thinking it would be cool to sleep at the judge's house, to be with Old Adam. How 'bout you?"

Adam nodded toward the shape under the blanket. "What about…?"

"What about 'What about?' You're my main man, Adam; let's us both go up and see if we can get some rest. It's been a long night. Damn these end-of-summer parties."

"Yeah."

"You like the fireworks?

"They were okay. Not as good as fourth of July, though."

"Yeah."

"But I don't get it; what's the point? Just because we're leaving?"

"I don't get it either, really. You know what I think?"

"What?"

"I think they end the summer with a bang because they know nothing but months of gray and mist lie ahead. It's a ritual, like they're trying to make explosions that'll get the sun's attention."

Adam looked back at the water. "Sounds like Dad ended it with a bang."

Justine started giggling and could hardly stop, thanks largely to the dope she'd been smoking.

"You're too little to know anything about that," she said when she caught her breath.

"I'm not little."

"No, you're right. I'm wrong. Know what? Sometimes I think you're older and smarter than me."

"That makes no sense."

"Yeah. Right. See what I mean?"

"No."

"You will, Adam. You will. Let's go."

They left the shape in the blanket by the beach and clambered up over the driftwood to the lawns above. Hand in hand, they ran to Old Adam's place, as if before a storm.

seventeen

THE STRONG COMPOUND was smaller than the Petersens' but, perhaps because of its slightly elevated position, always seemed to possess a certain graciousness that the more rustic Petersen houses never achieved. Where the Petersen cottages tended to ape the architecture of New England—weathered shingles and bleached white trim—the Strong houses were exemplars of Northwest vernacular, marked by wide overhanging rooflines and darker woods and stains, a design style that emphasized shelter and solidity against the region's notoriously foul winter weather.

The Strong family had arrived in Seattle by way of James J. Hill's Great Northern Railway. Thomas Strong, Old Adam's father, was a Hill protégé and a bright young legal advisor for the company. By the late 1890s, Thomas had moved from the railroad's headquarters in St. Paul to its terminus in Seattle, started a family, and become a founder of the now venerable Seattle law firm: Strong, Penfield & March. An ardent civic booster, a champion of organized labor, and a wise real estate investor in the bordering communities he knew someday would become a part of the expanding city, Thomas had quietly amassed a formidable fortune.

His son Adam, fresh out of Harvard Law, joined the family firm in 1935 and immediately made a name for himself as Seattle's lawyer of choice for difficult criminal cases. And in time, Adam Strong went from arguing cases to deciding them as a King County Superior Court judge. After several decades on the bench, he'd finally retired—respected equally in the end by both trial lawyers and the police, a rare combination.

JUSTINE SETTLED HER brother in one of the judge's guest rooms and looked in on her great-uncle. She found the bony old man propped up on his pillows, reading a Readers' Digest hardcover that included four novels condensed to roughly the length of his current attention span. Old Adam had always bored easily, but especially now, in his nineties.

"What are you doing up at this hour, you old relic?" Justine chided, giving his skeletal limbs a hug.

He winked. "Too old to have sexy dreams; might as well stay awake."

"You're disgraceful," the girl said, straightening his covers.

"So are you. It's our bond."

"Damn right!" she said, hugging him again.

"You're my favorite great niece."

"I'm you're *only* great niece, Adam."

"Well argued. Make a good lawyer, you would."

"Like my father? No, thanks."

"Your father's a terrible lawyer. Hasn't ever had a clue how to put together a case. Hasn't the focus or discipline. The firm's had to carry him for years. Embarrasses the hell out of me, tell the truth. Hired him because his own father, rest his dear sweet soul, was my kid brother. Family, you see. They'll boot him out when I'm gone, if not sooner." He shook his head like a dog shaking off a swim. Then he squinted at Justine. "You didn't hear that from me."

"Shit, Adam, if they do dump Dad, what happens next? What happens to Mom?"

"Pete's got her own resources, thank God. Old Robbie left her the shipping company. She's set—always assuming that nitwit absentee father of hers, 'the Pope,' hasn't signed the shipping company's assets over to the Knights of Malta or something."

"He's an Episcopal, Adam."

"Well he acts like the goddamn Pope…Mr. High and Mighty. When's the last time he came down from the Mount and visited the beach, huh?"

"When Two died, I think."

"And didn't that just do a world of good! Guy comes over from town, delivers a bunch of pious, empty homilies for a grandson he barely knew, then catches the next ferry back. Not a thought for what his daughter was going through. Pompous ass! Don't know how your mother puts up with him, frankly. Patience of a saint, that girl. You have any idea what a great mom you got?"

"I'm learning, Judge."

The old man sighed and shook his head, smiling. "For a smart girl, you're a damned slow learner."

Justine laughed. "I know."

"What the hell you think I'm hanging on for in this life? Waiting for you to happen, that's what! Don't know how long I can wait, tell the truth. I'm older than dirt!"

Justine looked away but the old man's eyes never left her.

Then he softened. "What're you doing here, anyway? Shouldn't you be shacked up with somebody?"

"Don't start, Adam," she said, wagging a warning finger, "I may be a girl but I know how to punch."

"So I hear. From the police. Heard you've cleared the bar a couple of times. Made me right proud, that did."

"Oh, shush," she said, flicking a hand. "No big deal tossing a couple of drunks. Speaking of which…"

"What?"

"Mom and Dad are drunk and fighting. Again. I brought Young Adam over here to sleep. Found him on the beach. He'd run away from the house."

"Great kid. Great name, too."

"Yeah…whatever. He overheard them fighting tonight. Mom said Dad is having it on with Peggy March."

The old man looked hard at the girl, then gripped the bedclothes and pulled them back.

"Son of a bitch!"

"Adam, relax."

"I should thrash him! Bad seed from that whore mother of his, pardon my French. Told her she wasn't welcome here, time she showed up with Richie's successor; imagine having the gall to come here at all! Her son's no better, is what I say. Watched him for years now. Loved his father, I did, such a gentleman, and a hero to boot. Never warmed up to that Tyler, though, even after he married Pete. Never seemed wrapped too tight, even as a kid, but after he killed Two—that's what he did, you know; his fault that boy died—he's got even more unhinged. Like those damned fireworks tonight: fine one minute, then *boom!* Unstable is what I think."

"Adam, hey. He's my father."

The old man snapped out of his rant.

"Right. You're right. Sorry. You're so terrific I forget that. Apologies, my dear.

"And besides, this is just what Young Adam said he heard."

"Tell you something, girl: whatever that kid brother of yours says, I'd believe. He doesn't miss a trick. Comes over here and borrows my books, did you know that?"

"He told me. Sherlock Holmes."

"What is he, third grade? Asked him why he didn't read the stuff they give him at school. Know what he said? 'Boring.' He's a pistol, he is. Just like you. Just like your mom, both of you. Sharp."

Adam suddenly remembered what they had been talking about and said, "Which is more than I can say for that father of yours. What the hell's he thinking? Peggy March? Okay, that's some set of water wings she's got on her, no question. A sweet enough girl, too, but not the brightest bulb in the chandelier. And Rob March—shit, he's practically family! Not to mention I hear Rob just took his old man's place as partner in the firm! And your father's banging his wife?"

"Adam had been asleep. They woke him up. Maybe he got it wrong."

The old man sank back into the pillows.

"You're right, counselor: insufficient evidence; jury'd never convict." The old man sighed; he'd run out of steam. Then his eyes narrowed. "Tomorrow! I want to see you and Young Adam in my chambers tomorrow morning, first thing! We'll get to the bottom of this case."

"It's already tomorrow, Judge."

"Then get the hell out of here, girl; you're keeping me from my beauty sleep!"

Justine leaned toward him, fluffed his pillows, kissed his cheek, and slipped out of the room.

She thought about returning to the beach, to the guy she'd picked up at the bar. No way. Loser. Doper. *Nothing new there,* she thought, *you're a loser magnet, you are.* No, that was unfair; she didn't attract losers, she sought them out. Nothing to do with them, really; everything to do with her: if you picked a loser, there was no risk of making a real connection, and therefore no risk of loss. *Smart,* Old Adam had said. *Yeah, right.*

Justine pulled an old Hudson's Bay blanket from the cedar chest in Adam's front hall and went out to the porch. She laid it on an Adirondack chair, slid in, and wrapped the scratchy wool flaps around her, like a mummy.

One thing about Old Adam: he said what he thought. And he was nobody's fool. But she'd never known he'd had so little respect for her father. It wasn't like it came as a shock when she thought about it—the old man had never been especially warm toward her dad—polite was more like it, out of respect for her mom, she guessed. Still, his anger shocked her. And he was right; her father changed after Two was killed. He'd always been moody—up one day, down the next—but after Two was killed it often seemed like his mind was somewhere else, like somebody walking down the street listening to an iPod: there, but not there.

Shit, who am I to talk?

It was in high school that she started "acting out," as one of the shrinks called it; running away, taking drugs, hanging out with older guys, men with criminal histories as haunted by past events as she was. Two had died when she was at the wheel of the speedboat. That was all you needed to know about Justine Strong. Grieving was her breathing. His death was her life.

All she'd really wanted, all those years growing up, was for someone to *see* her, to acknowledge her as the living child, as the first child. She wanted to be cherished, but instead she kept feeling sidelined by her parents' grief. Maybe she was just a painful reminder of what they'd lost. Maybe, had she never happened, none of this would have happened either. No Two being killed. No alienated, angry parents. No ghosts.

She had not made a great success of her life; as far as her parents and some of the public authorities in Seattle were concerned, she was a fuck up. But this summer, finally, she sensed something in her changing, turning like a sloop coming out of irons and catching the wind; she was moving, even if she didn't know yet in which direction. It was like she'd been trapped for years in the flat, still, weed-entangled Sargasso Sea, turning in an endless gyre ever so slowly and going nowhere. Then, suddenly, she wasn't in the doldrums anymore. She was making way.

She knew that the change was due partly to having decided to live permanently on this island, to become a part of its tight and supportive community. But it was also due to Janice Fradkin, the brassy owner of the bar where Justine now worked. Janice had been around, and her body and face showed it. Overweight from drinking, face a starburst of red veins, body worn from years of late nights, and soul wounded from men who were all wrong, Janice saw something in the girl who'd begged for work as a waitress at the end of May. What she saw was herself. She saw a second chance, a way to reverse what sometimes seemed an inexorable downhill slide. Here was someone young and bright and tough, someone who still had years stretched out before her. Janice had no children. In fact, she'd never married anything except the bar. But if she'd had a daughter, she'd have wanted her to become Justine.

After only three weeks of waitressing, she'd taken Justine aside, given her a crash course in mixology, and put her behind the bar where the tips were better. Then she sat back and watched the girl grow. It was almost physical, what she saw happen; Justine didn't tend the bar, she ruled it. She developed an instinct for limiting extraneous movement while mixing drinks, for husbanding her energy, for staying on top of the crowd late into the night. But something else, too: she seemed to think of the bar between her and her customers as a stage, a platform to entertain, console, encourage, and charm. Justine behind the bar was a civilizing influence; in no time at all Janice's oldest and most troublesome customers were going out of their way to gain Justine's approval and her genuine, if arm's length, affection. Justine was a tamer. And not one of those "heart of gold" types, either; no, this girl had a head of gold, too, and not because of her hair, either. She was wicked smart.

Justine had her father's height, which gave her presence, but also her mother's delicate features, which gave her class: same ash blonde hair, streaked platinum by the sun in summertime, eyes even bluer than a July sky, small breasts, broad shoulders, well-defined arms, legs that had gone, imperceptibly, from bony to lithe. She held herself with a certain unconscious authority...like a Siamese cat. Were it not for the fact that her preferred place to shop for clothes was the dollar rack at Auntie's Attic, the thrift store in town, she'd have been besieged with suitors, but her slouchy, shapeless wardrobe worked as a formidable barrier. She didn't display herself behind the bar, either, the way the waitresses did to get tips. She dressed conservatively but nonetheless managed, with the lift of an eyebrow, or a sideways smile, or a tilt of the head, to telegraph warmth.

She held them all in thrall, but the customers also soon learned Justine had boundaries you were wise not to cross. A lewd remark and you were cut off for good; get rude and you were out on your ear. More than once, she had leaped across the bar and slugged a customer. That was all she needed to do; her devotees did the rest and the guy was soon in the street.

It was only on the beach, in her faded black bikini, that anyone could appreciate Justine's native grace. There, on her solitary walks, you could see past the fake diamond nose stud, the eyebrow ring, and the tramp stamp tattoo that spanned the dimples at the base of her long spine. And what you saw behind the camouflage was near perfection.

The tattoo had driven her mother into a frenzy of outrage.

"What the hell is *that?!*" Pete exclaimed this year on their first day on the beach.

"Oh, Mom, relax, it's just a tat."

It was, in fact, a lovely tattoo, a fanciful butterfly executed with a Celtic twist: graceful, almost architectural.

"I can't believe you would do this to yourself!"

"You just can't cope with the fact that I'm different, that I don't conform."

"Oh, for Christ's sake, girl, don't you see? There's nothing nonconformist about it at all! It's like the piercings! You're not making a statement, rebellious or otherwise; you're just doing what everyone else your age does. That's what makes me crazy: It's so *common!* Your statement is, 'I'm just like everyone else!' And you're *not!* You're so much more, so much better!"

And that was the moment, on the Fourth of July, just two months earlier, when Justine knew her mother had a respect for her that Justine herself hadn't yet achieved. It was how she knew her mother believed she was unique and had value. It was how she knew her mother was her friend. She just hadn't figured out how to thank her yet.

Justine pulled the rainbow-striped blanket tighter and stared out over the dark water. It was very late. Or very early, depending upon how you measured time. The moon, which had silvered the wavelets on the outer harbor earlier, had slipped behind the hill to the west. She remembered a line from an old song. "And the darkest hour…"

She was asleep in seconds.

eighteen

MUCH AS HE longed to, Old Adam could not sleep after Justine tucked him in. He stared at the paneled wall opposite his bed—tongue and groove cedar planks gone orange with age—and played out the end-of-summer Labor Day weekend party on the wall like a flickering old home movie, the kind they'd all shot from jumpy Super 8mm cameras, long before cell phones could do the same thing.

He loved summers on the beach and had the gnawing fear that his were coming to an end. When his old friend Doc Stevens told him—what, fifteen years ago?—he had prostate cancer but that it grew so slowly he'd die of old age first. Adam hadn't counted on living this long, longer even than his doctor. In other respects, however, he was disgustingly healthy. But with a lawyer's attention to verbal details, he did notice that for some years now any upbeat declarative statement about his person—by doctor, relative, or friend—was followed not by a period but by a comma and the inevitable subordinate clause, "for someone your age."

Lately, though, he could feel himself weakening, especially in the knees; and the shiny blackthorn walking stick he'd long carried, a gift from that Irish vet, Colin Ryan, had become a necessity.

The damp months in Seattle were an indistinguishable blur, especially since he'd retired from the bench. He sat on corporate boards in meetings that left him certain they should be called "boreds." He walked a treadmill at the Washington Athletic Club downtown. But the long, wet Seattle winters left him feeling as unfocused and blurry as the perpetually rain-streaked windows in his den at the family home on Capitol Hill.

But the summers, the summers—they shimmered like gems, each one different, each precious. He took a special comfort from the certainty of the cycle that repeated each Fourth of July, generation after generation, here on Madrona Beach, cycles as regular as the moon and the sun and the tides.

This afternoon, for example, long before the end of season party had begun, he'd been sitting in a lemon yellow Adirondack chair on the porch of the Petersen Old House, sipping a tall glass of sun tea with spearmint his dear Pete had brought him. He watched the children in the water and thought about the magnetic properties of floating diving rafts. This was something science needed to look into; you built a wooden platform roughly eight feet square, attached floats to the underside, anchored it, and the next thing you knew kids were all over the thing—pushing and jumping, daring and diving, running from one corner to the other to make it pitch and roll. Shouts and shrieks of happiness all around, generation after generation.

He could see his childhood pal Robbie Petersen long ago, a bony kid if there ever was one, disheveled mop of Nordic blond hair, rallying the other boys to stave off a wave of girl cousins wearing those old black wool "bathing costumes" and threatening to occupy the platform. Four years older than Adam, Robbie and Adam's older brother Richie had been his idols. And despite the age difference, they always included him. He and Robbie had remained friends for life, and it was Robbie who got him through the horror of Richie's death. But then death took Robbie too, less than a year after his son Justin was lost at sea. Robbie was only fifty-five. Broken heart is what Adam put it down to, something he well understood. His wife Emily was gone by then, too: breast cancer.

He saw the years rolling past, and there was little "Pete" Petersen and her girlfriends in pink and green and blue bathing suits with tiers of flounces around their bottoms, shoving boys off the diving platform edge and piercing the air with screams of fake fear and real delight, the way only pre-teen girls do when they win—the boys, after all, not trying too hard to resist. There were lots of kids on the beach back then.

And today he could see, right in front of him and just off the beach, Young Adam, the apple of his eye, struggling with Rob and Peggy's son Mike to toss off Mike's sister Katerina and her friends from town—who were all older and bigger than the boys.

See, that was what most of these fretful parents never understood; all you had to do to provide seemingly endless opportunities for invention and mayhem at a beach was to build a floating platform. Even the plugged-in kids this summer, attached as they often were to their iPhones or video games or whatever the hell they were wired to like patients on life support systems—even they unplugged and became like all the other kids over the years when the sun was on that offshore floating platform. It was magical. Childhood was really as simple and reliable as an old wooden float.

There was a simple and reliable rhythm on shore as well, which gave him comfort. During the week, the mothers kept one eye on the children and the other on whatever novel their book clubs were reading, alternating shifts from time to time for tennis sets. Lunch was typically a do-it-yourself spread laid out by all three families in the kitchen of the Old House. But then, at five, the ladies had cocktails on someone's porch while the children bathed. Dinners were often communal.

Even in this day and age, the Madrona Beach mothers did not work in the city, and Old Adam considered this to be as it should be. He wasn't against women working—his law firm had already elevated three women to partner—but he believed mothers belonged with their children, and he was unapologetic about it.

When the men arrived at the beach on Friday afternoons, having left the city behind, everything changed: there would be a short but furious period of cutthroat tennis, or raucous touch football, or daredevil water skiing on the harbor. That was in the old days, though, before Two's accident. After that, there had been no more water skiing. The following summer, as if some silent signal had been passed, the families arrived on the Fourth towing simple aluminum fishing skiffs, not speedboats. Crabbing skiffs, they were. No one spoke of the change.

Then, when the sun dipped behind the low hills west of the harbor, the men would take to their grills. Slugging back cold bottles of Mac and Jack's African Amber or Redhook ESB, they'd sear thick burgers and brown bun-length hot dogs for the kids, the charcoal smoke curling into the air and resonating like a vestigial memory of the peat burned by his ancestors in the boggy levels of Somerset, in England.

Around the grills there'd be good-natured banter and insults about one another's culinary skills and, of course, flirting with the ladies. The women spent most of their time in the kitchen preparing side dishes, sipping fruity cocktails, trading gossip, and from time to time sashaying outside, ostensibly to replenish the beer supply, but also to remind the men what they'd missed all week.

The Labor Day weekend party was all of this, but magnified in a way the Fourth of July party wasn't, as if there were still torches of need, jealousy, lust, or anger among them all that had to be quenched before the houses could be closed up for the season.

It was also the unofficial but universally accepted day for the girls to get sloshed. Old Adam didn't remember when this had become the tradition, but as far as he was concerned, it made for interesting and revealing entertainment. All afternoon, the women, as if they lived in their mothers' era instead of the present, sipped old fashioned cocktails: martinis, whiskey sours, gin and tonics; the daiquiri that had become became a national fad during the Kennedy administration, as well as something new and pink that Adam had learned they called a "Cosmo." It was always something of an amusing mystery to him how anything got done in the kitchen when the women had only one useful hand with which to work, the other being wrapped around a condensation-bejeweled cocktail glass.

Then, as if on a signal, the women vanished. They repaired to their respective cottages to "freshen up" for the evening. The fathers fed the kids, bullied the reluctant ones to eat, gave them ice cream as bribes, sent the younger ones to the games room afterward and the older ones outside into the waning light. Eventually, the women emerged again, as if from chrysalises, dressed to kill. Sneakers and flip-flops gave way to heels that clicked across the painted porch floorboards and aerated the lawns, necklines swooped to reveal tans that glowed as if on globed lanterns, sleeveless print dresses swished on switched hips to the music from the Tacoma jazz and blues station playing on the radio, and the party kicked into high gear.

The season was ending; ripeness, ambiguity, longing, and finality flickered in the dusk like fireflies.

nineteen

OLD ADAM, DRESSED for the festivities in a cream-colored linen suit grown too big for his shrinking frame, an open-collar white shirt, and a weathered but still jaunty straw hat, had been given his customary bourbon on ice and a small bowl of salted peanuts, and been promptly forgotten. The delightful thing about being an old coot, Adam mused, was that you became invisible.

This evening, though, there was something new: Young Adam sat on the porch step next to him, his sun-burnished, blemish-free hand resting on one of Old Adam's polished brown brogues. He had not invited the boy to join him; the kid had just appeared, smiled, and sat, leaning slightly against the old man's leg, like a favored dog. They sat as if sharing the warmth of a fire in winter, inhabiting a small, insulated pocket of reality while the rest of the world swirled about them. For the most part they said nothing. They were observers of events, from two different ends of time.

There was quite a crowd this evening, Old Adam noted with pleasure; the families, of course, and their children, and their children's friends from the city, along with a new, younger couple, the Keatings, who'd recently bought a bungalow on the hill above Burton. They'd been invited, ostensibly, because their two young children had become playmates for Peggy and Rob's kids. But Old Adam guessed the main reason was because Jemma Keating, a Seattle psychotherapist in her late thirties, was immensely decorative.

Justin's widow Sylvia was expected, too. She'd never remarried, and Adam had always admired her—her resilience, her stoicism, her determination to make a life on her own terms after her husband's death. He'd also admired her big-boned frame and strong face, its cheekbones and jawline sharp and angular as if cut from granite. It was those Nordic genes, he guessed—centuries of weathered women standing on rocky shores, their Delft blue eyes focused on the leaden horizon as if by their intensity alone they could will their husbands' brightly-painted, snub-nosed fishing boats to reappear there.

Just now, Sylvia was across the lawn on her knees working in the border garden of her own small cottage: a woman not yet knotted by her advancing age, still fit, her graying long blonde hair braided and wrapped around her head like a crown. She would join the others, he knew, but in her own time. He looked forward to it.

Some years after his Emily had died, Adam had surprised himself by discovering he was attracted to Sylvia, but he never acted on the impulse. Oh, no, the age difference was too great. And yet, all these years later, he still fancied her. He shook his head; *the stubborn persistence of desire*.

Down at the beach, Adam watched Sylvia's leggy daughter, Alexandra, round up children for dinner. He suspected Sylvia and Justin had chosen the girl's Russian name because of all the time he'd spent on the Bering Sea. But Adam was a student of history and he wondered whether either Justin or Sylvia even realized that the girl's namesake, Tsar Nicholas's wife, had come to an unhappy end. Nothing unhappy about this girl, though; she raced along the sand behind the kids with her arms wide like trawler doors scooping bottom-fish into an invisible net, the children all shrieking with feigned panic.

Adam liked Alex, but she troubled him, too. The girl was closing in on forty fast, had married young, divorced soon thereafter, and bumped along in a series of either painful or unfruitful relationships ever since. Adam heard she'd recently moved to a co-housing development near the center of town, perhaps in search of reliable companionship.

Alex was a looker: trim and supple. A yoga teacher or something, he thought he remembered. Long strawberry blonde hair that may or may not have been natural; Adam couldn't tell and didn't care. He thought of it as pale fire. What worried Adam was that the girl nearly vibrated with the need for offspring. Over the course of the summer, he'd watched her eye every eligible man who showed up on the beach, single or married, family or visitor, and run through her own private calculus: Father material? Income? Potentially available? Desperation wreathed her like a fragrance, a scent most men caught immediately and fled from.

Damn shame, really. If she was anything at all like her mother, Sylvia, the girl had a lot to offer.

JEMMA KEATING STOOD behind the railing at the corner of the Petersens' porch, nursed her second Cosmo, watched her husband Todd wander among the linked beach families on the lawn, and admired yet again the ease with which he engaged virtual strangers. After twelve years of marriage and two children, it still amazed and pleased her. Almost six and a half feet tall and with a head of hair that always looked like dirty straw pitched carelessly into the corner of a barn, it was as if Todd's gangly, easy way of moving through the world extended, uninterrupted, from bone to brain. He'd wade into a knot of people he'd never met, smile his crooked smile, stick out a bony hand, and say something self-deprecating that directed attention away from him: *Hi, I'm Todd, the interloper. Now, how do you folks all know each other?*

She wondered if this quiet confidence wasn't a fundamental difference between tall boys and tall girls. Jemma was six feet tall in her stocking feet and had been since she was fourteen. She'd felt like a freak then, and despite the fact that she'd made a seamless transition from ugly duckling to graceful swan and become a beauty with lissome limbs, a feline smile, and anthracite eyes with hair to match, she still saw an awkward stick figure when she looked in the mirror. So, where Todd learned to lead, Jemma, the pale-skinned dark-haired skinny girl no boy would ever dream of asking to dance, had learned to stand to one side and observe. And because she was as bright as she was tall, her habit of being the observer had become, with time, training, and experience, a career.

The "cocktail hour" had begun at four and was still going strong at seven-thirty, as if it wasn't clear to anyone whether it or dinner was the main event. Initially, Jemma had gravitated to the kitchen where the other women were preparing side dishes. Most of them, she knew, had known each other all their lives. Perhaps all that familiarity bred contempt, though, because their banter seemed a language of insider jokes, sharp-edged jabs, and side-swiped, hit-and-run jealousies. It was an observer's paradise.

"Sylvia's Alex has certainly turned into a fetching young woman, don't you think, Pete?" Peggy March had been watching Alex as she rounded up the children on the beach. With her fingers, Peggy was turning mayonnaise, diced red onion, and fresh cut dill into the salted potatoes she'd boiled for potato salad, a process that seemed, as she did it, inexpressibly sensuous.

"Young?" Pete snorted, glancing out the window. "Girl's pushing forty!"

"Uh-uh; mid-thirties, as I recall. Still looks hot, though..."

"You would, too, if you'd never had kids and spent your days in a gym doing yoga contortions."

"Think so?" Peggy said, doing a mini-twirl by the sideboard.

"Actually, no, Peg," Pete said, laughing. "I'm guessing those two frontal cushions you've added as accessories would get in the way of all that twisting and bending."

"You're just jealous," Peggy said, arching her back and thrusting her chest skyward.

A short, sharp, laugh from Pete. "Between us girls, Peg, I never found that particular physical feature to be the main event anyway."

"Well, you wouldn't, would you, our petite little wren," Peggy countered, looking around to the others for affirmation and receiving only smiles and shrugs.

"But I commend you nonetheless," Pete continued. "It must take a fair amount of contorting just to get next to that rotund bedmate of yours...so maybe I'm wrong; maybe yoga is your métier!"

Jemma felt herself pulling away, as if rising up to a corner of the ceiling to watch the verbal fencing below.

"Ladies," Peggy's Seattle neighbor and guest, Lucia, interjected, "let us not be unkind, yes?" Lucia was Brazilian and there was still a Portuguese lilt to her English. "Besides, in Brazil absolutely everyone has these little surgical adjustments. Are we not like flowers that need a little pruning here, a bit of fertilizer there to flourish? Not to mention to be pollinated..."

Peggy flashed Pete a broad smile.

"Only in season," Pete grumbled, and everyone laughed.

Lucia had met Rob and Peggy when she and her American husband, Joe Robertson, a photojournalist, had moved into the small Craftsman cottage next door to the March's big "four-square" on Seattle's Queen Anne Hill, years ago. Lucia—"lush Lucia," as Peggy referred to her in private—was in her disgracefully vital mid-forties and had, as near as anyone could tell, never been visited by a surgeon's knife, but who knew? She had auburn hair that cascaded in loose waves well south of her perpetually bronzed shoulders. Her eyes were dark as baker's chocolate and surrounded by moats of white so brilliant it was as if the searing tropical sun radiated from them directly. You could be burned by those eyes, and many men had been.

On a walk one particularly shimmering Rio morning, the kind that presaged a stifling afternoon, she'd noticed a barrel-chested photographer picking his way slowly among the blankets and towels that quilted the sand along the beach at Ipanema. He wore khaki shorts, a white T-shirt, a multi-pocketed olive vest, and was armed with a big black Nikon camera to which was attached a foot-long, white telephoto lens. His eyes swept the sand not with the hungry voyeurism she'd grown accustomed to in this city of leering men and women in thong bathing suits, but with the intensity of a bird of prey. From time to time he'd lift the camera to his eye and quickly study a scene. When he saw something that held promise, he lowered the camera, smiled, handed out a postcard-sized piece of paper, mumbled something, and offered a pen. The person on the beach, or the group of people, would sign the release and the photographer would step back, smile again—a guileless, boyish smile, sweet and fresh and intoxicating as a lime caipirinha—and click off several frames. Then he'd bow slightly and shake hands.

A moment later, his radar picked up Lucia, who was strolling along the waterline. Though not tall, Lucia carried herself with a model's poise: an erect and knowing carriage that telegraphed confidence, and, of course, pride of body. She was fecund as a rain forest, and just as unselfconsciously natural. This time, the photographer lifted his camera first and asked permission second, handing her a card with the glossy image of a much-pierced and tattooed beach denizen on one side and his own name on the other. She looked at him without smiling, and looked again at the card...buying time. Then she signed the permission card, smiled, took his arm, and walked with him.

Thus, she and Joe began, and never looked back.

Pete liked Lucia immediately because she was so effortlessly honest, like a child to whom no one had ever said, "Hush." Peggy loved Lucia the way someone in a lawn chair in late spring loves the strengthening sun and basks in it gratefully; Lucia warmed her soul. Lucia reminded Peggy almost daily that a woman is born with special powers and needs only to cultivate and exercise them, like an athlete, to achieve her goals. The two of them could spend entire afternoons chatting and painting each other's toenails. Lucia teased that she was giving Peggy "girl lessons," and she wasn't far wrong. Raised in that commune by near strangers, Peggy had been improvising the role of a contemporary woman in the world for most of her adult life, mostly using women's magazines as her script. With Lucia she had a teacher. Lucia took Peggy shopping and helped her dress for public occasions with Rob, and private occasions with him, too. Lucia understood sensuality; she exuded it the way a hothouse plant emits oxygen.

It was just after Lucia had spread diplomatic oil on the choppy surface of conversation in the kitchen that Alex bounced into the kitchen in short-shorts, midriff-baring T-shirt, and sneakers.

"Kids fed," she announced to all and sundry. "Three bean salad next!"

"Alex, dear," Peggy said, "not all of us welcome bean salads at our age…"

Alex didn't miss a beat. "At your age," there was a momentary pause and a smile, "pulses, legumes, beans, should be a key part of what you eat and serve your families every day. They're at the heart of the Mediterranean Diet, which, as everyone knows, keeps your weight down and improves longevity, both of which would be of interest, I should think...at your age."

Alex smiled and tossed her hair, as if all she was doing was dispensing dietary tips. She lifted her left foot to the seat of the bar stool at the kitchen island, bent forward into a stretch, and touched her chin to her knee, then reversed and repeated the move with the other foot.

"Pete," Peggy said, "isn't that cellulite on the back of Alex's thigh?"

Alex whipped around to peer at the back of her legs, a move which, even with her "rubber lady at the circus" flexibility, was almost impossible.

"What? Where?!"

"There," Peggy said, pointing to a dimple.

Alex relaxed. "That's a scar! From rock climbing. But I expect the only rock climbing you've ever done is for that one on your ring finger."

At this, Pete couldn't resist a fit of the giggles.

"Pete!"

"I'm sorry, Peggy, but Alex's right; that's one hell of a rock you've got. I'm surprised your arm hasn't stretched from the weight."

It was true; her engagement ring was a massive stone that grew from her finger like a carbuncle and was guarded by a stockade of smaller stones.

"Just a measure of how much Rob loves me," Peggy said. She didn't give a damn that the ring was ostentatious; the moment he'd given it to her, she knew she'd left the commune behind forever.

Alex ignored this exchange, pulled a large Mexican green glass bowl from a Thriftway shopping bag, and began pouring out Tupperware containers of cannellini, garbanzo, and red kidney beans; thinly sliced red onion; finely chopped English cucumber; olive oil; crushed garlic; salt; pepper; a pinch of chili pepper flakes; cilantro; and balsamic vinegar.

"I can't wait," Peggy said, rolling her eyes.

"You'll just have to," Alex chirped. "I have to change."

"I think it will be splendid," Pete said as Alex jogged out of the kitchen. Pete was in peacemaker mode now. "I bet it will be yummy and good for us, all at once."

"Like sex," Peggy added.

Heads rose as if lifted by the same wire.

"Yes," Lucia said with enthusiasm. "It's what keeps us alive!"

"If that's the case, then I must be dead," Pete cracked.

Jemma descended from her imaginary observation post. "With respect," she said, nodding toward Lucia whose naive candor she found refreshing, "I don't think that's what keeps us alive. I think what keeps us alive is intimacy, which is something else altogether... it's to do with companionship, and trust. Sex is a product of that, not the source."

"Yeah. Whatever." Pete said to the salad she was preparing.

Peggy stepped over to where Pete was working and gave her a hug, "Shit, Pete, you've got Little Adam, and Justine, and Tyler; that's like the Trifecta!"

"I don't have Two," Pete said into the salad.

Peggy let her go.

Lucia interjected. "Pete...Mrs. Strong...how long has it been now?"

"Nine years."

"Nine. Almost a decade," Lucia mused. "How long before you let him go?"

'Never. I will *never* let him go!"

"Then your life is over."

"What?" Peggy snapped on behalf of her friend.

Lucia smiled and looked across the room and out through the multi-paned windows, as if reading a message on the waves beyond.

"Pete, forgive me, but is it not the case that today you have two children who need you and one who no longer does?" she asked. "Where do you focus your love and your life, Pete? On behalf of whom?"

"What do you know about loss?!" Pete snapped.

Lucia walked across the kitchen and kissed Pete lightly on the cheek.

"I lost both my father and mother. They were socialists who were assassinated during Operation Condor in Brazil. Many people were. I was a child. I raised my little brother alone. We begged along the beaches."

There was a moment of perfect silence, broken only by the distant voices of happy children eating at the picnic tables outside. Pete stepped away from the counter and put her arms around Lucia.

"Thank you, Luce. I did not know that. I am so sorry."

"As am I for your loss," Lucia said. "So, right now, here is our mutual task, eh? First, we finish the salads.

Then we all change. Then dinner. Then tomorrow. Then the next day, until forever, yes? We must live."

Jemma slipped out the side door to the porch and gulped air like a swimmer struggling to the surface from a great depth, as if the weight of tragedy carried by these women threatened to crush her chest. She was a therapist. She should understand this pain. But somehow its immediacy was stifling.

twenty

ALEX WAS THE first of the women to emerge dressed for the evening. As the men readied their grills to prepare the main courses, she swept down the steps to the cooking patio, wearing a body-hugging, calf-length crinkle rayon dress in the green of an unripe pear, a color that echoed her eyes and contrasted with her hair. She wore coral-orange fake snakeskin kitten-heel sandals, the short spikes of which were already stained from the clay that underlay the damp sod. Something about this besmirching only served to make her look sexier. As she approached the men and their grills, she bowed and presented Tyler with a martini, the chilled glass frosted like a winter window. A plastic skewer held three olives.

"Three!" Tyler noted with theatrical surprise. "That seems excessive."

Laughter all around.

"Excess is good," she purred.

Silence from the admiring men.

Rob March noticed Alex placed her palm on Tyler's hip for balance a moment longer than was absolutely necessary as she put down the drink beside his gleaming stainless steel gas grill.

After she'd picked her way back up the steps again, ever so slowly, and entered the house, Rob poked Tyler with his long-handled spatula.

"Goodness, old boy, how will you ever survive the winter without Miss Step-and-Fetch-It?"

"Cut it out; she's my cousin-in-law or something."

"No law against that," Rob countered.

"You should know."

"Hey, family and divorce law is an honorable profession."

"Like the oldest one?"

"Gimme a break."

"Not a chance. And anyway, how do you ever know who's telling the truth?"

"What, in a divorce proceeding?"

"Sure. Whatever."

"I don't. I'm not sure there's ever a 'truth.' The client presents his or her own take on reality; that's a given. The other spouse does the same. They seldom agree. You should know that; it's not all that different from any legal case."

"Truth. Lies. Reality. Fantasy." Tyler was staring off toward the house. "It's all like a hologram shimmering in space, all image and no substance. Hard to get your arms around..."

Rob squinted at his friend.

"Earth to Tyler?"

"What?"

"The thing is," Rob continued, "I'm not looking for absolute truth in a domestic case, and I don't think the judge is, either; we're looking for fairness in a situation that's fraught. Especially if there are kids."

Tyler was staring again. *Fraught.* Yeah. Things get fraught... with kids."

This was getting weird, Rob thought. He looked back at the door through which Alex had disappeared and lowered his voice. "You thinking about a divorce, Tyler?"

Tyler came back from wherever he was. "Don't be an idiot," he snapped, "I just wondered."

"And I'm wondering about you and that cousin-in-law or something... body like that? You lucky dog."

"Shut up, asshole. There's nothing going on there."

"Okay, okay; no need to get nasty. Just teasing."

"Teasing or jealous? You're not exactly a chick magnet anymore, counselor..."

This was true, if cruel. Over the years, Rob March had morphed from husky to corpulent. Tennis matches with Tyler were a distant memory. His only advantage over his former court rival now was recent, secret, and formidable: Rob had just been made partner in their families' firm and Tyler, as yet, had not...and, as Rob now knew, never would.

That had been decided by the partners at Strong, Penfield & March during a management meeting on Thursday—a meeting to which Rob was invited and from which Old Adam had abstained. The verdict had yet to be communicated; the senior partners decided that would be their newest partner's job. There would be a formal letter, of course, but they had asked Rob to pass the message on, gently and informally, since they knew he'd be seeing Tyler on the weekend. Rob suspected it was some kind of loyalty test. Whatever it was, it sucked. He'd put it off all weekend.

He'd put it off, in part, because he'd voted with the majority.

The discussion had been long, but polite. Rob had said little. Then the oldest partner present, Spencer Penfield, turned to him and asked, "So, Rob March, our newest member, how do you vote?"

Rob had assumed the vote would be silent. The question stunned him. For personal reasons, of course, he hadn't wanted to vote against a friend of so many years. But he didn't want to appear weak before the older partners. The plain truth was that while Tyler wasn't an incompetent lawyer, he could agree with the others that he wasn't a good enough one, either. As effortlessly skilled as Tyler had always been on the beachside tennis court and, for that matter, on the squash court at the Washington Athletic Club in town, as a lawyer he was erratic, even slipshod. Rob had worked with Tyler on cases only rarely—their specialties seldom overlapped—but when he did the experience left him irritated. In strategy meetings, tall, handsome Tyler would lean back on the rear legs of his chair and stare at the wall opposite, spinning out dreamy what-ifs: what if plaintiff's counsel takes this approach, or has this information, or brings that witness to the stand? This would have been helpful, had he known what he was talking about, but often he did not. "We need someone to look into that," he'd conclude with an airy wave. Tyler had no stomach for the grunt work of lawyering—the research, the case-building, the examination of possible cross-arguments, the rebuttals. He acted as if that were all somehow beneath him. The more likely truth, Rob suspected, was that Tyler couldn't find his way through the detritus of the problem, much less develop a strategy.

In court, he tried to charm juries and judges with his warm voice and patrician bearing, even as he skated on the thin ice of whatever argument he'd managed to piece together. Tyler used a certain animal cleverness to challenge juries. Or just confuse them. He was good at that. He'd make them as fuzzy about the facts as he was. He tied them in knots.

What galled Rob, and others as well, was that Tyler exuded a superiority that was entirely unearned. The senior partners noticed these sorts of things. So did the clients. You got to be partner by winning cases (Rob was very good at this, a bulldog; Tyler wasn't), by bringing in new clients (another of Rob's strengths), and by keeping the clients happy. His innate charm notwithstanding, the fact was Tyler's case record was mixed and his diffidence struck some clients as disinterest or, worse, a fundamental lack of *gravitas*. And in this, their instincts were accurate: he was a lightweight. Tyler rested upon his uncle's prominence as senior partner and son of a founder of the firm. Instead of growing into the job, gaining experience and skill, though, Tyler had become an embarrassment.

Rob knew failure to make partner was effectively an open invitation for Tyler to leave the firm. And he knew Tyler had nowhere else to go.

He looked squarely at Spencer Penfield and said, "I am opposed to Tyler Strong's elevation to partner, sir."

A nod from the old man.

Rob felt sick.

COLIN HAD JUST sat down after cooking burgers for the kids when Jemma Keating slid into an Adirondack chair next to him.

"Mmm," she said, "You smell yummy."

Colin laughed. "That's my aftershave. It's called Eau de Briquet. Comes in classic charcoal and mesquite."

"Oh, I'm all about classic."

She was, indeed, a classic beauty, but even in the late afternoon light, Jemma looked pale, and he asked her if she was okay.

"Women can be brutal," she said after a moment.

"To you?"

She shook her head. "No, no; to each other, to their oldest friends."

"Ah, you've been in the kitchen, then."

"Are they always like that? All claws and kisses?"

Colin laughed. "No, I don't think so. Maybe it's because it's the end of the season. Maybe there are scores to settle, or they're sorting out the pecking order for next year. You're the therapist; I'm just the vet."

"What, you didn't study animal behavior?" she countered, and now they both were laughing and the weight had lifted from her chest, only to be replaced by hiccups. She asked Colin for a glass of water and, when he returned, drank down the entire contents, holding her breath as she did so, and the spasms subsided.

When Tyler saw Jemma's empty glass, he bounded up the stairs to make her another Cosmo from the bar on the porch. This chivalry, however, was undercut rather severely when he stared, unabashedly, down the front of her sundress as he bent to deliver the drink. As Tyler returned to his grill, Jemma rolled her eyes at Colin. Colin shook his head.

"Animal behavior," he repeated.

She smiled.

He gestured toward the men at their grills. "It's the same down there; I've been watching."

Tyler and Rob were arguing now about local politics. Suddenly, their jibes began to seem like the script of some play. The topic of the moment was the state's proposed premium-priced option for a reserved car slot on the otherwise first-come-first-boarded car ferry from the mainland.

Rob: "It's anti-democratic and anti-American: why should rich people get to go to the front of the line?"

Tyler: "Oh Christ, March! Since when are you the proletariat? You'd be the first in line!"

Rob, raising his hands, unwilling to do battle: "I'm sorry, it's just wrong."

Tyler, viciously, if *sotto voce*: "You're sorry, all right…"

Rob: "I suppose you're also opposed to the increase in the island school levy?"

Tyler slamming the spatula on his grill: "Are you joking? You'd be a fool not to be! Shit, we're already paying a fortune in property taxes for this place and my kid doesn't even go to school here!"

Rob, annoyed: "Whose fault is that? While you're paying another fortune to send your son to that private school in the city, half the kids in West Seattle take the ferry over here because the island's public schools are so good!"

Tyler: "We don't live in West Seattle, smartass."

Rob laughing: "You could send Young Adam over here in a limo and *still* save money!"

Tyler: "Fuck off, March."

Rob, finally losing his patience: "Ah yes, the illiterate's inevitable resort to profanity. What the hell is it with you tonight?"

Tyler ignored him.

What intrigued Jemma was that this entire conversation was for Tyler apparently all about dominance, as if the man could not leave any declarative statement unchallenged. It spoke to her of a cavernous insecurity...and an underlying emotional volatility she found unsettling, even dangerous.

Finally, like rain refreshing a cracked desert floor, she heard Todd's voice.

"Okay, guys, I'll confess that I went to private school, too—one of the best: Lakeside. I was one of their charity cases, though they called it a scholarship. The thing was, my mother knew the public schools were failing and she wanted something better for her kid. Don't we all? Anyway, in the last couple of years, my company's been trying to strengthen the public schools. We've invested in them. Don't you think that's the way to go? Build them up?"

There was a guilty pause. From Tyler, a smirk; from Rob, a thoughtful nod. It was one of the reasons Jemma was so proud of her husband: he didn't need to win; he'd rather get warring parties to find agreement among themselves.

"You gonna cook those shrimp or just fondle them?" Tyler snapped at Rob, who was basting his skewers with marinade. The truce, apparently, was over. At his own stainless steel grilling temple, Tyler was slathering dill mayonnaise on wild Alaskan King salmon fillets as long and thick as hand-split cedar shingles.

Rob straightened to his full height, which wasn't much, smiled at Tyler like a lord to a subject, and said, "Stand back, amateur, and watch a master in action!" He laid the olive oil and garlic-infused shrimp, lemon, onion, and cherry tomato skewers across the grate above the charcoal in his modest Weber. The sizzle was like hail on a metal roof.

"While you embalm that beautiful fish in your customary—and may I add, utterly boring—supermarket coating," Rob taunted, "I have been preparing the precursor to tonight's fireworks."

"Behold, the chef..." Tyler said, ignoring Rob and focusing on his salmon.

Rob turned the seared shrimp skewers, reached for a squeeze bottle on the ground by his grill, brandished it grandly, and shouted, "Ladies and gentlemen and children of all ages: stand back! The performance is about to begin!"

There was a pause for effect, as if Rob had been about to stun a jury with some case-closing revelation about his client, and then, with a flourish, he squirted a stream of undiluted Greek ouzo on the shrimp skewers that lay on the grill above the hot charcoal. With an explosive whoosh, a four-foot column of anise-tinged alcohol vapor flamed into the darkening sky and instantly vanished, garnering a chorus of "Ooohs" from the kids on the lawn and, "Holy shit, Rob!" from Tyler.

Rob turned toward Tyler, grinning, his arms in the air, index and middle fingers of both hands splayed in a victory sign. The fat man did a little lumbering dance in a circle, then returned to his skewers.

Tyler shook his head. He shifted his overcooked, mayonnaise-slathered salmon filets to a large aluminum baking sheet and headed toward the kitchen.

twenty-one

HE COULD HAVE had Alex, of course. Tyler had known it not long after the families arrived in July. He always did know. His mix of diffidence and solicitousness, of engagement and distancing, disturbed the air around him and the women he met wanted to know more. They liked the way he unsettled them.

Tyler's greatest attraction for women, though, was unconscious and unaffected: he listened to them. He paid attention. Women shared secrets with him they wouldn't have dreamed of sharing with even their best girlfriends. He did not offer them advice, though he might ask questions. There was a profound grandiosity in this solicitude, of course, as if his attention were a gift he was bestowing upon them. But since no one had ever given them such focused and caring attention before, they didn't notice. Nor did they notice his mercurial mood shifts—there for them one day, absent the next. They gave themselves to him freely…and were baffled when, eventually and inevitably, he drifted away, as if bored.

Whenever Tyler Strong walked into a room—the living room of a friend hosting a party, a meeting room at a business conference, the reception line at a charity function, the hostess's podium at an acclaimed restaurant, an hotel bar where he was to meet someone, an airport waiting lounge, the aerobic machine room at the Washington Athletic Club—anywhere—he scanned for women. Like a vampire hunting for fresh blood, he was in continuous search for the attention of new women who could give him meaning, give him life. And he knew immediately which woman would do it for him.

It wasn't so much predator and prey as it was a meeting of the mutually needy.

IN THE PANTRY hall where the Petersens' dishes and serving plates were stored in old floor-to-ceiling, glass-fronted cabinets, Tyler slid his spatula under the salmon fillet, separated the crisped skin from the pink flesh, and transferred it to a large, chipped, cream-colored ironstone platter of uncertain antiquity. The way the old house was built, the pantry shelves were accessible both from the back hall and the kitchen itself. Through the glass doors on the kitchen side he saw Rob's wife Peggy bent over the kitchen's center island scooping her potato salad into a bowl. Slipping soundlessly into the next room, he grabbed her from behind so she'd jump. Then he reached around her warm body and swept the salmon platter to the counter before her.

"Tah-dah!"

"Very nice, I must say," she said.

"The salmon?"

"Not the salmon."

"The surprise?"

"As if you didn't know."

"You're looking exceptionally luscious tonight, neighbor, which is saying something…"

"And what is it saying?"

He pressed his pelvis against her soft bottom, briefly, then stepped away. "It's saying, 'Yum.'"

She backed up against him again to feel the bulge, just for a moment, then returned to her salad.

"Be careful," she warned.

"Hard, when I'm feeling dangerous."

Peggy shivered. "Um, yes. Hard."

Tyler was sure the word "voluptuary" must have been coined just for Peggy March. Tonight, she was wearing a vintage Diane von Furstenberg wrap dress in black and white diagonal stripes that guided one's gaze, like an airport's vector signal, to the golden declivity that ran southward from the cupped hollow between her collarbones to the shadowy chasm between her heavy breasts. A part of his martini-fuzzed brain wondered what piece of intimate undergarment engineering she had chosen this night to keep those luminous lobes upright. He decided he'd discover that later. Peggy, he'd learned in the last two months, had expensive taste in lingerie. And creative ideas about sex.

"Alex was here a few minutes ago; did you need another martini?" Peggy asked. There was just the slightest archness in her question.

He leaned toward her ear. "I need nothing but thee."

"Oh?"

He lowered his voice. "Hugely."

She smiled into the salad. "Good."

"You, too?"

"Me, too."

There was a commotion outside, and suddenly Peggy's fifteen year-old daughter, Katerina, flew through the door from the front porch with her brother, twelve year-old Mickey, in train.

"Why do I *still* have to eat with the babies, Mom? It's not *fair!*"

Mickey punched her.

"Oww!"

"I'm not a baby!"

"Okay, okay!"

"Stop it, you two!" Peggy ordered. "First of all, as your brother has just reminded you, there are no babies. Only kids, and you're not much older than most of them."

Tyler, observing Katerina's adolescent body and noting she was developing rather nicely, begged to differ, but did so to himself.

"Second," Peggy added, "it's a tradition. And on the last day of the season we observe traditions. You graduate to the adult table at sixteen. Next summer will be different. I promise."

"Next summer is next summer!" the girl wailed.

Tyler crossed the room, put his arm around the girl's shoulders, and leaned down, catching the warm, salty scent coming off her body.

"Look, it sucks, I know. But here's what I want you to think about," he said in his deepest, most seductive voice. "Right now you're Queen of the Hill with the kids: the oldest, the smartest, the most beautiful, the one everyone looks up to, the one in charge. I know you know that; I've watched you. You're terrific with them. A star. But step into the adults' group tonight and you'll be nobody. Poof! Just like that: Invisible. Loved, of course," and here he gave her a sideways hug that made her squirm, "but invisible. Now, which sounds better to you?"

Katerina hesitated. It was as if she was chewing the problem to digestible bits. Finally, she dropped her head and said into her sandals, "Yeah. You're right. But I don't have to like it."

"No, you don't. And next year you won't have to. I shall look forward to that."

Her head turned sharply, "You will?"

"You bet."

Katerina gave him an ear-to-ear smile, jumped up to peck him on the cheek, grabbed her little brother's hand, and danced out of the kitchen.

Peggy had her hands on her hips, which accentuated her décolleté. "You certainly have a way with the ladies."

He leaned across the kitchen island, ran a finger down her bare arm, and said, "I'd certainly like my way with one of them..."

Peggy blushed. She hated that she always did, that her need was so transparent. But tonight, after three Cosmos, she didn't care.

"West End? Two?" she whispered. "Under the Madronas? Rob will be asleep by then."

"Two."

At that moment, Pete burst through a swinging door from the back hall, her arms laden with plates.

"Two? Were you talking about Two? Please, let's not. Let's just get through this day without reliving tragedies—okay?"

As if someone had flicked a switch, Tyler shifted to attentive husband mode.

"No, no; the 'two' are just our new guests tonight, Todd and Jemma Keating."

"I like her," Pete said. "She's smart and thoughtful. But I keep thinking she's analyzing everyone."

Pete had changed into a simple spaghetti strap cocktail dress in bias cut black silk charmeuse that emphasized her shoulders, her summer tan, and her sun bleached hair, a dress that somehow managed to be both demure and sexy. Her high heels brought her almost to kissing height beside Tyler, but not quite. He slipped his arm around her waist, gave her a hug, and briefly kissed her hair, still damp from the shower.

"I know what you mean. But here's my signature salmon done, and Rob's flambé shrimps are on their way, the showy bugger. Colin's finished cooking for the kids and Todd's out there, too, scorching ribeye steaks and brushing them with some English brew called 'Daddy's Sauce.'"

"Right. I'll just take these plates out to the dining room," Pete said as Tyler held the door for her.

Peggy March, who'd busied herself with the potato salad, stole a look at Tyler and lifted an eyebrow.

"Daddy's Sauce?"

twenty-two

JEMMA KEATING STOOD behind her assigned seat at the dining table and willed the other chairs to stop moving. *Damn that Tyler's Cosmos!* There were place markers—little tents of manila from cut up file folders with names lettered with the practiced hand of a calligrapher. Pete, she wondered? Todd's place, she noted unhappily, was all the way across the table from hers. To her right, the little tent said "Rob." To her left, "Tyler." She would have preferred Colin. She wondered who'd arranged the seating.

She slid into her chair, hoping a lower center of gravity would steady things, which it did, and moments later the men swept in with platters of steak, salmon, and shrimp and the room filled with a rich fragrance of olive oil, garlic, citrus, oregano and charcoal. Jemma was suddenly ravenous. The women had already laid out salads. Tyler went to work uncorking bottles of wine: three chardonnays from Oregon for the fish eaters, two Washington pinot noirs for the carnivores.

Then Tyler sat, leaned toward her ear, placed an oddly possessive hand on her thigh, and whispered, "Welcome." She moved her leg. The wine was passed around and Tyler jumped up beside her.

"A toast, please, to both another season drawing to a close and to the company of wonderful new neighbors! To the Keatings!"

Jemma ducked her head slightly and Todd waved a disjointedly loose hand and pleaded, "Please, please, no fuss; lovely to be invited to join you all..."

Everyone else raised a glass, mumbling "the Keatings!" and "Hear, hear!"

Rob March had lifted his glass too, as if by reflex, but said nothing. The mass of him seemed to be pulling energy out of the stuffy dining room as if he were a small cosmic black hole. Jemma liked Rob: attentive to his kids, obviously besotted still with his wife. Despite his bulk, he had soft, doe-like eyes, eyes that spoke on his behalf even when he was silent, as he was tonight. Just now they seemed focused somewhere in the far distance, as if he longed to be elsewhere. Peggy March noticed, too, tilted her head to one side in silent question, but failed to catch her husband's gaze. The man was troubled; Jemma wondered why.

The volume of table chatter rose and platters were passed from hand to hand. Jemma was amused to see Alex's three bean salad speeding, untouched, around the table. Out of sympathy, she took a spoonful.

"So, Todd," she heard Tyler say beside her. "Did I understand you've already retired? You're not even fifty, dude!" It seemed to Jemma there was an oddly forced heartiness in his voice.

"Don't know about 'retired,' but I did sell my business. Maybe 'unemployed' is a better term..." Todd smiled.

"Happily unemployed?"

"Not unhappily."

"You're in computers, is that right?"

"Not really."

"Then...?" Tyler persisted.

"Software. We created applications for smartphones. Before we were bought out, by Apple."

"Way to go!" Tyler said, looking around the table for confirmation of the significance of this announcement and seeing none. "That must make you a zillionaire!"

Todd squirmed, as if the subject under discussion were wife-swapping.

Jemma stepped in: "Todd creates small technology firms—'idea labs,' he calls them—and then, when they've created something of value and taken off, he sells them. The smartphone applications are just the latest."

His embarrassment past, Todd grinned at the others. "I get bored and move on; I have the attention span of a flea..."

Colin, who was sitting between Todd and Pete, laughed and said, "Oh, I don't think we believe that for a moment."

"No, it's true; I work on something for a while with my team, really struggle with it, and then I'm done. I want it off my desk; I want to move on."

"Thankfully," Jemma said, smiling across the table, "that doesn't extend to wives."

"Yet," Tyler cracked.

Eyebrows lifted around the table but Todd ignored this and did a little bow toward his wife with his head and shoulders.

"I believe, Todd," Lucia said from the far corner of the table, "that whatever mathematical or programming skills you possess, you are nonetheless a man driven by a passion to create, yes? You get bored, as you say. Then you create again. You are an inventor, and in that sense you are a pioneer. So very American."

"Whereas Rob and I are merely parasites!" Tyler barked, so loudly and unexpectedly that it was like an explosion in the room. A few people looked at him; others attended resolutely to their plates.

He turned to Rob, grinning. "Right, old man?"

Rob glanced at him slowly, as if coming out of a trance.

Then Old Adam, seated at the head of the table with Sylvia to his left and her daughter Alex to his right, spoke up, his gravelly voice rumbling down the length of the table like a seismic shift. "I beg your pardon, counselor?"

"Come on, Adam; law school tries to brainwash us into believing that we're crusading advocates for the weak, defenders of the truth, upholders of the law, protectors of the damaged and downtrodden. But the plain fact is that we feed off other people's troubles. Without their miseries, we'd be out of business. We're maggots."

"Nonsense," Old Adam snapped.

"Do you forget your Shakespeare, uncle?" Tyler continued, his voice at too high a pitch for the small room, as if flirting with hysteria. "'...First thing we do, let's kill all the lawyers!'"

"A fine quip," Old Adam countered, "but your inadequate education is showing. Shakespeare did not say that; a scoundrel in *Henry VI* says it, whereupon he commits a heinous crime. Perhaps you missed the irony."

Colin had been watching Pete watch Tyler. Initially, there was the slightest hint of a frown, but then her face became expressionless, as if she were listening to distant music playing in her head.

Colin wondered whether this strange show wasn't all for Jemma's benefit; Tyler belittling his profession so that someone, like Jemma, would interrupt and say how noble it was. If it was a performance, it wasn't working. Though her head was tilted roughly in the direction of her tablemate, Jemma's body was angled away from Tyler and her eyes were focused on Pete, as if waiting for a parent to upbraid a wayward child.

It was Lucia's photographer husband, Joe, a bear of a man with a neatly trimmed beard just showing touches of gray, who finally was moved to speak,

"Surely, Tyler, you could not carry on if this was what you truly believed of your own profession."

Tyler widened his eyes in mock disbelief and smiled at Joe as if the man were an idiot. "We bifurcate, my friend! We pretend we're saviors but we're actually scavengers. We're not legal eagles; we're like the gulls and crows out there fighting for carrion," he said jerking his head toward the beach. "While we scavenge, we soothe ourselves by believing we are making the world a better place. It's all bullshit." He was speaking very loudly, very quickly, like a pilot making an emergency announcement just before a crash.

Rob March leaned forward and peered around Jemma to regard his colleague. He'd never known that Tyler had held their profession in such low esteem. And this behavior was bizarre, even for Tyler. Rob wondered how much Tyler had drunk already. Then, suddenly, he wondered if Tyler had already guessed the law firm's decision.

Colin stepped in: "Come on, Tyler; it must feel rewarding when you win a case, no?"

Rob responded before Tyler could, as if to calm the storminess that had swept the table. "I regret to say there is at least an ounce of truth in my colleague's bleak assessment. Look at it this way—if we win a case, somebody else loses, and no matter what you see on *Law and Order*, plaintiffs and defendants are seldom purely good or evil."

"It's about justice," Old Adam said.

"Exactly," Rob continued. "Consider the Innocence Project."

"What's that?" Alex asked, turning not to Rob but to Tyler and smiling with klieg light brilliance.

But Old Adam intervened: "It's a dedicated team of lawyers and researchers who've been using DNA evidence to prove that a lot of people on death row around this country never committed the murder for which they were convicted. What's more, in many cases they've found that law enforcement officials deliberately falsified or suppressed evidence to convict an innocent suspect just to get the case out of their hair."

"That's criminal!" Alex exclaimed.

Rob blinked at her word choice, then added, "No, it's consciously evil. Then again, the ambiguity of right and wrong is probably even more pronounced in my own specialty, family law."

This admission ran like an electrical current through the women at the table; they were suddenly attentive.

"There, everyone loses in one way or another, regardless of the verdict, regardless of who is right or wrong," Rob confessed.

He looked at Tyler. "And I don't think it's black and white in your corporate law, either, Strong."

"Bernie Madoff was certainly evil," Tyler crowed, as if he'd just hit a home run in a game no one else was playing.

Now Jemma spoke up: "No, I think Rob's point is still valid. Madoff was amoral, certainly, and deeply troubled in some way we may never understand, but not evil. It's almost as if he occupied two realities simultaneously: the exceptionally adept investor and the shyster." She turned slowly and leveled a look at Tyler. "Perhaps, like you, he bifurcated."

"But the man ruined hundreds of people!" Peggy nearly shouted, as if she'd been one of them.

"People ruin other people all the time; they betray each other all the time," Colin said. "My fellow New Yorker, Jules Feiffer, the famous cartoonist in the *The Village Voice*, called them 'Little Murders.' It was in a play he wrote years ago. But are those acts evil? Or just venal, or careless, or stupid, or self-centered?"

"That's it!" Tyler cried, missing the point entirely. "That's the lawyer's life every day: little murders. And the hell of it is, sometimes the jury will find on behalf of real murderers!"

"Feiffer's play was about domestic betrayal, Tyler, not the law," Old Adam corrected, his left hand supporting his forehead as it were weighted down by his nephew's performance. "A work of genius, frankly. I commend it to you all."

Sylvia put her hand on the old man's arm, not so much to silence as to calm him. He turned and acknowledged her touch and realized, as if a flashbulb had suddenly revealed what before had been darkness, that she cared for him. He was thunderstruck. Sylvia, who tonight wore a simple, scooped-neck, calf-length cotton dress in a corn silk yellow that deepened her tanned skin and returned color to her graying hair, squeezed his arm and smiled.

There was an uneasy moment when the only sound was the clink of silverware on china, a moment when, tortoise-like, the diners withdrew to their armored shells to check on the safety of their secrets.

Pete broke the silence. "So, Jemma, how's that house you've bought coming along?"

Her husband laughed and answered for her. "It's in the Mies Van der Rohe tradition, or perhaps I should say 'condition.'"

Everyone at the table turned.

"You know, the great Modernist architect, a minimalist who once said, 'Less is more.' The house is less than we thought it would be and needs more work and money than we ever dreamed it would. Maybe it's a Modernist masterpiece!"

Laughter all around, just a bit too loud, as if from a tension bubble bursting.

"That's the problem with many of the houses on this island," Pete said, relaxing into a favorite topic of island discourse: real estate. "They were built originally as summer cottages, little more than campsites, by people like my grandfather. Now we ask of them more than they were ever designed to be."

"And retrofitting is so much more expensive than new construction," Peggy added. "Who are you considering to do the work?"

"We talked to Randy Josephson. Friend of our real estate agent."

"There's a well-named chap," Tyler snorted, like an animal emerging from a hole.

"Excuse me?" Jemma said.

"Randy. English term."

"He doesn't have an accent…"

"Tyler," Pete piped up. "Stop."

Jemma looked around the table for clarity.

"Tyler's being mean," Peggy said.

"Word is," Tyler said, leaning again toward Jemma, "he has a way with his female clients."

"*A* way, or *his* way?" Lucia demanded, her question meant to expose not Randy but Tyler. "What are you suggesting?" This night, Lucia wore diaphanous olive harem pants tied at the ankle, gold sandals, and a lacy, spaghetti strap camisole in black that only a Brazilian would have thought appropriate in public. Her smile as she looked at Tyler was as wide and dazzling as a beach in Rio, as if to blind him to the sharpness of her challenge.

"Yes, Tyler," Peggy added. "What harm has Randy ever caused you? He did a brilliant job rebuilding the fronts of my cabinets."

She's confusing him with her plastic surgeon, Pete thought to herself. She didn't know exactly what had got into her; Peggy had been her friend for years. A defensive cattiness crawled beneath her skin tonight like poison oak.

"Ignore my colleague and neighbor," Rob said, waving his empty wine glass so someone would pass the chardonnay. The wine was dragging him out of his funk. "Everything Josephson makes, no matter how utilitarian, comes out looking like fine furniture. The guy's a genius—and with metalwork as well as wood."

"Then...?" Jemma asked.

"He's pricey," Tyler announced.

"The hell he is," Rob countered, "but he ought to be. Charges no more than any of the other carpenters on this island and none of them can hold a candle to him. Damned shame, actually."

"Slow, too," Tyler goaded.

"Look, there are three goals in any renovation job. I figured this out when Peggy and I fixed up the old Rutherford place. They're price, quality, and speed. The deal is, you can only ever get two of the three. You can get price and speed, but you won't get quality. You can get quality and speed, but you won't get a good price. Or you can get price and quality, but not speed. I'd go with that one every time. Randy'll give you a fair price and terrific quality. It'll just take a little longer to finish, because he cares more."

"Plus, that way he gets to spend more time with the lady of the house," Tyler sniped.

Jemma turned to the man beside her. "Is this reality or fantasy for you?"

"You go, girl!" Lucia called across the table, pumping her fist in the air.

"It's projection," Rob said.

"Bullshit! The guy's a letch," Tyler persisted.

"Projection," Rob said again.

Pete stood abruptly. "Dessert, everyone? We've got end of season blackberry pie with organic vanilla ice cream, thanks to Lucia..."

Lucia rose as well. "My specialty," she announced. "I trust there will be no one declining?"

"No one is that brave, Luce," her husband, Joe, said, laughing.

The mood around the table changed as if they had all released a collective sigh of relief.

"I have some lovely Prosecco from Conegliano, near Venice, already chilled," Tyler announced. "I propose we adjourn to the patio, where it's cooler, there to enjoy the death throes of the day."

The rest of the guests rose and headed, somewhat unsteadily, for the French doors leading outside.

"You're such a romantic, Tyler," Peggy whispered as she passed him.

twenty-three

ROB MARCH HAD put it off too long and he knew it. Part of it was anger. He was angry with the other, older members of the firm for ordering him to tell Tyler he would not be made partner. He was angry at himself for voting against Tyler, even though it was right. And he was angry with Tyler for making the decision inevitable. The truth was that he was amazed Tyler had lasted even this long; probably Old Adam's doing. Tyler wasn't a functioning attorney; he was more like a remittance man who hadn't the good sense to disappear to some distant tropical locale and live off his sinecure.

"Tyler, old man, let's us take a walk on the beach and leave the dishes to the ladies," Rob said after dinner and the beachside fireworks were over. They were on the Petersens' wide porch, waiting for their ears to recover. Tyler had amassed an arsenal for Labor Day weekend that had shattered the air and fired the darkness for more than half an hour. He'd raced around pyromaniacally, setting flame to wick, to keep the children gasping and the adults covering their ears. Dogs throughout the neighborhood howled. Rob thought him nuts. Colin and the Keatings had had the good sense to leave beforehand.

"Why would anyone in his right mind leave the ladies?" Tyler said, his long arm describing a wide, embracing arc as if encompassing all womanhood. "Only thing worth living for..."

Rob knew Tyler was drunk. Tyler always became effusive about women when he was inebriated, expressively grandiose. Rob wasn't sober either; what had started as girding his loins for this talk with a few stiff drinks had slipped seamlessly into overindulgence. He kept having to shake himself mentally to attend to the task at hand.

Rob lowered his voice. "Look, you and I need to talk."

Red flags went up at the primitive core of Tyler's brain: Rob knew about him and Peggy. Or she'd told him. Either way, it was trouble. Adultery is fine with strangers, he reasoned, using a calculus all his own, but with friends, lifelong friends, it was trouble. He'd known that from the get-go, but he had taken what was offered anyway and he and Peggy hadn't missed an opportunity all summer. He glanced back to the safety of the cottages, then turned to Rob.

"Okay. Lead on, old friend."

On the way across the porch Tyler grabbed another beer.

The tide had just begun retreating, and there wasn't much beach yet exposed. They headed west where the strand was broadest.

After a while, Rob said, "I've just been made privy to some information…"

"Privileged information, counselor?" Tyler joked. "Should you be sharing it with me?

"It's not privileged, Tyler. It's personal."

He knows, Tyler thought. *He fucking knows.*

"Well what is it, then? A matter of honor or something?"

Rob looked at Tyler's face in the reflected light from the beach houses, momentarily puzzled.

"Yes, I suppose that's what it is; a matter of honor."

"Look, friend; it's nothing. I promise you."

Rob was even more puzzled. "Nothing? You know already?"

"Know what?"

"That you won't be made partner in the firm."

Tyler stopped dead in the sand, his feet planted like pilings.

"What the fuck?!"

"The partners decided. On Thursday. They'll be communicating with you formally on Tuesday, but they asked me, as your friend, to tell you this weekend."

"As my *friend?* Or as my *Judas*?! You *bastard!* Did you vote *against* me?"

It was Rob's moment of truth and he didn't flinch. "I voted with the other partners; it was unanimous."

"You fat shit!" Tyler threw his half empty bottle of Red Hook at Rob, and the bottle grazed the side of the big man's head. The blow stunned him and he staggered.

Tyler seized the moment, charged his friend, and took him down so hard it knocked the wind out of Rob's chest. Tyler grabbed Rob's head and smashed it into the damp sand repeatedly.

"You son of a bitch; you fat, phony, fucking son of a bitch!"

Rob March found it in himself to throw the whole of his weight into a roundhouse punch to Tyler's left temple and it knocked the man atop him almost senseless. Rob scrambled out of Tyler's grip and stood. Tyler stayed down, a hand against his head. Rob was suddenly concerned. "Are you okay?"

"Judas! Fucking *Judas*!" Tyler rose to his knees, swayed, then fell to one side.

"Projection," Rob mumbled at the shape in the dark. Then he turned and trudged back up the beach and over the driftwood. He headed, automatically, toward the Petersen house, then changed direction and stumbled home. His head throbbed and his neck muscles were on fire from Tyler's thrashing.

When Tyler finally found his feet, he went after Rob, gave up, and stalked the dark beach too angry to understand how drunk he was; too drunk to comprehend how injured he was. He flung chunks of driftwood into the water so furiously he threw himself off balance, fell, got up, and did it all over again. He was ruined. Rob had betrayed him. The firm had abandoned him. How was he supposed to face Pete now, especially given the condition of Pacific Pioneer? Worse still, how could he face Amanda? His mother would never let him forget this, never let him live it down, never fail to hold him up against Richie and Jamie.

Rage seized him now like a tropical disease. He welcomed it. He gathered it into himself and nourished it. It was his armor. It would be his weapon.

JUST AFTER TWO, on the bluff beneath the Madrona trees, Tyler took it out on Peggy. She was waiting for him, leaning against one of the smooth-barked trees, looking seaward, and acting the part of the dreamy innocent, when he grabbed her from behind. She let out a feigned, "Oh!" and then giggled. Tyler yanked up her short striped dress and pulled her hips toward him. She'd already removed the lacy tap pants she'd had on earlier. She loved coming to him with nothing on beneath her skirt; it made her feel wild.

"You fucking slut," he growled. It was the kind of talk that always got her juices flowing. It thrilled her at some deeply primitive level; it went to an animal place within her that her husband, a good and gentle lover, never reached: a place that was her secret, a secret she'd discovered and shared only with Tyler. It was going to be the perfect ending to a magically erotic summer.

She tried to turn to embrace her lover, but he grabbed her shoulders and forced her head down against the tree. She heard him unzip and then he plunged into her, without a caress, without even a word. She was clinging to the trunk of one of the Madronas, stroking its cool, smooth russet bark with her hands and thrilling to Tyler's furious passion, pushing back hard against his thrusts. She felt flushed with both desire and desperation, because this was their last night together, her last chance for the validation that she, well past forty and a mother of two, was the woman who turned on Tyler Strong.

Then things went crazy.

"Lover, you're hurting me!"

"Shut up, bitch!"

"Tyler!"

"Shut up! You're getting what you've wanted all summer, what you beg me for, the down and dirty, right? *Right*?!"

"Yes! Yes, of course! But more gently, sweetheart, you're tearing me up!"

"Am I? Good. Because this is to make you remember me forever, and forget that fat-assed, pork-bellied, Judas husband of yours, the coward, the betrayer. You...will...remember!"

"Yes! Remember!" She cried. Her shoulder was being hammered into the tree trunk to which she clung. She felt as if some diabolical machine was bent on ripping her apart. This wasn't passion. This wasn't even sex. This was punishment. This was rape. She tried to twist away, but Tyler had her hair in his left fist. His right hand was clamped on her hip bone as he jerked her toward him.

Finally, Strong pulled out and flung her to the grass, face up. Her eyes were wide with panic and wet with tears. Then, like an animal marking territory, he ejaculated over her.

"A goodbye present just for you, my dear, my sweet. Take it back to that overweight eunuch bastard husband of yours and show him what a real 'partner' can do."

She curled to her right because she thought he was going to kick her, but instead, without another word, Tyler stalked into the woods and disappeared. She lay in the grass sobbing, as much from confusion as terror. Why was this ending this way? For weeks, she'd given herself to him with an abandon, with a fierceness she hadn't even known was in her. How could that not have been enough? Why was he punishing her?

And then it hit her like a belly punch: she was nothing to Tyler. Just as she was nothing to her father, who disappeared, or to her mother, who'd treated her as just another celestial being in the airy-fairy commune where she'd been raised. She'd hungered for Tyler for years, even before she'd married Rob. Tyler was her romantic ideal, right into middle age, her dazzling desire: tall, handsome, alternately aloof and boyishly playful. And finally, this summer she'd got him. She'd feasted on him; they'd feasted on each other. She hadn't expected it to go anywhere, of course, to continue beyond the season. She wasn't that self-deluded.

But she hadn't expected rejection either, and now here she was, her body brutalized and left behind as if a scatter of trash. That's all she was to him. Trash. To be disposed of. It was beyond comprehending.

What she did understand, with humiliated certainty, was that though she mattered not at all to Tyler, she mattered to Rob—the man who treated her as if she were composed of spun gold and silk and who, as a consequence of her own sense of inadequacy, she'd come to dismiss. She sat up, gathered the broken pieces of herself, and stood. Then she stumbled down the slope to the cluster of darkened cottages below, illumined by the moon-licked beach that once had been her haven, and to the husband who'd never stopped loving her.

SHE FOUND HIM passed out on their bed, still in his clothes, which were caked with sand. He must have been very drunk. In the morning, she would tell him everything, and beg his forgiveness. In the morning, she would start over and, if he would still have her, she would love him unreservedly. Because he was genuine. Because she knew, absolutely, that he would never abuse or betray her.

And because she'd risked losing it all.

She also knew she would never return to Madrona Beach.

twenty-four

TYLER STRONG PACED the porch and slugged back his fourth tall glass of orange juice and vodka. He'd changed into shorts and a black T-shirt. He wasn't sure when. Why hadn't somebody found Pete yet? Clearly the police hadn't found her or that cop would have called.

Maybe Two got sick during the night. Or Justine. Maybe that was it. She's gone to the clinic.

He padded into the kitchen, picked up the tiny island phone book, fumbled and dropped it, retrieved it again, thumbed through it and punched in the number for the Vashon medical center. He got a recorded message: closed for Labor Day. He cursed and slammed his phone shut. He looked at the phone for another moment, then snapped it open and hit redial, listened to the recording again, and followed the instructions to connect to the on-call nurse.

"This is the consulting nurse; how may I help you?" a live voice said.

"Um, hello." Tyler said, trying to frame words into sentences. "Has Martha Strong come to the health center this morning?"

"The center is closed today, sir; it's Labor Day.

"I know that, dammit, but you have a doctor on call, right?!"

"Of course. Are you all right, sir?"

"So has Mrs. Strong called him?"

"The doctor is a she.'"

"Whatever. Did she?"

"We're not at liberty to release that sort of information, sir."

"I know, I know; Privacy Act bullshit. I'm a lawyer. Also her husband."

"Let me just check her record and see if she has you on her list of people to whom information can be released."

"We're only here summers."

"Oh, the Strongs on Madrona Beach? I didn't recognize the name at first; I thought she went by 'Pete.' Just one moment, please, I'm checking..."

That was the problem with islands; everyone knew you and rumors about people and events flashed around at speeds that rivaled the Internet.

"No, she's just been here on occasion for little emergencies—sports injuries, kids' fevers, that sort of thing. But I don't have you on her permission list. In fact, she doesn't have a permission list in her record. That's probably because we're not her regular health services provider."

"Didn't I just say that?"

"Of course you did. Well, Mr. Strong, I don't think I'd be breaking any laws if I told you I've been the on-call consulting nurse all night and you're my first Strong. But are you, sir, you yourself okay...?"

Tyler had already hung up. He poured another vodka and orange, and went back out to the porch.

Nothing was making sense. It was time to be leaving, but the house was empty.

THE MORNING WAS still fresh as Young Adam pedaled back from the rowing club at Jensen Point. A car he recognized as Old Adam's spare pickup approached and he saw his sister Justine behind the wheel. The windows were open.

"Dammit, Adam, why didn't you tell me where you were going this morning," she shouted. "I've been looking all over for you. Old Adam wants to talk to us."

"I woke up real early but you were asleep. On the porch. I went home, and then I went to Colin's."

"Why?"

"He's my friend. Plus, Mom's gone."

"What?"

"Gone."

"I'm not getting this."

Adam shrugged.

"She's not with Dad?"

"Uh-uh. I checked. He was asleep. She wasn't there. They had a fight, remember?"

"Yeah, yeah, so what else is new?"

"New is, this time she disappeared. I thought maybe she was at Colin's."

"Why?"

"Colin's her friend."

Justine thought about this for a moment. Colin had always been in their lives. And she'd always sensed a kind of current running between Colin and her mom but she'd never thought it was about sex. There was something each of them gained from the other, some kind of sustenance.

What was it? Friendship? Companionship? Peace? Shelter? An hour with Colin was almost like a day at a spa for her mother; she returned refreshed. Justine had never known a relationship like that, and she realized she envied it.

"She wasn't there?" she asked the boy.

"Uh-uh. Colin wasn't either. I looked around, then waited. He came home a little while later. I forgot he does this early morning bike ride thing."

"You broke into Colin's house?!"

"No. I sat on the back deck. I go there to look for whales."

Justine shook off this line of discussion. "Whatever. Look, you. Old Adam's waiting. Maybe he can help."

Adam shrugged again, and Justine realized it was a shrug of hopelessness, not disinterest. She turned the pickup, and her brother pumped his bike ahead of her down the long hill toward the beach.

When they got to the old Strong house, Adam was dressed and drinking coffee on the porch, his walking stick at his side.

By way of "Good morning," Young Adam announced, "Mom's missing."

Old Adam nodded and continued to stare out across the harbor, as if he expected to see Pete walking back across the water.

"I know. Your father called a little while ago. Barely made sense. Said he'd called the police, too, the idiot. Man hasn't a lick of common sense."

"Uncle Adam..." Justine scolded.

He waved his hand over his shoulder. "Yes, yes. I know."

Before they'd arrived, Old Adam had been communing with his dead brother: *Richie, Richie, I could use some guidance here, okay? That kid you left me to look after is crazy Amanda's son, not yours, I swear. Erratic, fucks anything that blips on his radar, none too bright. Sound familiar? Amanda all over. Acts like a goddamn adolescent, no matter he's a father and a husband. Times I want to strangle the bastard, I tell you. Wonderful wife, a saint by God; great kids, too. But I swear he's off his rocker, and the hell of it is, I don't know what I can do to change any of it. So, if you're up there and not too busy flyin' around with the fuckin' angels, gimme a sign, okay?*

"Have you eaten?" Justine asked.

"What? No."

"Adam! You're a diabetic! You know better! Do we need to send you to the nursing home?"

"Young woman, I will not permit profanity in this house!" But the old man turned toward her smiling. It was a game they played, the nursing home threat: he acted up and she picked up the phone to dial the home.

When Justine went to get Old Adam something to eat, he turned to Young Adam.

"Counselor, explain to the court in your own words what you heard last night."

"About what?"

"Don't be obtuse, young man. About the… ah…disagreement between your mother and father."

"Jeez, Uncle Adam."

"That's great uncle, counselor."

"Okay, okay. They were arguing. It was like sometime this morning. Sounded like they were drunk. Mom said Dad had been with Mrs. March."

Old Adam wasn't surprised when Justine had told him about Peggy March; he'd seen the flirtations. One of the benefits of being old is that you see everyone; no one sees you seeing them. It's like being a ghost before your time. Mostly, it was amusing. Now it wasn't. He'd thought the principal object of Tyler's interest this summer had been Alex, who was younger and prettier than the March girl. Maybe that was just a diversionary tactic. Hard to tell.

Now, maybe Pete had just had enough. Maybe she'd walked away. Maybe to someone she trusted. Then it occurred to him that there was no one these days among the beach families Pete would consider "safe." Not Sylvia, because of her daughter, Alex. Not Rob, because of Peggy. And not him, because he was Tyler's uncle...not that that meant a damn thing to the old man. It was Pete he loved, and he wished desperately that she had come to him.

Justine returned with cereal and yogurt. He chewed a spoonful and then the light came on.

"Ryan," he said.

"Un-uh," Young Adam said. "That's what I thought, too. She isn't at Colin's."

"Damnation."

Old Adam had watched Colin Ryan slip into their lives over the years as gently as the tide on the beach. He liked the lad. The chap's broad New York accent, which never seemed to moderate, made him sound like some thick-necked, knuckle-dragging Mafioso hit man, but there was something quiet and caring about him. Folks on the island said he was a damned good vet and Old Adam had no trouble believing it. He saw how that rangy rescue dog of his, Eileen, doted on him, and it made him laugh. It wasn't much different from the way the man doted on Pete, come to think of it, except Colin didn't scratch behind Pete's ears, or anyplace else as far as he could tell. There was some kind of bond between them; that was obvious. But Colin reminded him of a theatrical understudy waiting in the wings to step into the lead role. Only it never happened, performance after performance, summer after summer. The call never came. Time that vet found himself a better prospect. He'd meant to talk to the boy this summer, but the weeks went by too fast. Everything did these days. Things slipped away.

twenty-five

"I KNOW WHERE she is," Young Adam said, almost to himself. He'd been staring at the water in the harbor.

"What's that?" Old Adam said, his cereal spoon suspended in mid air. "What's that you said?!"

"I know where she is," he repeated.

This was only partly true. Young Adam's deepest fear was that his mother was gone, that she was dead or had left them. But he couldn't accept that, so he had been deducing alternatives.

They'd all missed the obvious, is what he thought.

"She's with Miss Edwinna," he said, as calmly as if he were saying the tide was in.

Old Adam put down his spoon.

"Please continue..."

"It's simple, really; something's happened. She needed a break. But not with the families."

"Edwinna's family," the old man countered.

"Bullshit," Justine snorted. "The families never include her."

The old man flinched. "Point taken, though that's how she wants it."

He turned to the boy. "What's your reasoning, counselor?"

The boy rolled his eyes. "Look, only two people we know Mom's really close with—you know, more than just for tennis."

"Go on," the judge said.

"And that's Colin and Miss Edwinna. She's not with Colin. I proved that. So, like Holmes says, when you eliminate what cannot be…"

"…whatever's left must be," Justine said. "Jeez Adam, you'd think it was the Bible!"

The boy shrugged. It was an "I don't care if you believe me or not" sort of shrug. Young Adam had a whole language of shrugs.

"She's friends with Edwinna?" The old man was stunned.

"Edwinna's cool," the boy said. His sister nodded.

"I'll be damned. And I thought I knew what was going on around here," Old Adam chuckled. "Don't know squat. We'll then, let's pay her a visit."

"No way, Uncle Adam," Justine said, putting a hand on his shoulder. "That's too far for you. Me and Adam, we'll walk up there."

"Adam and I," the old man corrected.

"Whatever. I have my cell. I'll call you."

This was the part Old Adam hated most. His mind was sharp, his body unwilling…or, rather, unable. The arthritis was crippling and the old heart did dickey things—skipping beats, or racing. Not that he ever let on. It was embarrassing enough that he walked like a weaving drunk.

"Where's my phone?" he demanded.

"In the pocket of your cardigan," Justine said in a voice as soft as his cashmere sweater.

"I'll call Edwinna right now," he said, rummaging in his pockets.

"No, you won't," Justine said.

The judge stared at the girl. He wasn't used to being told what he could or couldn't do. But he always listened to Justine.

"Edwinna wouldn't tell you, for one thing. Plus, we'd lose the element of surprise."

The old man lifted a bushy white eyebrow. "Maybe the two of you ought to go into the detective business," he said. "All right, you win, Watson. Take Sherlock here and pay her a visit. But call me!"

"Let's take the beach," the boy said, "it's faster."

"No, she'll see us coming. We'll go through the woods."

The judge laughed. "If not detectives, then maybe spies!" he shouted after them.

And he prayed the boy was right.

COLIN EASED THE clinic's van down the rutted gravel drive that led to Edwinna's cottage. Eileen sat beside him in the passenger seat, concentrating on the road ahead like an anxious driving instructor.

The house was a simple two-story shingled bungalow perched on a bluff looking south over Outer Quartermaster Harbor and had broad porches front and back. He came to a stop on the gravel forecourt and opened the door. Eileen trampled him in her eagerness to get out, whereupon she leaped around, splay-legged, barking idiotically. Normally, he loved this, but not this morning.

"Hush! Heel!"

The dog responded immediately; she ignored him.

Edwinna met him on her front porch, which, like its owner, had a slight list to the west.

"Wake the dead, you would," she snapped.

"You ought to fix this porch before it slides into the sea. Is the dead awake?"

"She's asleep. Or was. Threw up again, no thanks to you."

He ignored this. "What have you learned?"

"Damn all. Last thing she remembers, she was arguing with Tyler on the patio of their place. Nothing after that. No question she was drunk, Colin, but I can't work out how she got so drunk we almost lost her. That's a mystery."

"Not if it was intentional."

"I can understand wanting to drink yourself to death because your husband's a serial adulterer, but..."

"He's what?"

Edwinna squinted at him. "You're joking right?"

"No! Look, I get it that you don't think much of him but, I mean, where does this come from?"

"Christ, Colin, you must be blind as well as dumb; the only woman on this beach he hasn't had is me!"

Colin couldn't help but laugh, but at the same time he was floored. He shook his head and looked around Edwinna's yard distractedly, as if searching for evidence in the trees. He remembered those months in London and all of Tyler's women. But that was years ago. He'd always assumed Tyler adored Pete, just as he did. He'd thought once Tyler married Pete, that was that...

"She never said anything to you?" Edwinna demanded.

"No. We don't, um, have that kind of...friendship."

"What the hell kind of friendship *do* you have?"

Like the fog dissipating earlier in the morning, when he found Pete in the road, Colin had begun to understand that he knew almost nothing about Pete and Tyler—nothing, that is, but what they revealed to him two months of the year. Nothing but what he had imagined. Pete never talked about her marriage. He'd always assumed she was happy. Wasn't that what the summer gathering was all about; the annual confirmation that, whatever other shocks or tragedies occurred, the Madrona Beach families persevered, the bonds between and among them immutable, their fidelity unwavering? He felt betrayed—not by Tyler, his strange and increasingly erratic friend, nor by Pete. No, he felt betrayed by the fantasy he himself had woven around them, around all these families, over all these years.

"Edwinna…I guess I don't know."

"Here's what doesn't make sense," he heard Edwinna saying. She'd already moved on. "She's drinking herself to death and then she up and decides she'll walk, what, a mile up the beach? Clamber over the rocks up to the Highway, then walk another mile to the foot of that hill, lie down, and hope someone will hit her?"

"I don't think suicide's sensible, Miss Edwinna," he said, yanking himself out of his dismay, "especially drunken suicide. But it's just as likely that she was running away and just passed out. Exhaustion and alcohol."

"Shit!"

Colin thought this was a comment on his reasoning but Edwinna was looking over his shoulder. He turned and saw Justine and her little brother emerging from the dark thicket of salal bushes beneath the second growth Douglas firs at the edge of Edwinna's overgrown yard. Eileen was off like a shot and ran gleeful circles around the boy.

"Now what, smartass?" Edwinna said to him under her breath.

"I thought you just said I was blind and dumb...?"

"You're trespassing!" Edwinna warned the approaching children, mustering her most belligerent voice.

Eileen barked and bounced vertically, landing splay-legged, a move so inelegant it turned her from queen to clown in the blink of an eye.

"Hey! We're family!" Young Adam shouted, chasing around after the antic animal.

"And not invited, you rude child," Edwinna countered, grabbing Eileen by her collar and hauling her in.

"Give it a rest, Edwinna; we know she's here," Justine said, her voice calm and even. She marched toward Edwinna's porch.

"Stop, Justine. *Now!*"

It was Colin's voice, and it was so authoritative, so unexpected, so out-of-character, the girl stopped in her tracks like a Border collie responding to a shepherd's whistle.

"What?!"

Colin sat on Edwinna's slanting stairs.

"Come here. Let's talk."

Justine approached like a truculent child. Adam played with Eileen. Edwinna, with a groan, settled next to Justine and put her arm around the girl.

"She's in there," Justine said, jerking her head backwards.

"Yes, she is," Colin answered. "And she's safe. But pretty sick. We need to let her rest."

Colin was about to elaborate, but Edwinna sensed this, lifted her hand from Justine's shoulder momentarily and rapped a bony knuckle on the back of his head to silence him.

"This is not a good time for you and Young Adam to be here, sweetie," Edwinna said.

Justine squared her shoulders. "With respect, ma'am, I don't think that's your call."

"Call me 'ma'am' again, girl, and I'm gonna fire your ass right out of here," Edwinna snapped.

Justine started laughing, then stood. "You're a kick in the pants, you are, Miss Edwinna. Look, you're old, okay? That means you're to be revered and respected. That's how I was brought up, anyway; or did you have some other system?"

Edwinna relented. "No, that system's fine with me."

"Okay, then, stop being a pain in the ass and let's start from the top, remembering our manners. You've got our mother in there, yes?"

"Right. So what?"

"Edwinna, stop."

It was Colin again. "What you're trying to do is noble and good," he said to the old woman, "but Justine's an adult, and Pete's her mother. For that matter, I think Young Adam's totally capable, too."

"Right, and we need to see our mother."

"Yes, you do," Colin said. "Let's go inside and see how she is. But if I sense a crisis, it's over, okay?"

Justine relented. "Deal."

Edwinna fulminated, but let it go, shoulders sagging. Colin was the one who could see clearly, now, she realized, and it occurred to her that love was what was clouding her vision; it drove her to her protective animal state, fangs bared. But these were not her enemies. Nor were they Pete's. These were Pete's allies, her children, her troops. She and Colin were just security, there to screen visitors. And these visitors were safe.

Justine was on her cell phone to Old Adam.

"She's here, with Edwinna and Colin. We're going in."

She snapped the phone shut.

Colin was smiling. "You make it sound like an ATF bust."

twenty-six

ROB MARCH AWOKE aware only that he hurt everywhere. His neck felt as if it had been wrung like a dishtowel, his head as if pounded by a pile driver. His ribs ached. His belly was sore. The index finger of his right hand was swollen. He turned slightly, groaned at the pain, and felt sand against his face. The sand yielded memory. The beach. The fight. Tyler Strong raging like a madman.

He turned the other way. He wanted to cushion his throbbing head on the pillow of his wife's breasts. That primitive comfort, that magical balm of her flesh. He would nestle there and she would stroke his head and he would feel better.

But she wasn't there.

He levered himself up on one elbow, groaned, and found his wife, fully dressed, slumped in an easy chair beside the window, the rising sun frosting her hair. Her eyes were open.

"Peg. What are you doing there?"

He expected her to smile at his condition, for he, too, was fully clothed, and a mess. But she did not.

"Waiting."

"For what, love? Have you not slept at all?

"No. I don't think so. What happened to you?"

He shook his head to clear it. Sand flew.

"Fight. With Tyler."

Peggy March lurched upright. "Oh, no!"

"I had to tell him the firm wasn't going to make him a partner. The vote Thursday was unanimous. The senior members asked me to tell him. I'd been holding off. I waited too long."

"You voted against him, too?"

"It was the right thing to do. Hard, but right."

"Oh, Rob…"

"Needless to say, he didn't take it very well. Called me a 'Judas.' Well, that was maybe understandable from his point of view. But then he proceeded to try to beat the shit out of me on the beach."

"Oh, Rob, I'm so sorry."

The woman in the chair began to sob. It began, Rob would later recall, like hiccups. And then it seemed his wife was gasping for air. And finally, she held her belly and rocked and howled like a wounded animal.

Rob rolled out of bed, body aching, and knelt beside her chair.

"Peg, it's okay," He promised, stroking her freckled arm. "Tyler was crazed. I shouldn't have waited so long to tell him. But I'm okay."

It took a few moments before he realized it wasn't about the fight on the beach. It wasn't about whether he was okay.

"Peg? What is it? What's this about, love?"

Peggy March struggled to control herself. Finally she grabbed both arms of her chair and looked directly at her husband. He noticed there was grass in her hair. Running mascara blackened her crow's feet. Her clothes were dirty.

"He raped me."

"What?! Who?!"

"Tyler. Last night. After you fought, I guess."

Rob was momentarily frozen in place. Then he leaned forward and wrapped his arms around his wife.

"Oh my God, sweetheart. Oh, my God. Wait. Are you okay? Why didn't you wake me?"

Peggy stared ahead as if mentally checking her own body, then nodded. "I needed to think."

"Shit, this is a nightmare, and I caused it."

"No, it's not your fault, Rob."

"You're right." Rob rose to his feet, looked out the window and across the broad lawns toward the Petersen compound. "You're right; he's a lunatic. I'm gonna kill the bastard."

He walked to the bedside table and picked up the phone.

"What are you doing?"

"Calling the police."

"No, darling, you're not."

"It's assault, Peg!"

"No, it isn't. Put the phone down, Rob. We were having an affair."

Her husband glanced at her and shook off the crazy words. "That's ridiculous; that asshole flirts with every woman he meets, not just you."

"You're not paying attention. We were having an affair. With sex."

Rob March stood staring at her for a moment, then put the phone down and sat on the edge of their bed. His face was as blank as a flat screen television waiting for a signal.

"In a matter of a few weeks I've ruined everything we spent our lives building," Peggy March said in a voice stronger and braver than she thought possible.

Rob stared at the carpet beneath his feet. It was the color of pale straw, tightly woven in a faint herringbone pattern. Peg had picked it out. Peg had wonderful taste.

"This is not happening."

"It is, Rob; it has. And I am sorrier than I can even begin to express. I hate myself."

Rob March fluttered his pudgy left hand, as if waving the white flag of surrender, but said nothing.

After several minutes during which the only sounds were their own breathing, Peggy March stood.

"I'm going into the bathroom now and I'm going to try to wash at least some of this filth off my soul. When I come out—and please don't be here—I'm going to dress, get in my car, and leave this island. I will never return to the beach again. When you and the kids have packed up and come home, I'll do whatever you want me to do, go wherever you tell me to go, including Hell. I have some money from Grandma Katie's estate. I'll survive. You've been nothing but wonderful to me from the beginning. I rewarded you with deceit and betrayal."

She turned, walked to the other side of the bedroom, entered the bathroom, and closed the door.

Rob March did not move.

twenty-seven

"MOM?"

Pete's eyes fluttered a moment, then settled on her son.

"Adam. Hello, sweetie."

"I couldn't find you."

"I'm sorry."

"I looked everywhere—around the house, in the neighborhood, over at Colin's..."

"Colin's?"

"He's my friend. He's your friend, too, right?"

She lifted her head and focused on the man behind her son.

"Yes. Yes, he is."

She saw her grown daughter beside her friend.

"Justine."

"We need to talk, Mom."

Pete looked at her daughter, the beautiful grown women she had become; the woman to whom she needed to tell so much.

"Soon," she said.

"Mom..." Justine pressed.

"Well, now that you've retched on every bed linen I own," Edwinna interrupted, sarcasm shouldering aside the worry in her heart, "how the hell are you, girl?"

"Shitty," she said. "Sorry, Adam."

"Mom," Adam asked from her bedside, "what are you doing here? Why aren't you home?"

Pete couldn't speak. All she could do was shake her head, moving it slowly back and forth across the pillows; and the tears came, as if the movement pumped them from a well. She reached a hand out from the covers and stroked the boy's hair once, noticed the bruise on her wrist again, and shoved it back under the covers.

"Okay, everyone out," Edwinna barked. "Visiting hours are over. Patient needs to rest."

"But…" Justine said.

Colin put a hand on her shoulder. "Not now, Justine," he whispered.

She turned on her heel and stalked from the room.

Edwinna shooed the boy out. Colin placed a hand on Pete's head, then withdrew, closing the bedroom door behind him. He found Justine on the back porch, staring out at the harbor.

Justine wheeled on him. "What the fuck, Colin! Where'd that bruise come from? What the hell's going on here?!"

"We don't know yet," he answered, hands raised in a gesture of helplessness.

"I don't believe you."

"Justine. How long have you known me?"

"All my life. What's your point?"

Colin, ever the diagnostician, noticed that despite the young woman's tan, the color had drained from her face. She wasn't angry with him; she was frightened.

"My point," he said, putting an arm around her shoulder, "is that I've never lied to you. I'm not lying now. I don't know what happened to your mother last night, but I intend to find out. Okay?"

Justine softened. "Okay. Thanks. But two heads are better than one."

"Agreed."

They went back into the house just as Edwinna brought a platter of glazed doughnuts and maple bars from the kitchen.

"Cool!" Adam said. He'd been playing with Eileen.

"I can't believe you eat such garbage!" Colin said to the old woman. "Do you have any idea..."

"Yes, I do, young man, and I don't care. At my age, I take my sins wherever I can find them. Doughnut?"

Colin made a face. Adam had a pastry in each hand. Colin leaned toward Justine and said, "Let's go for a walk, okay?"

The girl nodded. They went back out to the porch and then across the back lawn to the edge of the steep bank above the beach. As they descended the aged staircase to the sand below, they tested the strength of each weathered tread. The tide was retreating and the beach was sequined with the bleached shells of sand dollars.

"So?" Justine said.

"I'll tell you what I know, okay?" Colin said. "It isn't much."

"Whatever you have," the girl said, squatting to pick up one of the fragile white disks.

"I found your mother, unconscious, in the middle of Vashon Highway just before dawn this morning."

She sprang upright. "What?! Where?"

"I was doing my bike run. She was just around the curve at the bottom of that long hill as you come north toward Burton."

Justine stood rooted in the sand, her mouth open slightly, her head tilted to one side in speechless question. For a moment she reminded him of Eileen waiting for a dog biscuit.

"I know. Makes no sense," he said, shaking his head.

"No one speeding down that hill would see her until it was too late!" Justine said. She was very nearly shouting. "She was trying to commit suicide?!"

"I don't know. Looks like it, though. She was comatose when I found her. Acute alcohol poisoning."

"She was drunk?"

"Critically."

"Wait. That bruise on her wrist…"

"Both wrists, actually."

"Jesus Christ! Did someone rape her or something?"

Colin saw the panic in the young woman's eyes and had a sudden realization that this was a fear every woman everywhere on the planet carried in her heart every day. He wondered how they could bear it. He wondered how they ever found it in themselves to step outside into the world. Or to trust a man. It made him ache.

He reached out and gave her hand a squeeze. The truth was, he didn't know. It hadn't occurred to him. A GP would have considered this possibility instantly. He hadn't. He was a vet. He focused on the memory in his mind's eye—he saw Pete on the blacktop again. No, there were no stains; there was no dirt. Her position was decorous, almost relaxed, as if she'd just decided to take a nap. He said so.

"Then what's with the bruises?" the girl demanded.

"Justine, I don't know. I just don't."

"What happened next?"

"I got her out of the road and Edwinna arrived."

"You called her?"

"No. She just...you know...arrived. She knew, like she does sometimes. She's...I don't know what she is...she's amazing."

"If Mom was comatose, why didn't you take her to the medical center?" Justine demanded. "No, wait, I know why; forget it..." The girl looked out at the water. A harbor seal raised a glistening head, saw them, and flipped beneath the surface again. "Shame. It's all about appearances, and fear of shame, in this family—in all these families. Fear of what others might think. Fear that there might be a blemish on their glossy histories. They're ashamed of me, too, you know," she said looking up at Colin. "The family failure."

Colin took Justine by the shoulders, squared her up, and held her still for a moment. "You aren't, you know."

"So far."

"Not even so far. Your mother and I have been friends forever, right? Your father, too, I suppose. This morning I've been thinking about them both, and about this family, and all those years. And here's what I decided: You're the only one of the bunch with the gumption to go out and make your own way. I suspect Adam's another. You must both be adopted. For what it's worth, I'm very proud of you, young lady."

This brought a smile, and he let her go.

"So why didn't you take her back home?"

Colin looked at her but said nothing.

It took a moment, but finally the penny dropped.

"No."

"Can you think of any other explanation?"

She looked away. "You think Dad gave her those welts."

It wasn't a question. It was like a stale crust of bread she was chewing so it could be digested.

"I don't know, kid; it seemed to me my job was to make her safe first and discover facts second."

Justine nodded and looked at him. "You love her, don't you," she said, regarding him as if for the first time.

"Did once. Yes. Still do, I suppose, but differently."

"Meaning?"

Colin shoved his hands into the hip pockets of his jeans and looked up the bank toward Edwinna's house. From this angle, all he could see was the chimney.

"I used to think we were like two halves of the same being, or maybe like Siamese twins joined at the hip. And because we were connected in this way we would know and understand everything about each other. But that was never really the case. I realized this morning that I don't know much about your mother at all. And what I think I know is probably wrong, like a story I've carried in my head so long I believe it."

He turned toward the girl and smiled.

"Some friend, huh?"

"The kind of friend who makes sure she's safe, which is more than the rest of us seem to have done."

"But not safe enough, and too late. I feel like a failure in a legend of my own creation."

She slipped a hand into the crook of his arm. "Not to me and, I suspect, not to Mom, either. Let's talk to her, yeah?"

"Not yet. And I think we may need some help from someone who's not family."

"Who? I mean, who's left?"

They were at the foot of the stairs.

"Trust me, okay?"

twenty-eight

"PATSY? IT'S COLIN."

"This is the twenty-first century, Doc. I have caller ID."

"I need you, Pats."

"Another emergency? Why didn't my pager go off?"

"An emergency...yes, I think so. But not at the clinic. At Edwinna's."

"Shit, Colin; is Pete dying?!"

"No, no; nothing like that. But stuff has happened. I don't even know what all. I can't handle it alone. I thought I could, but I can't. Can you come?"

Patsy looked at the phone in her hand. In all their years together, Colin Ryan had never really asked anything of her. Oh, yes, she assisted him in surgeries and examinations. He respected her training and skill and often consulted with her about cases. But ever since the disaster with that girlfriend years ago, he'd kept his emotional life to himself. Fact was, though, if Colin Ryan asked her to step off a cliff for him, she would. Problem was, he never asked.

"Of course I'll come."

"Do you know where she lives?"

"Edwinna? Yes; I picked up her spastic cat once when that great white whale of a car she drives wouldn't start. On the bluff, east end of Madrona Beach, right?"

"That's the place. Soon, Pats?"

"Be there in fifteen."

Colin stuffed his cell phone into his pants pocket and stepped from Edwinna's porch into her knotty pine paneled living room. Justine was staring out at the harbor through a wide, multi-paned window, as if trying to see into the future. Young Adam was curled up in a slipcovered easy chair beside Edwinna's fireplace—a massive structure made of bowling ball-sized stones her mason had collected from the base of a storm-eroded bluff on the north end of the island—the twelve thousand year old detritus left behind by the last retreating glacier.

The slipcover of Adam's chair was frayed at every corner; the cat Desmond's apparent contribution to the cottage's "shabby chic" décor. The boy was thumbing an ancient copy of the *National Geographic*. Eileen lay on the hearth as if anticipating winter and a fire.

Colin found Edwinna rummaging in her kitchen pantry.

"What are you looking for; something I can help with?" he volunteered.

"What, you think you know my pantry better than I do?" the old woman grumbled without turning. "Chicken broth. Girl's gonna need something in her stomach soon, unless you have a superior suggestion, Mister Doctor…"

They were all as frayed, Colin realized, as that chair in the living room. Colin had given in to Justine's demand that they talk with Pete and it hadn't gone well.

THE FOUR OF them tiptoed into the bedroom and found
Pete curled in a ball on her right side, eyes open.

"Hi, Mom," Adam had said, with more jauntiness
than Colin guessed the boy felt.

"Hello, sweetie," Pete said, smiling as if the action of
lifting the edges of her mouth were painful.

Eileen plodded up to the bedside and nudged Pete's
arm with her muzzle. Pete's hands were beneath the
covers.

"Feeling better?" Edwinna asked.

"Not much."

"Well, no. I shouldn't think so."

"Edwinna, please; how did I end up here? I don't
understand."

The old woman looked at Colin, at the children, and
back to Colin. He nodded.

"Colin found you at dawn, on his bike ride. In the
middle of Vashon Highway. At the bottom of the hill
south of Burton. You were unconscious."

"How did I get there?"

"Good question, kiddo. Seems you walked to the end
of the beach, went up to the road, headed toward the
south end ferry, and just lay down on the double yellow
line at some point. Given how drunk you were, it's a
miracle you even got that far…"

Pete tried to sit up, thought better of it, and sank into
the pillows again, breathing deeply to calm her stomach.
The pain in her head was diabolical.

"We brought you back here," Edwinna said, as if that
were an adequate summation. "I've told you how and

where we found you; don't you think it's time you told me about those marks on your wrists?"

Colin wanted to throttle the old woman. They'd just got Pete talking, but there was no way she was going to reveal the source of her injuries with her son and daughter standing by the bed.

There was panic in Pete's eyes. She curled up again. Her chest convulsed as she sobbed.

This time Justine didn't need to be asked. She hauled herself out of the bedroom, dropped on the settee in the living room, and pounded a cushion against her thigh in frustration. Young Adam came out of the bedroom holding Colin's hand, like a child who'd been lost in a department store. Edwinna followed, arms in the air in exasperated impotence.

"I give up," she said.

There was a knock at the front door.

"Patsy. Thank God," Colin said.

"Who?"

"Oh, sorry; it's my assistant, Patsy Ashton. From the clinic."

"What the hell is this, Union Station?"

Colin ignored Edwinna and went to the door.

Patsy was still in her blue clinic scrubs. The sun was behind her and her backlit hair looked like a halo. He looked at his feet for a moment than back to her and smiled. It was a smile of defeat. "Thank you, Pats," he said softly.

She gave his elbow a slight squeeze as he led her in.

Patsy thought she'd never seen him so drained. Intuitively, she understood why: this was an emergency he couldn't treat. It wasn't a broken bone. It wasn't a tumor. It wasn't an abscess. It wasn't a parasite. It wasn't an infection. The deeply competent doctor she knew, the colleague with whom she shared her days, the man she loved, however privately, was out of his depth.

After he made introductions, she said, "I think perhaps I'll just sit with her awhile."

"Does she even know you?" Edwinna snapped.

"Not well," Patsy said, smiling. "But I think that may be an asset, don't you?"

Edwinna shrugged. Suddenly, the old woman had no edgy riposte. She was lost. The girl she loved as a daughter was beyond her help.

But she was also distracted; she was seeing a vision in her mind's strange eye, but the current crisis fogged it. She knew the vision was important, knew it was fraught, knew it had something to do with Pete. But it wouldn't coalesce and it troubled her.

twenty-nine

THE UPS MAN had come to the wrong house. At least that's who Old Adam thought the fellow was. The chap at the front door wore a brown short-sleeved shirt and matching shorts, knee socks and black shoes.

"I didn't think UPS delivered on holidays," Old Adam said, leaning his bony frame against the door jamb. He was surprised that the trip to the front door had tired him so.

The delivery man was in his mid-forties, Adam guessed; thick in the middle and none too tall. Head nearly shaved. No neck. Hands studded with knuckles big as lug nuts.

"Well, sir, to be honest, I'm not UPS. I'm with Jacobsen and Silverstein. We deliver important documents. Easier to find folks home on holidays, you know? And I have a package here for," the man looked again at the envelope, "Mr. Strong?"

"That would be me," Adam said, "but I can't imagine who..."

The man extended a clipboard and pen. "Just sign here, would you? Got a ferry to catch."

Adam, distracted by his other worries, did so. He thanked the gentleman and the fellow nodded and backed away from the door as Adam closed it.

The old man limped into the living room and sat in his favorite chair, a deep and worn Parisian brown leather club chair he'd found decades earlier at an antiques shop in Seattle's Pioneer Square. He looked at the package. It was a padded tan ten-by-fifteen mailer and it was thick.

He put on his reading glasses and discovered it was addressed to Tyler Strong. Wrong Strong. He was about to haul himself out of his chair to call after the delivery man when he noticed, in the upper left corner of the label, who the sender was: Soren Sorensen, his old friend Robbie's general manager.

He sat for a few moments regarding the envelope. Then he rose, hobbled over to his mahogany writing desk, its tooled leather surface beginning to crackle like alligator skin but the waxed wood still radiant, and opened the top drawer. He lifted out a leather scabbard that held a pair of slender, silver-plated, filigreed scissors for cutting newspaper clippings and a matching, sword-like letter-opener. He withdrew the knife and slit open the envelope. It took him only a few seconds to discover that Pacific Pioneer Shipping was ruined and Soren was resigning. Certain he must be misunderstanding something, Adam took the papers back to his chair and began re-reading.

At first, he was furious that old Soren, a man he'd always liked and trusted, had let the company founder. Then, as he scrutinized the contents of the envelope, he realized it had nothing to do with Soren; it was Tyler's doing. Soren had written repeatedly to his CEO about the failing company only to be either rejected or ignored. The company was buried in debt, had liens placed against its vessels by unpaid creditors, and was failing to meet its loan obligations. Worse, Pete was somehow a guarantor of the note. From what Adam could tell, the company would have to be liquidated and its capital assets wouldn't be likely to fetch much. Its ships were old and inefficient and he knew the waterfront land along the Ballard ship canal where the warehouse was located already was already plastered with weathering For Sale signs.

The old man pulled the cell phone from his sweater pocket and punched in Tyler's number.

All he got was the voicemail: *Please leave your name and number and the time you called...* It was Pete's voice.

WHEN PEGGY MARCH emerged from her bath, wrapped in an antique Japanese black silk kimono patterned with white chrysanthemums, she found her husband in the chair in which she'd spent the night. He had not changed his clothes. He had not left.

She said nothing.

Her husband looked at her for several moments. Neither moved.

"Take off your robe," he said, finally.

"What?"

"Do it."

Peggy untied the sash and let the robe pool at her feet. He gazed at her nakedness. Then he spoke.

"I know you, Peggy Rutherford March. I know your body. I know your heart. I know your soul. Because you have shared them with me. I know your true self, because I have seen it embrace our children in love and have felt that love myself. Your true self has nothing to do with whatever has happened between you and Strong. I'm not pretending it didn't happen. But I refuse to let it tear us apart."

Peggy March, who had steeled herself over the course of the long, empty night, who had made her exit plan and crafted her goodbye, who had used the hot bath as the first step in her cleansing and leave-taking, sank to her knees as if unable to resist gravity.

Rob March did not move.

"Get up," he said.

She struggled to her feet again.

"Come here," he ordered.

Suddenly, she was afraid. She hesitated.

"Come."

She stepped forward. She expected a blow. She believed she deserved it. Her husband rose, gathered her into his arms, and kissed her, tenderly and for so long that she gasped when he released her.

"You are going nowhere without me. Do you understand that?"

Peggy nodded, tears streaming.

He pulled her close again.

"We are human beings, and, as such, we are fools. Because we are fools, we do foolish things. The counterbalance to foolishness is forgiveness."

Peggy shook her head. "I don't deserve…"

"You don't ever deserve forgiveness; it's not something you earn. It's given, like a gift. It's given from the heart. From love."

Rob March stepped away from his wife, took her hand, and pulled her toward their bed.

"Later, I will deal with Tyler Strong. But right now, I want to hold the love of my life."

"You're filthy," she said, smiling through tears.

"So what?"

"Yes. So what…"

PATSY ASHTON STEPPED into Edwinna's living room, but left the door to Pete's bedroom ajar.

"Stuffy in there," she said softly to Colin, who'd jumped from his chair as if jerked by a rope. "I've opened the windows. She's sleeping." She looked around. Young Adam was on his fourth *National Geographic*. Justine was out on the back porch, pacing. Edwinna was dozing in her chair.

Patsy thrust her chin in the direction of the back door and walked silently toward it. Colin followed. Justine looked up when they emerged.

"She talked to me," Patsy began. "It was easy, like two girlfriends. She wanted to, I think. So I know more of what happened; not everything, but some things. It's not pleasant, okay?"

Justine nodded.

"Pete was quite drunk," Patsy began. "The guests had gone and Tyler had vanished. She'd seen him flirting earlier with her cousin, Alex, and assumed he was with her. She decided to wait him out and kept drinking. Sometime long after midnight—she's not sure when, naturally—Tyler finally appeared. She was about to take him on when she noticed he smelled like Peggy March's perfume. She flipped. I don't know, maybe she could deal with the idea of Tyler fooling around with Alex because the girl's much younger. But Peggy, her friend... well, that was too much. Anyway, they fought. She shoved him away and he fell. He was falling down drunk anyway. When he got up again, he grabbed her. Clamped both her skinny wrists in one hand, threw her down, and dumped the open gin bottle into her mouth with the other hand. Says she gulped until she thought she'd drown. That's all she remembers."

"Holy shit," Justine said. "He could have killed her. We learn that at the bar where I work: acute alcohol poisoning."

"Except that he didn't," Colin interrupted. "So at some point she must have fled. You were right, Patsy, she wasn't trying to commit suicide. She was running away, heading for the south ferry. And she collapsed before she could get very far."

Justine shook her head in disbelief.

"Let's talk to Edwinna about next steps...whatever the hell they are," Colin said.

When they reentered the living room, Young Adam was playing with Eileen, and Edwinna had roused herself and gone to the kitchen.

"Whatever else it is, it's also lunchtime," she announced from the door. "Peanut butter and jelly work for you?"

"Fine with me," Justine said.

"I had a late breakfast," Colin lied.

"I'd love a PB&J, Miss Edwinna," Patsy said. "Want a hand?"

"I think I can still cope with this particular culinary challenge."

Patsy ignored this and she and Colin followed her into the kitchen. "I've got the jelly," Patsy said. You handle the peanut butter; I always tear the bread with it."

"Hey guys?"

It was Young Adam's voice, in the next room.

"I think you should look at this."

The three adults drifted out into the living room again.

"What's up, bro'?" Justine asked.

"The dog."

"Huh?"

"Check it out."

Eileen was skidding around the polished fir floor, swatting at a woman's silver high heeled sandal with her front paws and watching it skitter around the room.

The adults watched the dog's pure joy in its play and smiled.

After a few moments, Adam became irritated.

"So what's wrong with this picture, people?"

"Excuse me?" Justine said.

Eileen picked the shoe up in her soft mouth and loped around the room, tossing her head.

Colin looked at Patsy.

Edwinna stared at the dog. Then she strode across the room and grabbed the shoe from the dog's mouth.

She turned the sexy sandal over in her hands a few times. Then she reached out and cuffed the side of Young Adam's head playfully. "Your mother didn't bring up no idiots, did she, boy?" She said.

Adam beamed.

"Somebody going to let the rest of us in on this?" Colin asked.

Edwinna tossed him the sandal.

"What do you see, big shot?"

Colin held the shoe for a moment and gave it back.

"It's one of the shoes Pete had on when I found her. So?"

Edwinna thrust the shoe at Patsy.

"What's wrong with it?" she demanded.

Patsy looked at the shoe for a few moments and then dropped her hand to her side, as if the shoe were made of lead.

"It's all wrong," she said.

Justine took the shoe from Patsy, turned it in her hand as Edwinna had, and finally the light came on: there were no scuffs on the sole. There were no scratches on the high silver heel.

"They've never been worn," she whispered.

"Which means?" Adam demanded.

"Somebody put them on her."

"And?"

"And left her there in the middle of the Highway. She didn't walk there."

"Elementary," the boy said. He was not smiling.

Patsy saw Colin was way ahead of them. He had his cell phone in his hand and was heading for the porch. As he passed her, he leaned down and whispered, "Would you look after Pete, love?"

She nodded and watched him slip out to the porch.

Love, he'd said.

thirty

HAVING FINISHED OFF a half gallon of orange juice and most of a half gallon of Stolichnaya for breakfast, Tyler Strong was now struggling to load the family Ford Explorer. An observer, had there been one, would have puzzled at the methodology, which appeared frantic and, at the same time, utterly random; Tyler was tossing whatever was at hand into the back of the SUV, talking to himself as he did so.

Suitcases: Got mine. Where are Pete's? Where's Two's? Where's that girl, Justine? She's old enough to help, dammit. Tennis gear. Got it. Water skis; where the hell are they? Can't find them. Emptied the fridge. Well, most of it anyway and filled the cooler. Shoved it to the back. Crammed stuff around it for insulation. Need more stuff. And the toys...never know which go and which stay... Shouldn't have to sort this all out myself."

He thought he heard his mother Amanda's low, cigarette-ruined voice, with its usual rasp of disgust:

"What the hell do you think you're doing?"

Tyler ducked out of the rear of the SUV to find not Amanda but Old Adam behind him. The old man was standing, legs apart for balance, in the middle of the crushed oyster-shell driveway, cane in one hand and a sheaf of papers in the other.

"Did you even hear me? What the hell do you think you're doing?" Old Adam repeated.

Given the extremity and baffling discontinuity of his present circumstance, a condition which made the space around him seem to ripple like heat waves off an asphalt road, Tyler had no idea what the old man was talking about, no idea even how he'd got there.

"Hello, Adam," Tyler said, buying time and trying to steady himself by leaning on the edge of car's rear hatch.

"Don't 'Hello' me, you bastard; do you have any idea where your wife is?"

"Nope." The younger man held his hands up in the universal gesture of helplessness and grinned, the picture of ease. "Went for a walk early this morning, I guess, and hasn't come back yet. Left me to do all the heavy lifting, her and those kids. How about that?" He wasn't at all certain this was the truth; he was finding truth to be elusive.

Old Adam was about to tell him where Pete was, but something—his old prosecutorial instincts, perhaps—held him back. Tyler was drunk; that must be it. But why would you be drunk on the morning you're supposed to be driving home? Crazy. He was also acting, or covering maybe; that was obvious, too. What was he disguising?

Adam switched subjects, an age-old technique to throw a defendant off his game: "Guess who just paid me a visit?" It was less a question than an accusation.

For a moment, for just a fraction of a second, for the merest blink in the stately procession of time from present to past and back again, he saw fear in Tyler's eyes. And just as quickly, Tyler's eyes went blank again.

"No idea, Adam. Is this a game? Maybe I should get Two. He likes games."

"Two? What the hell are you talking about?! Two has been..."but he stopped. He had no words for the craziness he was hearing.

Tyler didn't know. He didn't know where everyone was, why no one was helping. He looked around and listened for their voices, but the beach was silent except for gulls' cries and the distant keening of an eagle. He couldn't hear Amanda anymore either. Suddenly, he found the old man's questions infuriating, and the noisy dissonance in his head rose painfully.

"Get on with it, Uncle; I'm trying to pack the car."

"Odd how there's no one here helping you, isn't it?"

A part of his brain, the part on autopilot, agreed but he wouldn't acknowledge it. "Was there something you wanted from me?"

"Oh yes, there is. There is. A legal messenger just mistakenly delivered a package of documents to me. But they were meant for you. Guess who they're from?"

Tyler crossed his arms against his chest but said nothing. It was all a mystery to him, this entire encounter. He tried to be separate from it. It wasn't hard. He had only the slightest grip on the present.

"Soren Sorensen. Remember him? General Manager of Pacific Pioneer? Your wife's family's firm? Of which you're CEO?"

"Soren..."

"Now why do you suppose old Soren would resort to sending documents to you via a receipt-requested legal messenger service? Never mind; don't bother fabricating, I'll tell you. Thanks to your incompetence, Pacific Pioneer is effectively bankrupt and Pete is ruined."

Tyler slipped into another chapter of the present, found a bit of text, and waved a breezy hand. "Whole industry's in collapse, Adam. Nothing we could do. Fuel prices through the roof, customers dropping like flies, creditors snapping at our heels…"

"Who's 'we'?"

"Soren and me. And frankly, that old coot Soren—what is he, in his late fifties now? Older? He's lost it. Completely. Can't keep on top of the invoices. We're forever in arrears. Supposed to be the general manager but can't be trusted to make timely payments. Have to cover for him all the time."

"Curious of you to say that, Tyler, because these documents include increasingly desperate letters from Soren to you, pleading that you act to take charge of the company's financial crisis. If anyone's 'lost it,' it looks like you."

Tyler thrashed around in his crowded head for a response. "Oh Christ, Adam, the guy's a Chicken Little. The sky's always falling with him."

Adam leaned on his cane and fixed Tyler in his gaze.

"Funny how the sky never fell until Harlan gave you control of Pacific Pioneer…"

"That's my fault?"

"Well, you tell me. Whose is it, then? Harlan's? Maybe Pete's? Because you know what, nephew? I know you've made Pete the guarantor of the firm's loans. I don't know how you did it, but I'll find out. Pete's smarter than that. My guess is you forged her signature, but that's easily checked and you can be damned sure I'll have it checked. Now that the company's failed, you've left her holding the bag."

Tyler thought, *Hey, this is like being in court!* As if addressing a jury, he said, "Let us all remember that this is not my company; it's hers."

"Who's 'all?' This is you and me, and don't give me that bullshit! The general manager reports to you. The management decisions are yours to make, and what these documents show is that you've dodged those decisions for months. What the hell is wrong with you?"

Now Tyler suddenly felt himself in the witness box instead of arguing his client's case before the judge. He didn't like it.

He stepped out of the witness box and lunged for the documents, misjudging the distance. Old Adam pulled them away, stepped to one side, and swatted Tyler's back with his cane. Tyler went down.

"Let me tell you something else," Old Adam growled at the man struggling to his knees before him. "I'm not going to let you ruin my niece. I'm going to use every connection I have, every string I can pull, to exonerate her and make it clear that the burden of this failure rests upon your shoulders. What is more, *nephew*, I'm writing you out of my will. You got that? You've taken down the Petersen fortune; you won't take down the Strong fortune as well. Out of honor to my brother and love of your father, I've been carrying you for years. Pure dead weight. That's done. Over. Got that?!"

Old Adam turned toward his house.

Tyler decided he'd kill the old man before he got away. He found his feet, promptly tripped on the cedar driveway edging, regained his balance, and plodded after the hobbling old man. He had no plan; he dimly figured the cane would suffice as a weapon.

Then a hand gripped his shoulder and spun him around, and another slugged his face so hard he went down again, his head crashing into the slate-flagged path. The world swirled. A foot on the back of his neck kept him down.

"Judas? Isn't that what you called me, you filthy bastard? When all the while you were the real, live cheating Judas! How could you do it to her, to us, you depraved bastard?!"

Tyler tried to rise but the foot pressed him down again. It was so heavy he thought his neck would break. Even in his strangely altered state, he recognized Rob's voice.

"I can't breathe!"

"Best news I've ever heard, Strong. You fucking raped my wife, you son of a bitch. I'd kill you right now, but you're not worth the prison time." Rob pressed harder.

"What the hell are you talking about?"

"After midnight? On the bluff? In the Madrona grove?"

Another reality opened in Tyler's fragmenting brain: the mixed scents of the salt air and Peggy's perfume, the smooth-barked tree, the earth still releasing the heat of the day into the night air, the woman, the lush, eager woman, the thrusting, the fury.

"She likes it that way!" he croaked. It was all he could think to say.

Rob March lifted his foot for a moment and then kicked his friend's skull with all the strength he could muster. But Tyler was already twisting away, so the blow was glancing. Rob staggered to regain his balance as Tyler scrabbled, crab-like, across the grass. Rob saw that Old Adam had turned and was advancing on them and tried to wave him away, but the old man kept coming.

"Police! Hold it right there," a voice ordered. "All of you!"

thirty-one

CHRIS CHRISTIANSEN WAS still troubling over his conversation with Tyler Strong when the King County Sheriff's call center reached him just shy of noon and gave him Colin's cell phone number. He knew the vet, of course. Everyone did. Chris had lost his wife Harriet to cancer a few years back, and his daughter had given him a leggy, blue-point Siamese rescue cat as a companion. He loved his daughter too much to tell her he hated cats, and by the time he'd mustered the courage to do so the damned feline, which was smarter than most dogs he'd known, had him hooked. Colin Ryan looked after the beast, which the officer had named, "Sarge."

"Deputy Christiansen, here, doc. What's up?"

"Chris, hello. Thank goodness it's you. We have a situation here."

"A situation?"

"It may be attempted murder."

"Whoa, hang on there a moment, detective! Who's 'we?'"

"I'm at Edwinna Rutherford's house, with Pete—I mean, Martha—Strong. It's possible her husband tried to kill her last night by trying to stage a suicide."

"Okay, stop right there, doc. I heard from Strong earlier, saying his wife had gone missing. You say you've got her right there?"

"Yeah, but she's in rough shape, Chris."

"Meaning?"

"Acute alcohol poisoning."

"You're telling me a drunk told you her husband tried to kill her? We get that all the time."

"How many of them get their spouse deadly drunk and then leave them in the middle of the Vashon Highway to get run over, Chris?"

Christiansen paused, then said, "Be there in ten minutes."

"Wait! Don't come here. Go to the beach compound. I think that's where he is."

"Understood," the deputy said as he cut off the call and headed for his squad car.

Under normal circumstances, when a complaint has been made, his first step would be to interview the complainant, which was to say Mrs. Strong. But in this case, what with Tyler's earlier call—and what was that, anyway? Was it an honest inquiry or a red herring?—he was sure he could bypass procedure and speak directly to the husband.

Even without the siren and lights, which Christiansen had always thought unseemly on so small an island, he turned onto the lane along the beach within seven minutes of leaving the branch station. But he never made it to the front door. Off to the left, on the lawn between the Petersen main house and the Strong place up the beach, two men were shouting and fighting. A much older man was approaching them, brandishing a cane. Christiansen hollered for them to stop.

Everything that had been happening froze, as if someone had hit the "Pause" button on a video player.

He'd seen this happen time and again. It had something to do with the uniform, he guessed—the brown and tan military-like shirt and trousers, the black boots, leather straps and pouches, including the one holding his service pistol—which, in his entire career, he'd used only once, to kill an injured deer. It was as if the trappings had the power to hold time captive.

But it was, he knew, a fleeting condition. He needed to move fast to gain control of the situation. He crossed the lawn quickly and stepped in front of Old Adam, who had his cane raised. He knew all three men. Tyler Strong sat on the grass holding his head; he looked dazed. Portly Rob March was bent over and breathing heavily, hands on knees.

"Morning, gentlemen," Christiansen said, as if he were greeting them on the street. "Mr. Strong; Mr. March; Mr. Adam, sir. What seems to be the difficulty here?"

For a moment, no one said a thing.

"Bastard raped my wife," March finally gasped.

"Bullshit," Tyler replied, struggling to his feet and then staggering to keep his balance.

"What?" Old Adam was dumbstruck. *Bankruptcy and now this?*

Christiansen, part of whose brain had been trying to work out the link between this fight and Strong's report of his missing wife, and failing, switched gears quickly. "Will the lady be filing a complaint, Mr. March?"

It was Tyler who answered.

"Can't...consensual...having an affair," he said with a bizarre smirk that seemed almost triumphant.

"Oh, well; that's all right then," Christiansen said, doing little to disguise his disgust. Chris Christiansen was old-school, a regular at the Unitarian church and, before she died, a devoted husband to Harriet. He stared at Strong for a long moment, then took Rob March's elbow and said, "Let's us have a chat, shall we, Mr. March?"

Rob nodded.

"I wouldn't be going anywhere if I were you, Mr. Strong," he said over his shoulder.

After Rob caught his breath, he said, "It's true, officer; we can't press charges; they'd been having an affair, apparently. Imagine: one of my oldest friends…"

"You said 'rape.' Was she assaulted, sir?"

"You mean does she have bruises or something?" Rob again saw his naked wife, fresh from this morning's shower. He shook his head. "No. He brutalized her last night, all right, viciously, but there are no external signs of violence. Look, officer, we are not going to press charges. I'm a lawyer, okay? She admits they've been lovers. There isn't a judge in the county who'd convict the bastard of rape. And I am certain she would never consent to go through that process anyway. But keep me away from him, officer; I want to kill him."

Christiansen nodded. "I hear you. But I didn't. May I suggest that you return home?"

"Sure."

Rob had just turned when Christiansen said, "By the way, have you seen Mrs. Strong this morning, sir?"

"Pete? No. Why?"

"Mr. Strong called 911 this morning to report her missing."

Rob stopped. "I don't understand…"

"I don't either, Mr. March; I've been trying to think of a connection."

SYLVIA PETERSEN TOOK Old Adam by the hand and led him away as the policeman, who she thought she recognized from town, began talking to Tyler. She had seen the altercation from her garden a few hundred yards away, seen Adam turn back, and had dashed out to keep him from becoming embroiled.

"Come on, dear man, I don't think there's anything you or I can do here that this officer can't do better, whatever the problem is."

Adam hobbled alongside her, almost grateful to be removed.

"What time is it?" he asked his companion.

She looked at her watch. "Just noon."

"So much destruction in so few hours."

"What do you mean?"

"First, Pete goes missing…"

"What?"

"But we've found her, at Edwinna's. Then I discover Tyler's bankrupted Pacific Pioneer."

"How?"

"Sheer incompetence, as near as I can tell. Huge debts, plummeting income. Company should have been reorganized or shut down long ago; instead, my idiot nephew's apparently been hoping it would all go away. Can't even liquidate its assets; the ships are rust-buckets, probably worthless. And that's not the worst of it: he's taken Pete down, too; she's personally liable for the company's debts. I can probably save her home, but the creditors will come after everything else."

They'd reached the flagstone patio in Sylvia's waterfront garden. She stopped and looked over her shoulder. The sheriff's deputy was leading Tyler toward the Old House. "Is that what the fight was about?"

"Hell, no. Rob says Tyler's raped Peggy."

"Jesus, Adam!"

"Maybe that's why Pete disappeared. I don't know."

The old man looked at the woman beside him.

"Everything's going crazy, Sylvia. Everything's coming apart."

Sylvia gathered the old man into her arms and held him there.

"Not us, Adam. We're coming together."

Adam looked at his old friend, his leathery face creased with bewilderment.

"And that's one more thing about this weekend that makes no sense," he said. "Why would someone as young as you be interested in an old codger like me?"

Sylvia chuckled. "Me, young? Lord, Adam, you must be senile, too…"

"Forgetful, not senile. Like they say: Forgetful is not remembering where you put your keys; senile is not remembering what keys are for."

"All right, then, I confess: I'm in it for the money."

This time the old man chuckled. "Too late. It's all going to Pete and her kids eventually."

"Thank goodness for that." She squeezed his wiry hand. "Shall I tell you the real reason?"

"I'm dying to know."

"Please don't. Not just yet, anyway."

"If you insist."

The two of them settled into Adirondack chairs Sylvia had painted the color of seawater on a day just like today.

"I've been thinking a lot lately, Adam, about the missing."

"The what?"

"The missing. Think about a family tree, okay?"

"Okay."

"We use 'tree' as an image for families because, with each generation, its span increases. It starts with two people, at the roots, and then spreads: thick limbs, smaller branches, twigs, with new fruit each season. Right?"

"I'm with you so far."

"Now look at our family trees, Adam; the Petersens, the Strongs, the Rutherfords, too. What do you see?"

Adam looked out over the water as if he could see the legions of the missing out there in the sparkling distance.

"They're upside down," he answered finally.

"Pardon?"

"The trees. They're not spreading, they're shrinking, as if back to the roots. This beach used to be crammed with all of us. Lots of branches in the past; now there's just a couple of stems. Shit, Sylvia, we're almost gone."

"I hadn't thought of it as 'upside down,' I was thinking of blight. But yes, that's my point. We're almost gone. So many of us are missing. And more to the point, you're almost gone, Adam."

"How very kind of you to remind me."

"Oh, shut up. What I mean is that men like you—*gentlemen*, Adam—are almost gone. You might be the last of the breed. I don't think I've ever heard you utter an unkind word, or say something unfair or mean-spirited in all my days in your presence...which, let's face it, is a lot of days. And while you sometimes pretend to be a cranky old chauvinist, in fact you have always shown women the deepest respect."

"Well, I've known a lot of stupid men in my time," the old man said jerking his head back in the direction of the Old House. "It's always been my belief that women are proof than man was just God's first draft."

"Stop kidding and pay attention to me."

"Yes, ma'am."

"Adam Strong, I should be honored to spend my remaining days...and nights...with you, sir."

"Isn't that something I'm supposed to say?"

"Shall we return to the subject of stupid men?"

Old Adam smiled and stroked Sylvia's sun-spotted hand. "Is it too early for a bourbon?"

Again, she looked at her wristwatch.

"Not in London," she said.

thirty-two

"I THINK I have a concussion."

Chris Christiansen looked at Tyler without sympathy. "I was at some remove, Mr. Strong, being in the squad car and all, but I don't think Mr. March fully connected with that kick."

The two men were seated in chairs on the broad waterside porch of the Petersen Old House. The officer had just pulled a small notebook from a pocket of his tunic.

"If you feel dizzy, Mr. Strong, I'd go with the more obvious explanation: you're falling down drunk. People believe vodka has no smell. But they're wrong. Pull over enough DUIs, like I have, and you can sense it: something oily and aromatic in their sweat."

Tyler shook his head, as if to jerk himself out of some other internal dimension he'd been occupying. *Where the hell are Pete and Justine and Two?*

"Remind me, would you, officer, why we're having this conversation?"

Christiansen thought for a moment that Strong was being sarcastic, but the man's confusion seemed genuine. He was beginning to question Strong's grip on reality. It wasn't just alcohol.

"I stopped by to inquire after your wife."

"Pete? Why?"

The deputy stared at the man in the chair before him.

"Do you recall, sir, contacting the 911 call center and, in turn, speaking with me this morning? To report your wife as missing?"

Like a fast-moving squall, a cloud of confusion passed over Tyler's face and, just as quickly, moved on.

"Well, of course, I do, Christiansen!" Tyler lied.

There was something about being called by his surname that galled Chris Christiansen. It was like being treated as a serf by a member of the titled aristocracy. But his face was as neutral as a blank sheet of paper.

"Have you heard from her since, Mr. Strong?"

"Not yet."

The officer watched as Tyler looked around, as if his family were simply loitering on the beach somewhere. Chris nodded toward the half packed Ford Explorer, its rear hatch still open. "Gone when it's time to close up for the season?"

Tyler shrugged, but the cloud was back. "It's a mystery," he said, as if to himself.

There was a crunch of gravel in the lane leading up to the Petersen compound as a white van arrived.

After a moment of complete silence, Tyler's mystery began to unravel.

Eileen boiled out of the van's passenger's door and raced around the grounds chasing chimera. Martha 'Pete' Petersen Strong climbed down after her as if every movement was painful. Colin Ryan stepped out of the driver's side door and Justine and Young Adam slipped out the sliding side door behind their mother.

Pete stood for a moment gripping the door for balance and scanning the scene, as if the houses, the lawns, the beach, the water—all these features she'd known since childhood—were suddenly alien. Then she began walking toward her house. Justine caught up with her mother and took her arm. Adam walked beside his mother on the opposite side and held her hand. Colin stood beside the van. Patsy stepped out the side door and joined him. Then they, too, followed. The sun was high overhead, the sky sun-bleached, almost white.

Tyler Strong jerked from his chair as if he'd been given an electrical shock and stepped to the edge of the porch.

"Pete!" he called. "Where have you and the kids been? I've been worried sick! I called the police!"

Pete stared at Tyler as if he were some curiosity in a museum. Finally, she blinked and said, "They found me in the middle of Vashon Highway."

"What?! Who's 'they'?" There was a flash of panic in his eyes.

If she heard him, Pete didn't acknowledge it. She shifted her gaze to address the officer who stood beside her husband.

"Deputy Chris, hello. I am sorry to call you out on a holiday."

Chris Christiansen nodded. "My job, Miss Martha."

"You called him?" Tyler said. "He said I did…"

"Thank you, deputy," Pete continued. "This man, my husband," she said, inclining her head momentarily toward Tyler, "and I had a fight last night."

"It was one of those moments," Tyler suddenly interjected, "when, after perhaps too much to drink, tempers briefly flare." His hands were splayed in a gesture that managed simultaneously to suggest the insignificance of the incident and a modicum of regret. It was the first coherent thing Chris Christiansen had heard him say since he'd arrived. And, given that the man had just been in another, different fight, it was simultaneously bizarre.

"During this fight," Pete continued, "my husband — and let me confess that I, too, was drunk — my husband restrained me and poured gin down my throat. All I remember, officer, was thinking I would drown. After that, nothing."

She stopped there and looked at Tyler, as if challenging him to correct her account. But Tyler's gaze was miles away, as if his brain had checked out of his body. *"They" found her. What was "they?" She isn't hurt, so nothing actually happened...did it?*

"It would seem that other things happened after that," Tyler heard his wife continue, "but I have no memory of them. I was unconscious. My friends, here, may be able to help you sort that out."

As if suddenly drained empty, Pete Petersen Strong sank to one of the porch stairs. Her son joined her, wrapping his skinny arms around his mother's legs.

"Might I have a word, Chris?" Colin had his hand in the air like a student at school.

"Would you excuse me for a moment, Miss Martha?" the deputy asked. "Perhaps you'd like to step inside out of the sun?"

Pete nodded. She was staring through her husband, as if he were made of tissue, toward the constant, reliable, glittering water beyond.

Justine came to her mother's side and helped her into the house. Young Adam followed. Tyler sat immobile, his face vacant as an empty room, his eyes focused somewhere in the far distance.

Colin walked across the lawn toward the driveway. Chris Christiansen followed and met him beside the squad car.

"What's this about 'attempted murder'?"

"I can't think of any other explanation," Colin said.

"Any chance you might start from the beginning?"

"I'm sorry, Chris. Of course."

Colin described finding Pete on the highway at dawn, her condition, and his decision to have Edwinna look after her.

"Not your smartest move, doc."

"So I've been told."

"Should have taken her to the medical center and called us."

"Perhaps."

"The attempted murder?"

"It's all about the shoes."

"Excuse me?"

"I would never have noticed."

"Doc?"

"Sorry. When I found Pete on the highway this morning, she was wearing the same black dress she had on last night—the one she has on still—and there were silver sandals on her feet, okay?"

"Uh-huh."

"Edwinna and I, well, we assumed Pete had either decided to commit suicide or was running away from something." He looked over his shoulder. "Or someone."

The deputy nodded, "Keep going."

"To end up where I found her she'd have to have walked the full length of the beach and then another, I don't know, half mile south along the highway."

"And?"

"It was young Adam who worked it all out. He's been reading Sherlock Holmes, you see."

"Look, Ryan…"

"Sorry, yes. I found her at the bottom of that long hill, right?"

"Right."

"She'd have to have walked a long way to get there, right?"

"So you said."

"But the shoes have no sign of wear, Chris."

"So how'd she get there," the deputy said, nodding. It wasn't a question; he'd already got it. He pulled a cell phone from a pouch on his leather belt and punched in a number.

"That kid worked this out?" he said.

Colin nodded.

"Too bad we have child labor laws; I could use him on the force."

The call connected.

"Give me the supervisor."

The deputy waited a moment, staring at the Old House and shaking his head. *Some kind of morning…*

"Sam? Christiansen on Vashon. We need the Major Crimes Unit to send a detective over here a.s.a.p. I know it's a holiday, Sam. It's also an emergency. Maybe attempted murder. Marital dispute of some kind. No, I have no direct evidence, but we can hold the guy on an assault charge his wife's already made to me. Yeah, an official 'excited utterance,' with witnesses. No, I didn't prompt her; she made the statement independently. The judge will buy it."

Christiansen filled his superior in on what little he knew and was about to ring off when he heard shouting.

"Colin!" It was Justine, screaming from the porch of the Old House. "He's leaving!"

At almost the same instant both men heard the roar of an outboard.

"Shit!" Christiansen yelled. "Sam! Stay on the line. We've got a situation here. Hang on."

The two men raced across the lawn and reached the lane that ran along the beach just as Tyler Strong gunned his aluminum fishing skiff and pointed the bow south toward the distant harbor's mouth.

The deputy yelled into his phone, "Sam, get on to the Coast Guard. We've got a suspect escaping by boat. South out of Quartermaster Harbor at high speed. No, I don't have the goddamned registration number. Aluminum skiff, open outboard. Suspect wearing khaki shorts and black T-shirt. No hat. Got that? Good. No, Sam, I didn't have him in custody; I had nothing to go on, okay?!"

Justine had run into the house and returned with binoculars just as Colin and the deputy climbed down to the beach.

"Son of a bitch," Christiansen said between breaths as they reached the water. "I'm getting too old for this game."

"He's stopped." Justine said as she reached them.

A quarter mile or so out, in the deepest part of the channel, the outboard's silvery wake suddenly softened and then vanished. The skiff slowed and, no longer under power, turned slowly on the tide.

"May I have those binoculars, Miss?" Christiansen asked, employing a calmness Colin knew was forced.

Even at this distance, they could see Tyler standing at the skiff's bow.

thirty-three

WHEN DID EVERYTHING begin breaking into shards? Tyler wonders as he stands at the skiff's gently rocking bow, coiling the anchor rope. *Maybe it's always been in pieces, or maybe prisms, like one of those kaleidoscopes. Yeah, that's it: Kaleidoscope. And what happens is you paste the shards together so they make some kind of sense, so you can move from one day to the next without getting lost. It's like landmarks: visions you can hold on to. But if that's the case, everybody's reality is different. The landmarks are arbitrary. Illusions.*

Only I can see the pieces distinct from one another, keep them in their separate places. That's why I know the Truth of them. Nobody else sees the Truth but me. They can't distinguish the pieces within the whole. They're too busy trying to make an airtight case, or a story, or something—beginning, middle, end. Squeezed between covers, or presented in court, as if that would force them to make sense. That's why the law is bogus; it's always about fixing boundaries. And punishing those who cross them. About containing. But there are no boundaries, because the pieces have independent lives. Yeah, like these jellyfish out here in the harbor, each its own independent reality, its own universe. But people can't leave the jellyfish alone, oh no; they keep trying to make something from them—careers, families, relationships, futures. Fools. It doesn't work; you can't hold them. One goes, they all go. Dominoes. Crazy to try to make something of them. Illusion. Illusion.

He looks back at Madrona Beach and sees several figures gathered along the shoreline, like actors at the lip of a stage. This must be a comedy, he thinks, and he starts laughing. He laughs so hard he has to sit down. He laughs so hard the pieces in his head rattle.

A cast of amateurs. That's what I've been cursed with. Idiots! Look at them--Old Adam's pissed because Pacific fucking Pioneer is a goner. Shit, the company's like that French character, Camille; it's been dying for years. Keep it alive? Futile. What a joke. But he's getting no laughs. His act is a flop. Let it go. What the hell does he care, anyway; he's a goner soon, too. And Rob's pissed his wife's been fucking me. Another comedy. He wants to make it a tragedy, so it's 'I raped her.' He doesn't get that he's only ever had a piece of her and I found the rest. Man, it's every which way with her. Girl never gets enough. Got enough last night, though. Ride of a lifetime. Oh yeah. Audience loved it.

He smiles as he thinks back to that woman on Madrona Bluff. He hums a bawdy song he learned long ago at overnight camp, and rocks the boat from side to side: *Roll me over, roll me over and do it again...*

Pete's pissed, too. Thinks I tried to drown her with gin. Already three sheets to the wind, she was; how the hell would she know? Frigid bitch. Partner, partner. Partner in marriage. Partner in a company. Partner in law. Partner in firm. Bit parts, trying to join. More illusions; more jellyfish, trying to be what they can never be, more than they are.

Double yellow stripe on a black dress. Where's she got to? Where are her shoes?

On the distant shore, he sees another figure, a woman, stepping from a white limousine, and recognizes

her immediately: it is the play's director, his mother
Amanda. She watches, expressionless, and he
understands this is it, the grand finale. He must soar in
his role, he must triumph.

Just watch, he shouts to his mother across the still
water. *Watch what I can do!*

"DID YOU HEAR that? That shout?" Justine asks.

"No. Well, maybe." Colin says. "Something, anyway."

"He's standing in the bow again," Christiansen
reports.

"Even we can see that," Justine says, fear making her
voice harsh. "What's he doing?"

"Nothing. Not a damned thing."

"This is crazy," Colin mumbles. He looks back at the
house and sees Pete and little Adam standing at the
porch rail. Pete has both hands on her head, as if trying
to keep it from flying away. To his surprise, he also sees,
parked at some distance away along the beachfront lane,
Edwinna's ancient white Cadillac. She is standing by its
open driver's door, but does not move. Off to the east,
the blinds are down at Rob and Peggy's house, their
driveway empty. Along the beach to the west, Sylvia
Petersen and Old Adam, having noticed the commotion,
approach, arm in arm, at roughly the speed of a
Dungeness crab crossing the seafloor. In fact, it is as if,
here under the hammering noon sun, everything has
crawled to a near halt, and the day itself holds its breath.

HERE, AT LAST, Tyler rejoices to himself, *is the one true symmetry, strands of history knitting together, an eternal reality. This is how the broken drama is completed, how the gap between Papa Richie and sweet Two is closed by Tyler I in the final act. You two should not have had to wait so long,* Tyler whispers. *Sorry. So sorry. My fault. Always my fault. Never measured up. But I am now. I'm coming now. The director will be amazed. Amanda will cheer.*

Tyler Strong balances again at the bow of the skiff and, with the care of a master rigger adjusting the jib sheets on a schooner, wraps three short lengths of anchor line around his waist, taking care to finish with a neat clove hitch, the one knot that only gets tighter the more it's tugged. Then, with the skiff's heavy galvanized anchor grasped in his right hand, Tyler Strong lifts a hand to his audience and steps off the bow.

"SHIT!" CHRISTIANSEN LET the binoculars drop to his side. It had been in his head from the moment he saw the skiff stop in mid-channel: *Why does an escapee cease his escape? Because a superior escape presents itself.*

He walked away from the beach and called the sheriff's office in Burien again. The same supervisor was on duty.

"Christiansen here, Sam. Tell the Coast Guard we need divers. Suspect has entered the water. With an anchor. We've got a suicide."

"What the hell's going on over there, Christiansen?" the supervisor demanded.

"Sam, I haven't begun to fill you in. But I will, I will."

"Damn straight you will, deputy."

Christiansen looked at the phone for a moment, then returned it to its pouch. He looked out at the harbor. The boat was still adrift. There was nothing else moving, no disturbance on the surface. There were no other boats in sight.

It was, after all, the end of the season.

WHAT I DIDN'T understand, you see, Tyler explains to Richie and Two, as the fractured green-blue surface of the outer harbor rises above him, *is that the broken pieces only join at the very end. It is only then we become whole. All else is fragments. Bits of dialogue. Rehearsal. Only this is real. Only this...*

The breath Tyler had taken on entering the still water begins expanding in his chest even as its benefits collapse. Bigger and bigger his chest seems to grow; thinner and thinner the contents. For a moment, an involuntary moment born of reflex, he struggles with the knot at his waist. He tries to release the anchor, but yanking on the rope only drags him deeper into the cold, green water.

All at once, he ceases struggling. As the darkness thickens, there is a distant sound of welcome, a kind of music that shoves aside the pain of pressure in his ears and on his eyes as he descends. He unclamps his throat and takes in the cool water, salty and sweet as a lover's skin.

Dad?

It is Two. He hears him. And his heart sings as its pounding ceases.

"GOD! DAMNED! SON of a bitch bastard!" Justine cried, hammering Colin's chest with her fists. "Fucking coward!"

Colin Ryan did not move. He let the young woman's anger flare and burn out. It didn't take long. After a few moments she was sobbing in his arms. He looked again at the porch of the Petersen house. Pete had disappeared. Only Young Adam remained.

"Justine," he said, "we need to look after Adam."

"Let's both do it, Justine," a voice said. Colin turned and it was Patsy. Calm, capable, lovely Patsy. She touched his arm, took Justine's hand, and the two women walked away just as the deputy returned.

"Any other boats here, Colin?"

"It's Labor Day, Chris; everyone else is gone. The boats have all been towed or stored."

"I need to get out there. Coast Guard's already notified the island's fire and rescue team. They have a Zodiac, but they're still twenty minutes out."

"Chris?"

"What?"

"It's over."

"Shit, doc..."

"Yeah. I know."

Christiansen turned away from the beach, defeated, and walked back toward his squad car.

Colin noticed Edwinna had left her car and was walking toward the Old House. He caught up with her on the lawn.

"What are you doing?" he asked.

"Going to look after Pete."

"That's not what I mean and you know it. You saw it all, didn't you?"

"Of course I did."

"You know what I'm talking about, Edwinna."

The old woman stopped and looked out toward the water.

"Yes. I did."

"When?"

"Just after you all left my place in the van. I saw a man jumping into water. I started getting it earlier today, but it wouldn't come together."

"And you drove over here."

"Yes."

"And did nothing."

She turned again and looked directly at him, arms crossed at the chest.

"That's right. I stayed by my car. Now, unless you have any further questions, young man, I'm going inside to see to Pete."

She did not wait for a reply.

epilogue

"HERE'S WHAT I still don't get..." Patsy said.

She and Colin sat side by side on his rear deck high above Tramp Harbor. The small weathered teak table between them held the remains of a Caesar salad and a nearly empty bottle of Palouse "Golden Pearl" Viognier, a gift from one of their clients, who owned a new island winery. The sun had just dipped behind the ridge to the west and while the sky directly above was flushed with fire, the eastern margins of the island below were shifting into shades of violet. Far to the north, near the Canadian border, snow-clad Mount Baker had taken on the antique pink of a fading English rose about to drop its petals. On the south side of Colin's house, the tomato vines were heavy with fruit.

"...I don't get him trying to kill her."

Colin took a sip from his glass and looked out over the water. The wind was shifting from southerly to northerly and the surface of the shipping channel shivered far below. It was the Saturday after Labor Day.

"Humiliation," he answered. "I talked to Jemma Keating about it."

"Meaning?"

"Tyler was the only one who knew everything, who knew all the betrayals."

"Help me out here."

"Okay, think about it. Old Adam learned Pacific Pioneer was finished, but no one else knew, except Tyler. Rob knew Tyler would not be made partner in his own family's firm, but no one else did, even Old Adam, until Rob told Tyler that night on the beach. And though Pete may have suspected an affair, only Peggy—and later Rob—knew Tyler'd assaulted his wife."

"Okay, I get that. I can see those as reasons for killing himself, maybe; he's ruined. But why try to kill Pete?"

Colin was smiling.

"What?" his companion demanded, punching him playfully on the shoulder.

"Do you remember what you said last Monday morning, when I told you I'd found her in the middle of the Highway?"

"I must have had too much wine tonight; I don't."

"You said she'd gone there because she knew I would find her on my bike run."

"Oh, yeah; right."

"But you were wrong She didn't think that, Tyler did. She didn't put herself there, he did."

"Huh?"

"Tyler laid her there in the road, before dawn, knowing I'd be along before the ferry traffic started."

"You mean he wasn't trying to kill her?"

"I don't know, Pats. Honestly. Given his mental state, he could have been. All he knew was that he was finished, and, in a sense, I think he didn't want Pete to ever know how finished he—and they—were. The weight of everything he was hiding, everything he'd packed into little boxes and kept separate and locked away in his head, finally broke him. I keep thinking of a wave cresting on the beach, but it's a tsunami and everything will be engulfed.

"Maybe some part of him wanted Pete to die before she could discover all the ways he'd failed her, okay? But I'm thinking that that part of him didn't win. So he hedged his bets. He left her precisely where he guessed I would be the first to find her. I think he was trying to save her from himself. If she was hit, it would look like suicide. But if she wasn't, he knew she'd be found and looked after."

"Jesus."

They sat quietly for a few moments, watching the expanse of water below fade from blue to silver.

"What about Young Adam?"

"Do you know what? I think that may be the happiest outcome."

"I'm listening…"

"That kid's resilient. But the good news is that, for the time being, Justine's going to take him under her wing, while Pete recovers. I think the two of them will thrive. They're two of a kind."

"Two."

"Yeah. I know. That boy, that bright young thing: he haunted them all, but maybe Tyler, I think, far more. Much as he may have struggled to keep Two's death in a separate box, he knew it was his carelessness that killed the boy, the golden haired son so like himself and in whom Tyler saw his second chance at life."

"And Pete?"

Colin shrugged. "Old Adam says she's been so busy sorting out the financial mess Tyler's left her in that she hasn't even had time to deal with his suicide. It's horrible for her, though…has to be."

Patsy looked out at the water far below. "I need to ask you something, Colin."

"No, you don't. I know it's about me and Pete, and the answer is no. I'm not running off to rescue her. I've spent so much of my life in a box of my own construction, in a fantasy—about her, about loving her, about those families and their life. So stupid; such a waste…"

"I'm not sure it's ever a waste to love someone, even from a distance," she said.

"But I feel…"

"What, Colin?"

He was about to continue, when it dawned on him she was talking about herself, about her own lost years.

"I feel like such a fool."

"That would make two of us, sweetie."

Patsy lifted the nearly empty bottle of wine.

"Remember that bottle of Dom Pérignon we shared at the end of our first year?"

"Yes. I made a fool of myself then, too."

"No you didn't, darling man; I did."

The statement hung in the air, shimmering. Colin turned to her.

"May I share something with you?" he said.

Patsy nodded.

"I think you are the loveliest, smartest, most grounded and wonderful woman on this entire island."

"Big deal; it's a small island."

He held up his hand to silence her.

"You know what else I think? I think I'm the dumbest man on this island: a swirling pit of dimness. Not to mention blindness…"

"I'm liking this part," Patsy said, grinning. "Do go on."

Colin paused, then took a breath.

"Yes, exactly; 'go on.' I'd like to go on with you, Pats. On and on, forever and a day. If you'll have me. Though why you would is a mystery."

"To you, doc; only to you."

Patsy reached her hand across the table and placed it atop his. She patted it gently, as one might the hand of an errant child.

"You're right about one thing, you know," she said, turning to him and smiling.

"Only one?"

"One."

"And that would be…?"

"You are, without a doubt, the dumbest man on this island."

"Why, thank you."

"And also the best."

"It's a small island."

She gave his hand a slap, and they rose and went indoors. The air was cooling quickly; the marine layer was creeping in from the sea.

Keep reading for an excerpt from **Harm None**, Book 1 in the Davies & West Mystery Series.

Harm None
A Davies & West Mystery

An excerpt from Book 1
in the Davies & West Mystery Series

The Major Crime Investigating Team

Detective Chief Inspector Arthur Penwarren

Detective Sergeant Morgan Davies

Detective Sergeant and Crime Scene Manager Calum West

Police Constable Terry Bates

An ye harm none,
Do what ye will

From the "Wiccan Rede"

Some There Are Who Know

prologue

I KNEW BEFORE Tamsin did. I had one of my seeings. Gave me a shock, I can tell you. The problem with seeings is they fade fast, the way dreams do when you're just coming awake. Seeings aren't dreams, though. Uh-uh. In a dream, you sort of know you're asleep. Seeings happen when you are awake. Suddenly I can only see the normal world around the edges of my eyes, because there's like a video going on in the center, like suddenly I'm at the cinema on Causewayhead.

Clearness was the problem with my seeings of Becca those first few weeks after she'd gone off to…well, wherever she went. They were ever so dark and muzzy, like looking through a grimy window into one of those old miners' cottages up on the moor above Penzance. I knew she was trying to get through to me, but I couldn't see her true.

Tamsin says my seeings are a gift. I can tell something's gonna happen before it does, or sometimes after it has but I wasn't there. *Clairvoyance*, it's called. That's French and means "clear vision," she says. But mine aren't so clear. Tamsin tells me, "Don't worry, Tegan girl, they'll get clearer as you get older." That could be long wait; I'm only ten.

I heard once that people who lose an arm or a leg can still feel it. That's Becca to me. I feel her so often, and I know she's still here, somewhere here in West Penwith. That much, at least, I can see. I just don't know where, you know?

Anyway, today I'm at Tamsin's cottage. Tamsin Bran's the village wise-woman in St. Euny. She never uses the word "witch," though other people do. Her cottage used to be a small mill for grinding grain, powered by the fast stream that gathers on the moors and races down through this narrow valley. Ages ago, someone built a long, level, stone-lined leat into the side of the valley to divert some of that stream water to a flume where it tumbled over the mill wheel. Tamsin says when she bought the place it was a ruin, but she's fixed it up nice and tight with the help of those she's done spells or healings for. One of the huge old grooved millstones now sits atop a granite pillar in the middle of her kitchen as a work surface.

That's where I'm standing today—Monday—measuring herbs for a powder. I love this room. It's a modern kitchen and all, but there are also shelves and shelves of labeled glass jars filled with all manner of herbs and stuff. There's a massive granite hearth in one wall with a big copper pot hanging from an iron arm set into the stone. It's for when she needs to cook up a spell. Beside the hearth is where she leans her tall staff, the one she always walks with. It's wood and it has two short branches at the top, like horns. Tamsin says the branches represent the duality of nature. I had to ask her about that; it means the two-ness, like day and night, good and bad, black and white, male and female. That's what she says anyways.

There are also two handmade brooms: one of skinny stiff hazel branches, the other—my favorite—made of snowy swan feathers bound to a stick with cord. And there's a short stick with a hook at the end, a "hook wand," which she says she uses to pull in good energies when she's doing a ritual. I never saw her do a ritual, so I don't really see how a stick could hook energies, but there's a lot I don't know.

There's also stuff I'm not to touch, ever. Like a sacred pottery bowl with the image of a hare inside, a cup made from animal horn she says is a chalice, and a knife she calls her *athame*. It has a carved black handle and cutting edges on both sides. She says it does good things, but honestly it scares the death out of me.

I'm here doing cleaning and tidying to earn pocket money. My teacher at school arranged that, as a summer job, like. She's friends with Tamsin. I live nearby, just a twenty minute bike ride over the moor-top. But Tamsin also lets me help her with her work, too. She writes the ingredient amounts for powders and potions on a slip of paper and I put them together for her. It's brill that she lets me do this now, like she used to let Becca. And she says I have "more promise."

Today, I'm putting together a Go-Away Powder for Brian Tregarren. He's the captain of the Lady B—that's for "Brenda," his wife—out of Newlyn. It isn't to make him go away, of course, but to banish the fogs. Out on the cuttlefish grounds, he's been bedeviled by sea fogs and his catch is falling behind the other vessels in old man Stevenson's line, which isn't good as the Tregarrens have three kids to support. So he's asked for a spell.

Tamsin's cat, Desmond, who's black but for the one white paw, like he stepped in paint or something, is watching me from atop the herb shelves, as if my measuring is a test he's judging. Some cats, you know, they just seem to wander aimlessly in their own little dream world, or they're asleep in the sun somewhere. Not Desmond. He's a watcher. It would be creepy if he weren't such good company. He also has some kind of glitch in his brain that makes him twitchy, and sometimes he rockets around the cottage for no reason I can figure, howling as if he's possessed. But Tamsin says he's not really bewitched or bedeviled, just different. Desmond doesn't like most people, but he likes me, which is brill. When I ride up to Tamsin's cottage on my bicycle he races out through the cat flap to greet me, whirling around in circles and talking a blue streak, as if he needs to fill me in on everything that's happened since the day before.

But he's not worried today; we both know Go-Away is a simple powder to measure out, nothing like as complicated as some others. It's just three teaspoons of benzoin, one each of mullein and St. John's Wort, two of wormwood and salt, and two blackthorn tree thorns. I don't grind them, though. Tamsin does that bit: seven grinds clockwise, seven counterclockwise in her big black mortar and pestle, over and over till it's ready. I don't know how she knows when that is; I reckon that's part of the witchery, part of the Old Craft. That's what Tamsin calls her work: the "Old Craft."

Anyways, the tide will begin ebbing just after midnight, Tamsin says, and there's also a full moon which is a good thing. So tonight, after the grinding is done, she'll drive down to Newlyn in her funny little Morris 1000 estate wagon with the polished wood trim, which is way older than me, from the Fifties, she says. She'll scatter the powder onto the sea from the end of the ancient stone jetty that protects the anchorage, the tide will pull it out, and Captain Tregarren will be right as rain. Or at least not in fog.

I'm new at this, and I do wonder sometimes about these powders and such, but Tamsin's been the wise-woman in St. Euny for quite some years. Her mum was the wise-woman before her and I guess she passed the knowledge on. Folks come by all the time, and not just from the village, either; from all over. Maybe they have love trouble, or have a nagging pain somewhere, or a cow that's poorly. Sometimes they're under a spell from someone and they want it lifted. Or the other way 'round, though Tamsin's not much into the darker stuff, is what she says.

Except for Desmond, Tamsin's all alone, and I don't really get that, because she's really pretty. She's got these nearly black eyes flecked with golden speckles and when you look into them it's like looking up into the sky on a clear night, all sparkly and limitless, like you could see through them into the whole universe. She uses a lot of black mascara and liner, which really highlights those eyes in a way you can't look away from, and I've asked her to show me how she does that but she says I'm too young. She says that a lot. It frosts me, but then I think, well, at least she cares. More than Mum does, that's for sure.

So here I am, measuring under Desmond's glazy-eyed gaze, when out of nowhere, there's Becca. Well, not here in the kitchen, but somewhere, and this time she's clear as day. And naked as a babe. And she's screaming. I can't hear it, but I can see it in her face, in the twist of her mouth. Scares me senseless and I drop the bowl I'm filling. Desmond hisses, leaps to the stone floor, and speeds out of the room yowling. And then the phone rings.

"I've got it, Tegan girl," I hear Tamsin sing out from upstairs where she's sorting laundry.

And that's how it all starts.

one

DETECTIVE SERGEANT MORGAN Davies slid her white, unmarked Ford estate wagon to a stop in the yard of Trerane Farm, a few miles shy of the south-westernmost tip of Cornwall. She yanked up the emergency brake, shoved open the door, and made to get out but pulled her low-heeled navy blue pump back just before it reached the manure-splattered ground.

"Bloody hell," she muttered.

She looked at the mess in the farmyard and at the steep climb to the top of Dewes Tor, made a face, pulled off the heels, and reached into the rear seat for a pair of black rubber Wellies.

Several hundred feet above the farmyard, Bradley Hunter, professor of archaeology at The Pennsylvania State University, watched the new arrival beside his site manager, assistant professor Amanda Jeffers. Hunter was a slender but weathered forty-five-year-old with longish curling salt and pepper hair that danced in the wind off the Atlantic as if it had a life of its own. Amber-tinted aviator glasses hid his mahogany eyes. He wore heavy work boots, khaki shorts that revealed calves taut as knotted hawsers, a vented white safari shirt, and a multi-pocketed canvas vest more suited to fly-fishing than digging. It had belonged to his father, a digger of another sort: a Pennsylvania coal miner and avid fly-fisherman. Hunter would never admit to being superstitious, but he'd worn the vest on every successful expedition since his father had died of black lung disease a decade ago.

Behind Hunter and Jeffers, as if it had grown out of the ground, lay the stone foundations of Carn Dewes, a prehistoric walled settlement dating from the Iron Age, but which Hunter had just discovered could be far older, and far more important than a mere settlement.

THREE DAYS EARLIER, in a bell-shaped stone chamber several feet beneath the Carn Dewes settlement, Hunter stared at the screen of his ground-penetrating radar and felt the hairs on the back of his neck rise. The equipment was aimed at a ground-level granite niche roughly two feet wide and three feet high set into the wall of the chamber. Behind the slab at the back of the niche, the screen revealed a wavy anomaly; something that should not have been there.

Hunter scrambled through the tunnel to the surface and called out to the nearest graduate student, "Find Jeffers and get her down here!"

Amanda ducked into the chamber just as Hunter began prying out one of the short upright stone columns at the side of the niche.

"Jesus, Brad, what are you doing? English Heritage will have our heads!"

"Look at the scanner's screen," he ordered without pausing.

"Oh, wow."

"Give me a hand here—we need to get behind the back face of the niche without causing the chamber wall to collapse. I think the lintel above will hold."

Together, they loosened and removed the other vertical stone and, with a short steel pry bar, inched the rear slab outward as if opening a creaky door. Three-thousand-year-old dust drifted into their hair.

"I can't imagine why no previous researchers thought to take this niche apart," Hunter muttered. "It's been described as a hearth in the old literature, which is laughable...a hearth with no chimney?"

"Maybe originally there was a hole in the peak of the chamber through which the smoke escaped, like the cone-shaped roofs of the houses in the settlement above?"

"Think about that. This stone chamber is a dome, cruder but architecturally little different from St. Peter's in Rome. Its structural integrity depends entirely on the keystone at the very top which directs the compressive force of gravity outward along the curve to the base, rather than straight downward. Remove that keystone and the whole chamber collapses."

"Right; so no hole."

Hunter ran his hands over his scalp and twisted his neck until she heard a cervical vertebra pop; a habit he had when he was anxious.

"The niche is an altar is what it is, raised slightly from the floor of the chamber. It's not a hearth. And where is it situated?

"Directly opposite the chamber entrance."

"Precisely one hundred eighty degrees around the circumference of the chamber, the space between perfectly bisected. Why? Because before the late Iron Age tunnel outside the chamber was built, this chamber's entrance would have been set into the hillside and would have faced the very point on the horizon where the sun rises at the winter solstice, the moment of the rebirth of life, the return to the season of fertility after the season of death. At that moment, the altar would have blazed like a fire in the new light, at least for a few magical moments. That's why the altar looks like a hearth."

"But an altar to what?"

"I think we're about to find out."

Working together, they pulled aside the rear face of the niche, only to find another cavity, much smaller this time and, nestled within it, a figurine, obviously female, carved in white quartz that glittered, jewel-like, in the beam of Hunter's flashlight, its rough surface shooting shards of light around the shallow niche.

For a moment, neither of them said a word.

"Get me latex gloves and some bubble wrap from the operations tent, would you Amanda?" Hunter finally said. "And tell no one."

"On it," Jeffers said, backing out.

What Hunter could not tell her, what he did not understand himself, was that the moment the back wall of the niche had been opened a charged energy had vibrated within him like a tuning fork. She apparently hadn't experienced it. He'd read about Egyptologists experiencing something similar when opening a tomb, but this was a first for him and he tried to come to terms with it. He sensed no threat. If it was a message, he could not comprehend it.

But a part of him, a distant, primitive part of him, wished he'd never opened the niche.

DETECTIVE SERGEANT DAVIES was halfway across the farmyard and pulling on a rainproof jacket when she heard a second vehicle approaching at speed along the narrow country lane that led to the farm. Moments later, a Ford Fiesta hatchback, its side panels plastered with the neon blue and lemon yellow grid of squares emblematic of the Devon and Cornwall Police, pulled into the farmyard.

"How did she get here before us?" Special Constable Trevor Williams asked the woman behind the wheel.

"Always does, is what I hear," Police Constable Teresa Bates said. "We'd better get a move on."

Bates stepped out, ignored the muck, smoothed her black uniform, adjusted her equipment belt, tucked her short ginger hair beneath her regulation PC's black bowler hat with its checkered headband, and hurried to catch up with Davies. Everyone at the Penzance nick knew better than to keep DS Davies waiting. Williams followed, shrugging on his waterproof jacket which, like the Fiesta, was patched in reflective blue and yellow.

They met the detective at an iron stile set into a stone wall at the foot of a stony footpath that climbed up the eastern flank of the tor through thickets of gorse, bracken fern, and heather.

"You lot should have got here first," Davies snapped.

Bates came to attention and introduced herself and Williams. "We were on foot duty for the Golowan Festival parade, ma'am. It took us a while to get through the crowds to the Penzance BCU and requisition a car.

"Bloody Golowan. Bunch of drunken pagans in fancy dress clogging up the streets just because it's the longest day of the year."

"Actually, ma'am, it's also the feast day of St. John," Williams volunteered.

Davies shot him a look that would have blistered paint and began climbing.

THANKS TO THE Golowan celebration, which drew hundreds of pagans to Penzance, Davies had had the gloriously empty CID office to herself. Given Golowan, she might have been out on the streets managing crowds like the rest of the Force, but Morgan detested the Golowan revelries. The event, the dancers, the musicians, the fancifully-constructed giant paper and wire creatures, and the crowds that thronged the streets of Penzance on Golowan weekend were, as far as she was concerned, ardently to be avoided.

Instead, she'd been going over, yet again and just as fruitlessly, the case files on the murders of two very young prostitutes in nearby Newlyn, the fishing port immediately adjacent to Penzance along the broad sweep of Mount's Bay. Both had been strangled (apparently in the throes of sex, given the forensic evidence) and then dumped, two weeks apart, like so much rat bait in the maze of cobbled alleys that climbed the hill above the port. So far, and despite door-to-door inquiries, Morgan had got no closer to a perpetrator. And the other Toms catting around the port were keeping mum. So when the emergency call about the Carn Dewes find came in from Comms, Davies welcomed the distraction.

Minutes later she was blasting south along the A30 in her staff car. At Drift, she veered right onto the minor road through Sancreed and headed up into the high moors. The entire trip took twenty minutes, half of it extracting herself from the one-way traffic pattern in Penzance.

"THIS IS GOING to shut us down, dammit," Hunter mumbled as he watched the police ascend the tor.

If Penn State's highly-regarded archaeology department had a "star," Brad Hunter was it, though he would have rejected the label. He was known as a mesmerizing lecturer and a caring mentor. He was also uncommonly successful in his expeditions. His reputation pulled in streams of talented graduate students. But, in his field, that reputation was only as good as the latest find. Now he had a new one, a stone figurine that could rewrite the history of the Neolithic,

Bronze, and Iron ages in Britain. But a second discovery now threatened to bring his dig to a halt.

The trouble had begun less than two hours earlier.

Hunter had been in the operations tent poring over data on Neolithic figurines on his laptop when he caught sight of his second in command pounding across the gently sloping ground within the settlement's inner ramparts. An athletic brunette just turned thirty, Amanda Jeffers had the honed frame of the distance runner she proved herself to be early each morning, arriving long before the rest of the crew and racing over the moorland paths. She ran effortlessly, her body fluid, like water flowing. Not for the first time did he consider what that athlete's body would be like unadorned by her usual uniform of Vibram-soled work boots, olive drab multi-pocket expedition trousers, khaki spaghetti-strap knit cotton shirt, and muddy gray rain jacket; a beauty in mufti, but one who signaled "Keep Your Distance" as if in blinking neon.

"Brad!" she yelled. "Something you need to look at. Now!"

Hunter had never quite got used to the curiously commanding nature of his assistant. Her clipped attitude ruffled feathers among his graduate students and the internal tension at the dig would have been lessened by her absence, but he respected Amanda's professionalism. She wasn't autocratic, just focused and precise. In that regard, at least, they were well-matched.

Jogging to keep up, he followed Jeffers across the settlement. To his surprise, she carried on right out through the only gap in the Iron Age walls. Beyond the entrance, a narrow path led through wind-stunted gorse and dense heather thickets across a finger ridge that ran southwest from the hilltop. Roughly two hundred yards along stood Dewes Quoit. A hulking Neolithic stone structure far older than the settlement, the quoit looked out toward the seething Atlantic a mile or so to the west and far below. Three massive, five-foot-high granite megaliths stood like the legs of an elephantine tripod, and atop them lay a two-foot-thick granite capstone crudely shaped in an elongated oval. Roughly twelve feet long and eight feet wide at its widest point, the almost unimaginable mass of this capstone was perfectly balanced across its uprights.

There were quoits like this one crowning hilltops elsewhere in West Cornwall, as well as Ireland, Wales, and Brittany in France. They were thought to have been tombs for revered Stone Age chieftains and would originally have been covered in earth after being erected. But thousands of years of weathering by Cornwall's relentless storms had eaten away at the soil and rubble cover and left the great support stones exposed. Obvious as the naked monuments were upon the skyline, all had long since been plundered for whatever artifacts or grave goods might have been interred with the chieftains. They remained today simply as engineering marvels, silently bearing witness to the skills of a primitive civilization in a mysterious, ancient time. No one fully understood how the great capstones, weighing tons, had been placed so precisely that, millennia later, they remained in place. Given the absence of sophisticated tools in the Neolithic, the quoits beggared explanation.

"I was just policing the quoit," Jeffers called over her shoulder as Hunter caught up. "Walkers like to picnic up here..."

They squeezed beneath the hulking mass of the quoit and in the dim light, Hunter saw it: the curled first two segments of a skeletal finger rising from the ground. Working with a bristle brush from Amanda's tool belt, it took him only a moment to conclude the bones could not possibly be ancient. The site had been excavated more than once at least a century earlier and the soil around the exposed finger wasn't compacted enough to be even that old. It was everything he could do to keep from unearthing more of the remains. Instead, he had Jeffers call the police from her mobile.

DS DAVIES ARRIVED atop the summit ridge flushed, sweating, and disgusted. She hadn't planned on mountain climbing this particular Saturday afternoon—or any afternoon, for that matter. On any other off-duty Saturday, she'd be at home watching some romantic old black and white movie and nursing a vodka tonic. Bodies, she grumbled to herself, showed up in the most inconvenient places—reservoirs, mountaintops. Inconvenient.

Handsome in a strong, Katherine Hepburn sort of way, albeit with a bit more heft, Davies was as fit as any largely desk-bound detective might be, but lately she had begun feeling her forty-five years. When PC Bates reached the summit ridge behind Davies she grabbed Williams's coat and waited while Davies, pretending to take in the view, caught her breath. The afternoon was waning and the western light had reached that burnished gold peculiar to higher latitudes in high summer.

After a moment, Davies turned, approached the archaeologists, and flashed her warrant card.

"What have you got?" Morgan Davies wasn't long on pleasantries.

Hunter pointed to the quoit. "You'd better have a look," he said, leading her there.

Holding on to one of the upright megaliths, Davies lowered herself to her knees and peered into the shadowy space beneath the capstone. Hunter was beside her, his sunglasses removed. In her twenty-five years of service in the force, she'd seen her share of bodies, but this—this single skeletal finger, curled as if desperately clawing its way free of the earth—raised the hackles at the back of her neck. She shook the feeling away.

"Who's the fool's been digging under here?" she demanded.

"That would be me," Hunter said.

"SOCOs won't be pleased," she said as she backed out and stood. She steadied herself on one of the uprights. Davies hated confined spaces.

"SOCOs?"

"Scene of Crime Officers. You've mucked up their site."

Davies turned to Special PC Williams and barked, "Get Ms. Jeffers away from here, take a statement, and caution her about saying anything about this to anyone else."

Williams nodded sharply and marched the unwilling young professor across the ridge toward the settlement and the dig's operations tent.

"I'm issuing you the same caution," she said turning to Hunter, "and I want you to give the same instructions to anyone else who's working with you here. Got that?"

Hunter nodded.

Davies smiled. What she saw was a man accustomed to controlling events but for whom events had suddenly spun out of control, a man of certainty newly faced with uncertainty. He was also arrestingly handsome in a weathered sort of way. On another day, in a different situation, she would have fancied him. Any woman would.

"A word, then, if you don't mind..." She took his elbow and led him a short distance along the ridge from the quoit, leaving Bates at the quoit and out of hearing.

"You're in charge here, I gather?"

"Yes, it's my project, sanctioned by English Heritage and the Duchy of Cornwall."

"Means sod all to me, professor. Look, I'm a detective; you're an archaeologist. What I want to know is what do you make of this?"

"The bones can't be ancient; that's why I had my assistant call 999."

"Why not?"

"Okay, the bones are already skeletonized, but that's not surprising; the conditions up here are brutal. If I had to guess I'd say this body—if it is a body and not just a hand—has only been in the ground, shallowly buried, between one and two years. The soil is too loose for it to be much older. But I'm no forensic expert."

"You'll do in a pinch. And for what it's worth, since I am even less of an expert, I tend to agree with you, based on other cases. I appreciate your expertise."

As if clicking off a switch, she turned and left him, rummaged in her shoulder bag, pulled out her mobile, and clumped off along the ridge toward the settlement. He watched her go with a curious combination of awe and interest. He'd seldom met a more compelling woman; tough-minded, bordering on belligerent. Not his type at all. And yet...

Davies leaned against one of the granite megaliths flanking the entrance to the settlement and described the situation to the on-duty senior investigating officer at the Bodmin police hub, who turned out this day to be her former superior in Penzance, Detective Chief Inspector Arthur Penwarren.

"All right, Morgan. You know the drill. Get the response unit to cordon off the site until the SOCO people arrive. Comms called West just after they called you. Knowing the way he drives, he'll only be minutes away by now. Wait for him, will you? I'll notify Penzance their constables will be there a while. We'll have a Major Crime Investigating Team meeting first thing tomorrow: eight o'clock, Camborne nick."

Davies rang off and found Bates at attention behind her. Discipline and intelligence radiated from the young woman's eyes. Her body language said, *I await your orders.* Davies liked that she'd said nothing yet.

"I'm guessing, Constable, that you're the one with brains here..."

"PC Williams is a novice Special, ma'am; a new volunteer. Just a bit green is all."

"Very charitable, but you're confirming that he doesn't know what he's doing, so I'm putting you in charge. The SIO's already on to Penzance. Cordon off the scene; keep others out. After that, I'm afraid you and Williams will be here all night."

"Nature of the job, ma'am."

"Hours of boredom punctuated by moments of bloody terror, that's us," Davies said. Bates smiled and nodded in a way that said she relished the task.

Then, as if controlled by wires, the two women's heads suddenly pivoted east at the sound of another approaching car, this one's engine deep-throated and roaring. Almost immediately a big Volvo estate wagon executed a perfect four-wheel power slide and came to a halt in the farmyard at the base of the tor next to Morgan's car.

Davies shook her head, smiling. "West."

"Ma'am?" Bates asked.

"Calum West, SOCO crime scene manager and would-be race car driver. And, as he's also part of the national anti-terrorism unit, he gets issued that fire-breathing Volvo: top cruising speed one hundred forty. Thank god he's a brilliant driver is all I can say.

"While I wait for him here, tell the professor I'll want to take formal statements in Penzance as soon as possible from him, his assistant, and anyone else involved in this discovery. Have him dismiss the rest of his people."

"Ma'am."

Davies watched Bates stride across the summit toward the operations tent. It was like watching a shade of herself, twenty-five years earlier. But it was a bittersweet image. She had learned so much since then, been through so much. She remembered her optimism, her sense of mission, her passion to make the world, or at least a small part of it, safer, more secure. A quarter century later, she knew the best one could hope for was to beat back the forces of chaos to a stalemate.

CRIME SCENE MANAGER Calum West, lugging a pre-packed SOCO kit, took his time ascending. A balding, genial middle-aged chap, quick to smile, West was at the top of his game, but lately his heart had taken to fluttering like a very small bird trying to escape his ribcage. He'd told no one. But Davies noticed he was pacing himself.

"Ah, this is indeed my lucky day," he crowed as he reached the ridge-top and caught his breath. "Human remains *and* the ever-lovely and talented Morgan Davies!"

"You're lightheaded from the climb."

"And you're so gracious in accepting compliments. Where's the body?"

"Finger."

"One is ever hopeful."

They regarded each other for a moment and Davies finally smiled. She led West across the ridge to the quoit and filled him in en route. When they reached the site, West climbed into a white Tyvek jumpsuit he pulled from his kit bag and put paper booties over his shoes. Then, stepping only where others had, he entered the space beneath the giant capstone and examined the exposed finger. He took several digital record photos of it and the rest of the dim interior which he'd later download to the laptop in his car. Then, he slipped a clear plastic bag over the exposed bone and backed out.

"Have you spoken to Mister?" he asked as he shed the coverall. Davies nodded. "Mister" was what they all called DCI Penwarren, at least in private. The chief inspector was admired by everyone in the force except those who resented his complete disinterest in the politics of the Devon and Cornwall Police. He was a detective and he liked being one. He hadn't sought promotion; he'd been elevated to DCI for the simple reason that his accomplishments could no longer be ignored.

"Major Crime Investigation Team meeting tomorrow morning. Camborne," Davies said.

"Well then, much as I may wish to tarry with you in this scenic spot, Morgan, I'd better line up the experts."

"Duncan's already been notified."

"Our best pathologist by far, but we'll also need a forensic anthropologist and a forensic archaeologist. I'll call them in from the Penzance BCU. Long night; even longer for those two PCs you've got up here, poor devils. Creepy place, you want my opinion."

"Mine, too; not fit for man nor beast."

acknowledgments

I HAVE THE GREAT good fortune to live on a beautiful island in Washington's Puget Sound populated by talented, warm, and good-natured neighbors and friends. It is the kind of place where I consider it a bad day unless at least four people driving the other way wave to me on my way to buy groceries. My fellow islanders are a big part of what makes this such a magical place to live and work, but a special bowing and scraping is due the regulars at the Burton Coffee Stand with whom I spend a raucous hour every morning: laughter is a great way to start the day and the hilarity there is as rich and vivifying as the coffee.

Let me hasten to add, however, that all of the characters in this story are fictitious or—in one or two potentially recognizable cases—are used fictitiously.

There are writers' resources aplenty here and I owe special thanks to the staff of the Vashon Public Library, the Vashon Bookshop, and the Vashon-Maury Island Heritage Museum. On matters of police procedure, I had the help of several officers in the Vashon Substation of the King County Sherriff's Office. For background on the shipping industry in Alaska, I thank James Soriano, and for commercial law, Gayle Bush at Bush, Strout & Kornfeld, Seattle.

I am grateful, too, for a team of early readers I can trust to give unvarnished comments on early drafts. For this book, they include: Francine Tanguay, Kate Pflaumer, Martin Mann, and Clare Stebbing.

Finally, my deepest appreciation to my extended family: Eric, Baker, Nancy, and Tom. They understand that when they talk with me, some part of me will always be AWOL—working on the latest book. Thank you for your patience and love. And to the late Marion and Ron Robbins, who were as dear to me as surrogate parents, I extend my enduring affection.

And finally, a deep bow of gratitude to the entire creative team at Northstar Editions: my project manager and steadfast advisor, Stephanie Konat; gifted cover designer Laura Hidalgo, proofreader Hunter Richards, and book formatting genius Adam Bodendieck.

—Will North
September, 2017

* also by Will North *

The Long Walk Home
(Romance)
Forty-five year old Fiona Edwards answers her Welsh
farmhouse door to a tall, middle-aged man shouldering a
hulking backpack—he is unshaven, sweat-soaked and
arrestingly handsome. What neither of them knows is
that their lives are about to change forever.

Water, Stone, Heart
(Romantic Suspense)
Nicola and Andrew have each come to the Cornish
village of Boscastle to escape their troubled pasts. When
they meet, they're bristly and sarcastic—yet are attracted
to each other. What neither of them knows is that a
ferocious storm is brewing, one that could destroy them,
and the entire village. And that storm is about to hit.

Harm None
(British Murder Mystery/Davies & West Series: Book 1)
When an American archaeological team discovers the skeletal remains of a missing child, British Detectives Davies and West unearth a growing list of suspects. Just as they close in on their prime suspect, another child goes missing.

Too Clever By Half
(British Murder Mystery/Davies & West Series: Book 2)
The naked, maimed body found bobbing in the English Channel presents a vexing puzzle to Detectives Davies and West. Post-mortem confirms the body's wounds were inflicted by torture, but without a name or a crime scene, Davies and West are stymied. Unraveling this mystery of betrayal, deep secrets, and revenge will test their skills as never before.

Trevega House
(British Murder Mystery/Davies & West Series: Book 3)
Three years after surviving a catastrophic flood (***Water, Stone, Heart***), twelve year old Lee Trelissick has settled into a safer life with her adoptive parents. But before long, preternaturally wise Lee announces "Someone wants to do us harm. Someone evil." She's right. Can Detectives Davies and West protect the girl and stop the killer before it's too late?

find more great books by
Will North at:

www.willnorthnovelist.com/books.html

Made in United States
North Haven, CT
01 October 2023

42250839R00192